london love

by Clare Lydon

First Edition July 2015
Published by Custard Books
Copyright © 2015 Clare Lydon
ISBN: 978-0-9933212-3-8

Cover Design: Kevin Pruitt
Copy Editor: Gill Mullins
Typesetting: Adrian McLaughlin

Find out more at: www.clarelydon.co.uk
Follow me on Twitter: @clarelydon

Acknowledgements

Like any book, this one wouldn't be in your hands without the help and support of many people — so without further ado, I give you my stellar supporting cast.

Gratitude and thanks to my beta readers for your constructive and ever-so-useful feedback which is greatly appreciated: Jeremy Cope, Gary McKee, Tammara Adams, Angela Peach, Rachel Batchelor, Sheryl Scott and Emma Young.

Also thanks to my niece-in-law, Gemma Bicknell, for her invaluable floristry advice — everything I know about being a florist, I learned from the best in the business. If you are in or around Malton, North Yorkshire, do call into The Topiary Tree for some fabulous flowers and say hi to Gemma!

Thanks to my awesome cover designer Kevin Pruitt who pulled this one out of the bag when I was tearing my hair out — you are a superstar. Heaps of plaudits also to my copy editor extraordinaire, Gill Mullins. Finally, a tip of the hat to my typesetter and all-round cheerleader Adrian McLaughlin — I simply couldn't do this without any of your help, so all three of you stand up and take a bow!

Much love and thanks to my wife Yvonne for reading this manuscript once, twice, a zillion times and for being an unfailing support in every way possible.

And last but by no means least, thanks to you for reading. Every email, Facebook message or tweet makes me smile and gives me the encouragement to keep going. I hope you enjoy this book and let me know what you think of it!

Connect with me at:
Tweet: @clarelydon
Email: mail@clarelydon.co.uk
Sign up for my mailing list at: www.clarelydon.co.uk.

For my gorgeous wife, Yvonne.
Our London love keeps me going.

1

Kate Carter picked up the bottle of Veuve Clicquot and refilled her glass. She pulled down the cuffs of her egg-white shirt, flexed her calf muscles under her black trousers and waited for the laughter to die down. She'd been at her company's awards ceremony for over an hour now and the woman hosting wasn't quite as funny as she thought she was.

The team from Kate's magazine — Female Health & Fitness — were sitting at a round table in a swish Mayfair hotel, surrounded by at least other 50 tables, all filled with an excitable media crowd and an endless supply of Bordeaux, Chablis and Champagne. It was August, and the room was awash with summer excitement, along with a healthy dose of anticipation and sparkle.

Kate didn't do dresses, so she'd opted for a black tuxedo, the first time she'd ever done so. It sat well on her tall, slim frame — she should have done it years ago. She leaned back in her chair and rolled her ankle, the light catching on her black patent brogues. More dazzle.

"Kate. Kate!" Her colleague Henry was not doing a good job of keeping his voice down, such was his eagerness for more booze. "Kate! Psst! Pass me the bottle!"

Henry held out his hand, his cheeks already alight with Champagne splotch, his pupils periodically sparking then slumping. Kate could tell that Henry's lovingly conditioned hipster beard was going to be hiding some food by the end of the night, and if he didn't lose his phone as he did on most of these occasions, she would eat her bow tie. But she passed him the bottle anyway — Kate wasn't a killjoy.

On stage, music blared as the winner of Feature of the Year trotted up to collect her gong. Kate had seen her walking the corridors in their building and she wasn't a fan. The woman never held the door open if you were behind her, and Kate had witnessed her being rude to staff in the canteen on numerous occasions. Never trust people who are rude to serving staff, life lesson number one.

True to form, the woman shook out a speech with almost as many words as her lemon dress had sparkles, and Kate let her eyelids flutter shut. She didn't mind these occasions, but the speeches could be a bit of a bore.

Kate opened her eyes again when she got an elbow in her ribs.

"Are we next? I thought they said we were first half?" Magazine editor Dawn was chewing the side of her cheek and fidgeting with her red napkin. In recent years Dawn had never come to one of these ceremonies and not won anything, so Kate hoped she wasn't let down today. The March issue of Female Health & Fitness was up for Cover Of The Year and they all thought it stood a fighting chance, adorned as it was with a Hollywood actress, a UK sprint sensation and the promise of a new you for summer. Something for everyone, as Dawn had rightly opined at the time.

Kate nodded. "I think so. Do you think if we win, management will spring for us to go abroad for a week?" She fixed her gaze on the air above her, painting the picture with her hand. "Sun, sea and sangria on them? What do you reckon?"

Dawn spluttered. "I'm sure it'd be no problem at all."

Their conversation was interrupted as the winner on stage got a huge cheer for something she'd said. The woman grinned and waved at the crowd.

"And finally, thanks to my darling fiancée Hugo —
you're the best and I can't wait to marry you next year!"
To a cacophony of cheers and whistles, the previous winner
tottered off the stage in heels the height of goal posts and the
next award flashed up on the screens — Cover Of The Year.

"This is it!" Dawn dug her fingers into Kate's arm in
excitement.

Kate watched as the company's art supremo, Simon, was
called to the stage to present the winner. In all her years working
as a designer, Kate had never won Cover Of The Year. It was
something she was desperate to remedy, even if she was trying to
underplay it tonight. She bit her lip and ran her hands through
her platinum-blonde hair as Simon began to speak.

"It's true what they say — people judge a magazine by its
cover. If the image, coverlines and overall ethos don't appeal
to them, they'll move on and you'll lose a sale. The magazine
market is a cut-throat, fickle business, so snagging consumers
is all important in the battle to stay alive."

Dawn turned to give Kate her best knowing nod, combining
it with the raising of both eyebrows.

On stage, Simon continued: "All of these next five covers
fulfilled that brief in terms of having vibrant imagery, must-do
coverlines and engaging the reader, and thus improving sales.
Let's take a look."

He stood back in his Armani suit as the covers flashed
up one after the other on the giant screen, receiving rounds
of applause and whoops from the appropriate tables. When
it was the turn of Female Health & Fitness, their table lit up,
glasses clinking, whistling and applauding.

A minute later, the screams had died down and the tension
settled once again on the room.

On-stage, the envelope was ripped and Simon smiled,
moving his mouth closer to the microphone. "And the winner
is truly well deserved and a personal favourite of mine...

Well done to Female Health & Fitness magazine for its March cover!"

Kate's heart rate soared and her mouth dropped open — they'd only gone and done it.

Dawn flung herself at Kate. "I can't believe it — we bloody won!" When Dawn released her, Kate looked around the table at her team, arms raised in the air, volume ratcheted to the max as they celebrated in unison.

On stage, Simon was speaking into the mic. "Come on up, art editor Kate Carter and editor Dawn West!"

Hearing her name called, Kate finished high-fiving her co-workers but found her grin was stuck solid to her face. She shrugged on her jacket and straightened her bow tie, before taking Dawn's hand and pulling her up towards the stage.

Dawn brushed imaginary crumbs from her blue sparkly dress as she followed Kate, tottering like a pro on her extra-high heels through the sea of applause. "Have you prepared a speech?" she muttered in Kate's ear.

Kate turned and shook her head. "Thought it might jinx it."

They were at the stairs leading up to the stage now and Kate had goosebumps all over.

"How's my hair?"

"Gorgeous and ultra lesbian." Dawn kissed Kate on the cheek. "If you don't pull tonight in that tux and with this award in the bag, the world's gone mad." Dawn gave Kate a wink, then she was up the stairs, taking Kate with her.

They reached the debonair Simon, who was holding the glass trophy in one hand. He went to give it to Dawn, but she shook her head and gently pushed Kate forward.

Kate bashfully accepted the award and Simon kissed her on both cheeks. Then he stood back and applauded, while Dawn got on the mic.

"Thanks, you lovely people!" Dawn had never been shy of public speaking and she wasn't about to start being shy now.

"I'd like to say a massive thank you to my whole team, who are all brilliant, but mostly thanks to the brains behind this cover, my dear friend, Kate Carter."

Dawn turned her clapping in Kate's direction, before darting back to the mic. "Oh, and even though he's not here, thanks to my husband Nick for being a saint and putting up with me!" With that, Dawn backed away.

Kate replaced Dawn at the mic and held the trophy aloft — the crowd applauded, and through the dim lighting, she saw Henry and features editor Hannah clapping madly, arms above their heads.

"Like Dawn said, this is a team effort, but thanks again for the award — it means a lot." Kate was shaking slightly, and she felt Dawn's soothing hand on her back. "I'd like to thank my editor Dawn, my deputy art editor Henry and everyone on the magazine!"

Kate felt the love in the room embrace her as she held the trophy aloft again. But then it hit her, as she looked out across the room and the smiling swathe of people, most of whom had somebody to go home to, to celebrate with. For Kate, that was not the case. Sure, she had her editor and her team to toast with tonight. But there was no girlfriend or wife who she could dart back to the microphone and thank as the previous two speakers had. Being single didn't ordinarily bother her, but at this moment she could feel it clogging her arteries and slowing her breathing. In this lifetime, right now, Kate was flying solo.

But, ever the professional, she styled it out, never losing her grin, glossing over the fact she had nobody to say she loved as a footnote on such a grand night. Instead, she made an 'after you' gesture to Dawn, who took her hand and held it aloft as they made their way down the stairs and back to their team, placing the trophy in the middle of the table as they both sat down.

"Incredible — I still can't believe we won!" Dawn simply couldn't wipe the smile off her face.

"I can — it was a brilliant cover," Henry said. "Made all the more brilliant by my addition of the gloss to the headline, didn't you think?" Henry had his serious face on, which made Kate burst out laughing.

"It was all about you, Henry," she said, patting his shoulder.

Pulling her chair up to the table and rubbing her hands together, Dawn smiled round at her team, the adrenaline clearly still sparking in her veins. "Right, now that's over with, let's have a great night! Nobody has to be in tomorrow till lunchtime at the earliest." She paused and pulled the Champagne from the bucket, then frowned in Henry's direction when she saw it was empty. Dawn looked around and accosted a nearby waiter.

"Two more bottles when you're ready, please."

2

Mr Davis clicked his fingers together as he stood at the counter of Fabulous Flowers and pointed at Meg. He looked very pleased with himself. "A young Sharon Stone — that's who you look like! Was she the bunny boiler in that film?"

"I don't think she boiled any bunnies, but she was definitely a bit unhinged." Meg gave him a thin-lipped smile.

"That's it, then." He paused. "Not that you look like you'd boil any rabbits soon either, but you get what I mean." He looked Meg straight in the eye. "It's a compliment, by the way. Sharon Stone — she was a looker in her day. Not so bad now, either."

"I'll take it as a compliment, then." Meg smiled and willed her mum to come out of the back of the shop, where she was just putting the finishing touches to Mr Davis's flowers.

Mr Davis was a terrible flirt who came into the florist every Saturday, rain or shine, to pick up flowers for his wife. Every week, he told Meg she looked like someone new. Last week it had been Cameron Diaz. The week before, Marilyn Monroe. Meg was always amazed he knew who all these actresses were as they spanned many different eras, but Mr Davis was something of a film buff. Plus, being newly retired, he had a lot of time on his hands.

As far as Meg could see, the only similarity she had with any of these people was she was female and had blonde hair — but she didn't like to point this out to Mr Davis. Meg knew his first name was Clive, but neither she nor her mum had ever called him that. Always the formality of Mr Davis.

Just in the nick of time, her mum, Olivia, appeared with his flowers.

"Here you go, Mr Davis," she said, handing him a fat bouquet dressed with silver ribbons. "Seasonally bright and gorgeous. Sheila's going to love them."

"Perfect — they look beautiful, just like the two of you."

Meg could never quite work out who Mr Davis flirted with more — her or her mum. She hoped it was her mum but she could never be sure.

Olivia waved his comment away, smiling. "Flattery will get you everywhere."

He bid them both farewell and left the shop, the bell over the door ringing as he did so.

"I swear he gets more flirtatious by the week," Meg said.

"He's a solid, regular customer, so he can flirt all he wants," Olivia replied. She disappeared into the back of the shop and came back with a cup of coffee for both of them: hers white, one sugar, Meg's pitch black. Meg liked her coffee like she liked her martinis — straight up and minus the olives.

"I might shoot off after this." Meg blew on her coffee and took a sip.

"Sure — you doing anything special? Moving perhaps? Getting rid of that good-for-nothing ex of yours?"

"Mum…" Meg shot her mum a warning glance, but Olivia chose to ignore it.

"Wasn't that your birthday resolution in June? Turn 32, sell the house and move on? Only, now it appears to be September and you *still* haven't even got the house on the market. And don't get me started on you going back on the dating scene and meeting someone new."

Olivia held Meg's gaze, but Meg couldn't take it and looked away.

Meg knew the drill, she'd heard it many times before.

"And don't give me that look. After the year I've had —
surely that should be a warning to you. Live life now. Live it
to the max. Get rid of the dead wood."

Meg smiled. "Mum, *I know*. I know I have to change things,
but you're beginning to sound like a never-ending stream of
those terrible positive-thinking slogans people frame and put
on their walls."

They both laughed at that.

"Actually, I've got to catch up on the accounts, so I thought
as you said Anya was available this afternoon, I'd do that at
home." Meg paused. "She is still coming?" Anya was their part-
time help in the florist.

Her mum nodded. "As far as I'm aware."

"Good."

Olivia took a sip of her coffee and stared at Meg once
more. "But you will think about what I said?"

Meg nodded, looking down into her coffee as if it might
hold the answers. "I think of nothing else every minute of
every day, believe me."

"Good." Olivia paused, before putting an arm around
Meg's shoulders and giving her a squeeze. "I'm your mum, it's
my job to worry. And I want my only daughter to be happy. Is
that such a crime?"

3

It had been a month since the awards, and this week had been a time for the Female Health & Fitness magazine team to put their autumn and end-of-year-plan into action. There was going to be a whole slew of new features and impressive cover gifts in the run-up to Christmas, all leading to a full-scale redesign of the magazine in the New Year.

The day had been a non-stop whirlwind of meetings for Dawn and Kate as they'd explained their plans to all their connected departments, telling them how they expected the various teams to run with them. Kate was pretty sure they were all on-board so far — now they just had to deliver on the editorial and the rest would fall into place.

Kate had arrived home to her first floor converted flat in central London's Old Street around an hour earlier. The balmy September air was seeping in through the windows along with traffic fumes, car horns and the low hum of commuter chatter.

Kate's commute was a short one — Southwark to Old Street taking just 15 minutes tonight on her trusty bike, Beryl — and for once, she hadn't been nearly mown down by a lorry or an impatient driver. Her bike was now safely stowed in the hallway downstairs as she relaxed into her distressed leather sofa, admiring her newly installed light fitting crafted from reclaimed metalwork and jam jars. Fresh-cut tulips sat in a blue glass vase on the coffee table, while on the TV, Kate was watching an American cookery show where a man was paid to visit a slick succession of diners and eat as much meat as possible. Every time she watched it, Kate thought it was a job she could well handle.

Her phone ringing broke the silence. Kate picked it up and stared at the glowing screen — it was her mum. Kate sighed. Her batteries were drained after her busy day and while she loved her mum, the only reason she'd be calling was if she wanted something. Mums normally did.

Her flatmate and sister-in-law Jess poked her head into the lounge and gave Kate a quizzical look. Jess had been for a haircut today and it looked particularly lesbionic — short, jaunty, brown. Kate wouldn't tell Jess, but her cut was straying worryingly close to looking identikit to her girlfriend, Lucy. She'd have a word with Jess about her and Lucy merging into dyke-alikes later.

"Your phone's ringing," Jess said.

"I know. It's my mum." The phone's cry was still piercing the lounge air.

Jess raised an eyebrow.

Kate sighed. She'd have to answer it now. She picked up her Samsung and swiped her finger across the screen.

"Hi, Mum."

"Hi, love," her mum replied.

Kate's breathing stilled. "What's wrong?" She remembered the same tone from when her mum had called nearly five years ago, to tell her Dad had died in a car crash. Sometimes, that day five years ago seemed like it happened to someone else entirely. But sometimes, like now, it seemed like yesterday. Kate sat forward and dropped her head between her knees. If her mum had some terminal illness, she might vomit onto her grey carpet.

"It's Uncle Mike," her mum said. "He's... He's dead."

Uncle Mike. Kate knew it was wrong, but relief flooded her body. Her mum and sister were fine. But Uncle Mike was not. Kate tried to remember what Uncle Mike looked like, but the image was hazy. His smell wasn't, though — tobacco and motor oil. Uncle Mike liked smoking and cars. Well, he used to, anyway.

"God, that's awful. How?"

"Heart attack. At work today." Her mum let out a small sob. "It's so awful. Can you come over?"

Kate was already on her feet. "Course. Let me get changed and I'll jump on my bike."

Her mum sucked in a breath. "Can't you get the tube? You know I don't like you riding your bike in the dark."

Kate smiled. "It's fine, Mum — I have lights and everything."

"Just for me, not tonight."

Kate relented. "Okay. Have you eaten?"

"No."

"We'll get something from that nice Indian you like. I'll pick up some wine and we'll toast Uncle Mike. Should be there by 8pm." Kate paused. "Have you told Vicky yet?"

"She's going to answerphone."

A likely story. "I'll call her on the way. See you in a bit — go make a cup of tea."

"Okay, love. See you soon."

Kate hung up and marched down the hallway, pausing in the kitchen doorway. She pulled at the bottom of her black denim shirt and leaned her head against the white doorframe.

Jess was making ribs for dinner and the flat was filled with the smells of roasted meat and sharp, smoky spices. She was wearing a blue apron with white pinstripes — a classic, cheffy look. Before Jess had begun working in a café over a year ago, she'd been allergic to cooking. Now, you couldn't get her out of the kitchen. Not that Kate was complaining.

"Everything okay?" Jess slotted an earthenware dish into the hot oven and shut the door, before casting a wary glance towards Kate.

Kate shook her head. "I'm going to have to bail on dinner — my uncle just died, so I'm going over to Mum's."

Jess covered her mouth. "Shit — how's Maureen?"

Kate shrugged. "A bit shaken."

Jess cocked her head. "Hang on, you've got an uncle? I met your Aunty Viv at the wedding, but I never knew there was an uncle."

Jess's brother Jack had married Kate's sister Vicky nearly six years ago, so Jess had met most of Kate's extended family at big occasions and summer barbecues.

Kate smiled. "That's because he wasn't at the wedding. Or at the christenings of our two gorgeous nephews. Let's just say Mike wasn't really a family man. For all I know, he could be gay or have a few love children scattered around the country. But he was still my mum's big brother."

Jess leaned against the counter-top, wiping her hands on a tea towel. "So duty calls," she said. "Shame, as these ribs are looking delicious."

"They don't smell too bad either." Kate pushed herself off the kitchen doorframe. "Maybe you should call Lucy and tell her you've cooked her a special treat."

Jess shook her head and folded her arms across her chest. "My gorgeous girlfriend is out on the tiles tonight, so this is just for me. I'll save you some for tomorrow night."

"It's a date." Kate kissed Jess's cheek before heading to her bedroom to grab her jacket.

"Give Maureen a hug from me!" Jess shouted after her.

* * *

Two hours later, Kate was sitting on the sofa at her mum's house in Finchley, chicken bhuna eaten, glass of Malbec in hand.

"It's weird to think you can just drop dead at any minute, isn't it?"

"I'm hoping you won't," Maureen replied. Her mum was normally a ball of energy, but she was understandably subdued tonight.

Kate smiled and ran her hand through her short, platinum-blonde hair. "You know what I mean. One minute you're here, the next minute you're not."

Her mum nodded. "I think we learned that the hard way five years ago, didn't we?" She paused. "I wish I'd seen your uncle more, but you know what he was like." Maureen twisted her wedding ring as she always did at times of stress. "Anyway, will you be able to help with some of the arrangements? Viv's coming tomorrow to sort the funeral, but could you sort the flowers? There's a place down the road that's reasonable."

"Sure — just give me the details."

"Thanks, love."

The doorbell interrupted their conversation and Kate got up. She opened the front door to her sister Vicky, car keys dangling off her right index finger, her face drawn with tiredness. She stepped into the house and gave Kate a hug.

"How is she?" Vicky shrugged off her blazer and threw it down on the bottom of the stairs.

"She's okay — I've calmed her down with wine."

"Good plan."

They walked back through to the lounge, before Kate disappeared to the kitchen to make Vicky a cup of tea. When they were all resettled, the memories of being in exactly the same position five years previously came flooding back.

"It's strange how it never leaves you, never goes away," Maureen said. Despite the food and wine, she was still pale and drawn. "You're doing okay, but then something like this happens and it knocks you back."

Vicky leaned over and hugged their mum, while Kate took a sip of her wine.

"But you haven't gone back, Mum," Kate said. "You've

got on with your life, and you're doing really well. And we'll deal with this together, as a family, just like before. Right?" Kate directed the last bit at Vicky, who nodded.

"Absolutely. All of us together — the intrepid threesome. Just let me know what I can do and I'll do it." Vicky nodded her head again with defiance.

Maureen took each of her daughter's hands in hers and squeezed tight. "I don't know what I'd do without my lovely girls, I really don't." She shook her head and her lip trembled.

Kate and Vicky squeezed right back.

4

The next day Kate was late into work, but she knew it wouldn't be a big deal. The magazine was in the first week of its four-week schedule, which meant her day would be light on work, heavy on personal chores — which now included funeral flower arrangements. Kate had no idea what that might involve, but she wasn't looking forward to it — visions of Six Feet Under floated through her mind.

She sat down at her desk near a window overlooking the Thames, taking in the open-plan floor which housed six magazines in total. Laughter floated through the rows of desks and occasional pot plant, and someone was playing old-school Eurythmics. The mood was light this morning, with the September sunshine ensuring everyone was embracing the last dregs of summer.

Kate had worked in magazines for the past eight years and she loved her job. She'd previously worked on titles involving food, horses and cars, before moving onto Female Health & Fitness a year ago, following Dawn from their previous foodie magazine, Scrumptious. When Dawn had announced she was leaving to launch a fitness magazine, she'd convinced Kate to come with her — and Kate was glad she had. Their publisher Ben called them the dream team, which they both loved.

Kate had learned a whole lot about how to stay fit and healthy during her time on the magazine, and she tried to follow its advice as much as she could. The women she stared at on its pages seemed to glow with health and vitality, probably through eating salmon and blueberries all day, and drinking only spring water. Well, that and the aid of Photoshop — it was amazing what their touch-up artists could do these days.

"Morning, sunshine." Her editor Dawn sat on the edge of Kate's desk and grinned at her. Dawn was dressed for the season in a yellow sundress and thin cardigan.

"Morning — how are you?" Kate stretched her arms over her head and let out an audible yawn.

Where Kate was blonde, tall and lithe, Dawn was dark-haired and pint-sized, but still slim. Kate doubted Dawn would have got the job if she was overweight — the magazine had an image to keep up, after all. But what the readers didn't know was that while Dawn looked virtuously healthy, she actually survived on a diet of Kit Kats, coffee and the occasional sausage baguette with extra ketchup.

"I'm good — very good in fact. I was ovulating last night, so it was a long night for Nick and I, if you catch my drift." Dawn winked at Kate.

Kate stuck her tongue out and made a gagging sound. "Not before I've had my first coffee, please."

Dawn shook her head. "You're so heterophobic."

"Before my first coffee, I'm everyone-phobic."

Kate got up and walked towards the kitchen, with Dawn following close behind. She pressed the cappuccino button on the enormous coffee machine and watched a plastic cup the colour of tan tights fall into place.

"How about you — how was your night? Wasn't Jess cooking up some fabulous meal?"

Kate shook her head. "That was the plan. But then my uncle dropped dead, so I had to go round to my mum's instead." The coffee machine stopped whirring and Kate took a sip. She recoiled as the liquid burned her tongue, a daily routine.

"I'm so sorry!" Dawn's face creased with concern. "Were you close?"

Kate waved a dismissive hand. "Last time I saw him was about ten years ago, so not really. But I might have to leave early to arrange flowers, just to warn you."

Dawn nodded. "Of course, whatever you need. Is your mum okay?"

"She's coping. Her sister's there today so they're doing the coffin, funeral and all of that." Kate paused. "So well done you, having a night of sex." She pointed her finger at Dawn. "We could all die any time, you know."

Dawn smiled. "That's what I like about you — your cheery disposition." She wagged a finger back in Kate's direction. "We've got to get you a night of sex before you die too, that's my mission."

Kate nearly spat out her mouthful of still-too-hot coffee as they walked back to their desks. "I hope I have sex again before I die. It's been nine months already and that seems like a lifetime."

Dawn grinned as she sat in her seat and pulled out her desk drawer. Inside were four two-finger Kit Kats and a Penguin. She selected a Kit Kat and picked up her tea.

"I'm going to take a picture and tweet you having breakfast one of these days." Kate swung round in her chair.

Dawn grinned. "I'd just say it was for a dare, then send a follow-up tweet of me holding a banana and a stick of celery." She paused. "Are we having a meeting this morning?" Dawn looked around the office but only half the staff were in — features editor Hannah and deputy art editor Henry were missing in action.

"Henry's at the dentist. Root canal," Kate said, pre-empting Dawn's question.

"And Hannah?"

Kate gave Dawn a wide grin. "She had a date last night, so I couldn't possibly say."

Dawn rolled her eyes. "What it is to be young and free."

* * *

That morning, Kate's mum called with the details of her favoured florist — Maureen was insistent because Barbara down the road had used them for her husband's funeral and the flowers had been beautiful. Neither of them mentioned they could have just used the florist they used for Dad, but Kate imagined Mum didn't want to be reminded of that dreadful day.

Kate clicked on the Fabulous Flowers website — tastefully done, with pastel colours and flowing fonts. Whoever was in charge of this particular florist knew about design. It was one of Kate's bugbears — bad colours and fonts, especially on the web. Having been trained in print design, seeing so many rules flaunted online broke her heart daily.

She checked their opening hours — till 7pm. It was 2pm now, but the art department had nothing in their in-tray and her deputy Henry had his legs propped up on his desk, reading a copy of their sister magazine, Male Health & Fitness. Kate tapped the top of the magazine.

Henry duly lowered it. "Yes?" His dark beard was a little out of control, but Henry also possessed killer green eyes which made women swoon.

"I'm going to bugger off early — you think you can handle the rush?"

Henry swept his eyes around the half-empty office and nodded slowly. "I think so, although keep your phone on and I'll call if there's an emergency." He paused, before raising his voice. "Like if Daisy gets the letters page over to me that was due this morning."

Across the office, staff writer Daisy didn't even raise her head, but simply extended a middle finger in Henry's direction.

"Great." Kate patted Henry's leg, shrugged on her jacket and slotted her phone and wallet into her grey canvas bag. "Can you tell Dawn I've gone when she gets back too?"

Henry saluted her. "Consider it done."

5

Kate arrived in front of Fabulous Flowers just after 4pm. Like their website, the shop was tastefully designed with impressively modern signage in soothing green and an inviting window display. Maureen had just called to ask if Kate had organised the flowers yet, and Kate had told her she was on her way. She forgave her mum for being a little overbearing seeing as she was dealing with a family death — but seriously, she'd agreed to do this less than 24 hours ago.

Kate pushed the door and heard the bell as her senses were overwhelmed by a wave of fresh floral scents. Colours and vibrancy jumped out at her from every angle, with familiar flowers and the more exotic jostling for attention. The floor on either side was taken up with chrome buckets stuffed with blooms, and every other available surface — wooden crates, stands and boxes — was overtaken too. Far from being chaotic, though, the overall effect was an artful, sensory overload.

On a wooden stand against the wall to her left were sheets of tissue paper in cool shades, and the large, retro counter straight ahead held multi-coloured ribbon and string, along with a cash register, phone and thick appointment book.

Even though she was a graphic designer, Kate had never really been drawn to flowers as an art form. However, this shop showed it could be done and she was impressed.

"Mum, I know that wasn't how you did it back in the day, but this is how I do it now, so you're going to have to trust me."

The conversation was out of sight but Kate could hear every word. Rich, smooth voice and the unmistakable hint of an adult child being peeved with her parent. Kate could well sympathise.

"Yes they wanted them for every table." Pause. "I know, but it's their wedding. Look, I have to go, someone's in the shop. Let's talk about this tomorrow." Pause. "Yes I know, we'll talk tomorrow. Bye."

Kate turned briskly and focused her attention on a bucket of delicate pink flowers. She had no idea what they were, but she was certain they'd be a winning choice if your favourite colour was shocking pink. Which hers wasn't. But Barbie would love them.

Kate heard footsteps come into the shop, a sigh and she looked up. But she was not prepared for the sight that greeted her. Standing behind the counter was a woman around her age with short hair the colour of sunshine, deep, greenish-blue eyes and miles of tanned skin running down her neck. She gave Kate a grandstand smile as their eyes met, and Kate stopped breathing for a second. Perhaps two. How had she never stepped into this florist before today? She'd passed by it often enough on the way to her mum's house.

"Hi," Kate managed. She was impressed her words sounded level, normal. Her words did not give away the fact her heart was thumping, her ears flushed, her buttocks clenched. No, Kate was fairly sure these were facts only she knew. Her brain instructed her legs to move forward and thankfully, her legs obliged.

"How can I help?"

Kate's mind was blank. The only thoughts whizzing round her head had nothing to do with her uncle's funeral. Kate forced herself to focus.

"It's my uncle — he died." Kate winced. That was not a slick opening sentence.

"Oh my goodness," the woman said. "I'm so sorry. Would you like a seat? A cup of tea?"

"I'm fine, really." Kate batted the offer away with her hand. "We weren't close." *Did that sound like she was a heartless wench?* She ploughed on.

"But my mum's asked me to organise the flowers, so here I am." Kate paused. Her throat was dry. She needed liquid. "But now I come to think about it, that's all the instructions she gave me. Do you have a set thing you do for funerals?" Kate looked at the florist, baffled. "Because the only other person who's died in my life is my dad and I didn't do his flowers. My sister did. She did all the arranging really, she was great. Just took charge. I was a bit shell-shocked, like my mum." *Oh. My. God. Why couldn't she shut up?*

Kate wished she'd remembered to take her cool pills this morning.

Clearly though, the florist was used to it — she didn't look alarmed. "I can well imagine." Her eyes radiated kindness and sympathy. "Wait there," she said, and disappeared into the back of the shop.

Did Kate have time to check her appearance in her phone camera? She put her hand in her bag, but before she could grab her phone, the florist reappeared, this time carrying two chairs. She arranged them around the corner of the counter and motioned for Kate to sit down.

"Please." She flashed Kate her grandstand smile again which flooded her eyes, and Kate could do nothing else but comply, her heartbeat pulsing in her ears.

The florist sat in the other chair and pulled across a couple of books from the end of the counter.

"First things first — I'm Meg." She held out a hand to Kate.

Kate took the hand in hers, trying not to dwell too much on the long, slender fingers. She shook Meg's hand slowly and brought her eyes up to meet Meg's again.

Was Meg looking at her fingers too? *Of course she wasn't.* Honestly, no wonder Kate's mum thought she needed checking up on. Here she was, tasked with sorting out her uncle's flowers and she was trying to hit on the undoubtedly straight florist. *Focus.*

"Kate," she replied, still holding onto Meg's hand. "And I'm sorry I just blurted out half my life story to you. It's just a weird situation, ordering flowers for a funeral." Kate wasn't sure she'd made it any better.

Meg smiled back. "Believe me, you did not blurt out your life story." She fixed Kate with her gaze. "Besides, us florists are like therapists — confidentiality is key. What goes on in Fabulous Flowers, stays in Fabulous Flowers." Meg let out a low chuckle that reverberated all the way down Kate's body.

Suddenly, Kate had a new plan of action: the quicker she could get this over with, the better.

Meg, however, had other ideas, getting to her feet and licking her lips. "So how about that tea, now you know you can trust me. Or I have coffee if you prefer?" She smiled at Kate as she waited for an answer.

Kate was still focused on Meg's lips. "Coffee would be great."

"Gimme two ticks."

Kate watched Meg's trim form disappear — she was tall, perhaps taller than her, and Kate was no slouch in the height department. Kate's cheeks reddened and her eyes darted around the shop — she needed a distraction. Lilies. Were they appropriate funeral flowers? Kate thought she'd read it somewhere. There were some intriguing black flowers on the far side of the shop, but she could just imagine her mum's face if she ordered those. Maureen would not be amused.

Meg came back a few seconds later with two white mugs of coffee. She put them down on the counter, then disappeared again, coming back seconds later with a two-pint carton of milk in one hand, her phone in the other.

"Wasn't sure if you took milk." She handed the milk to Kate. With her other hand, she fiddled with her phone, frowned, then put it back in her pocket.

"Everything okay with you?" Kate was glad to have a moment where she was the one who looked in control.

Meg smiled, but her face didn't light up this time. "Fine — just dealing with my mum. We run the florist together and we're having a difference of opinion." She shrugged and held up both palms. "But anyway, back to you and your uncle's funeral. Do you want to have a look at some popular funeral choices?"

Kate nodded and Meg pulled open a couple of books to show her. Meg spoke about arrangements, seasonal flowers, popular choices and budgets. But all Kate registered was a silky voice, a musky perfume, professional confidence and strong arms. *Really strong arms.* Kate was thrown. Was Meg single? Was she a lesbian? But then, whoever heard of a lesbian florist? Besides, Kate's gaydar was not going off, so she should just back away.

Then again, Meg *did* have short fingernails.

Meg shut the books with a flourish, then stood up and put them back under the counter. "I'll mail you with all the details — options, prices, the flowers we talked about. You can check the website, too — everything's on there."

Kate's chair scraped the floor as she stood up too. "My mum will be happy at least." She flicked her eyes up to Meg, who was staring intently at her.

There was a beat as neither of them said a word.

But then Meg forced a smile. "And my mum will be happy I've got another customer, so it seems we're golden daughters today."

Kate chuckled. "First time for everything." She slung her bag over her shoulder and held out her hand. "Thanks, you've been really helpful. And you've got my email."

Meg shook her hand warmly. "Yep — I'll be in touch."

Desire shot up Kate's arm and through her body. Goddamn it, it was like she'd been cast in some kind of corny movie. But after a few seconds, she noticed Meg seemed frozen to the spot as well — and they were still holding hands.

They both swiftly dropped them.

Kate reached into her bag and brought out her wallet. "Just in case you need to call me about anything, here's my card too."

Meg took it with a smile. "Thanks." They walked towards the door together. "Really lovely to meet you," Meg added, opening the door for Kate.

"You too." Kate gave Meg a wave that resembled a windscreen wiper, then stepped onto the street.

Outside, the world looked the same and life carried on. Had anything happened or was it all in her head? Kate glanced back into the shop, and Meg, who'd been watching, swiftly turned her back.

Kate flicked her head up to the sky and exhaled, breathing in the September sunshine. It was a gorgeous day to be alive and she was glad she was. She was also glad her Uncle Mike wasn't, otherwise she'd never have gone into Fabulous Flowers.

"I'm going straight to hell," Kate muttered as she walked along the High Street. She could be at her mum's house in ten minutes if she walked quickly. However, dealing with her mum and Aunty Viv when she'd just met a gorgeous woman, who was surely straight, wasn't top of Kate's list.

Instead, she turned and walked the other way, back in the direction of the main road and the bus stop. Her sister Vicky's house was within 15 minutes and the thought of a cup of tea with her was more appealing.

* * *

Twenty minutes later, however, standing on Vicky's doorstep, Kate wasn't sure if she'd made the right choice. Perhaps she should have just gone home and spoken to her flatmate, Jess? But she was here now. She rang the doorbell and waited.

Her three-year-old nephew Freddie was the first to arrive, pressing his face against the frosted glass and licking it. Kate knew that his four-year-old brother Luke would be sat on the sofa engrossed in some TV show and would pay no heed to her arrival. Eventually, Vicky arrived at the door and her eyes lit up when she saw her sister.

"Hello stranger — anyone would think someone had died." Vicky gave Kate a hug and invited her in.

Vicky and Jack lived on a new build estate near Mill Hill, bought just after giving up on their dream of staying central after the necessity of space overtook the necessity of having a cool postcode. They were now safely ensconced in suburbia along with all the other commuting young professionals, their house boasting a garden, stairs and a garage. In London, that was true luxury.

"Yeah, well — I've just sorted the flowers, so that's one less job to do." Kate followed Vicky into the kitchen and hung her jacket on the back of a dining chair as she sat down. She deposited a loitering Freddie onto her lap, and he picked up a glass of orange juice from the table and took a swig, smacking his tiny lips together.

"Very tasty," he told Kate, nodding.

"Is it, sweetheart?" she asked, kissing the top of his head.

Freddie nodded. "Yes it is. Very tasty."

"It's his new phrase," Vicky said. "Everything's very tasty, isn't it Fred?"

He nodded. "Very tasty, Mummy." He paused and eyeballed Kate. "Did you bring me any sweets?"

Kate laughed. "I didn't, I'm afraid," she said. "I'm a terrible aunty, aren't I?"

Freddie thought about it. "Not terrible," he said, before jumping off Kate's lap and running into the lounge.

Kate got up and walked over to Vicky. "Your son's very forgiving."

"Takes after his mother."

Kate snorted. "Has Mum been on to you today?"

"Onto me? All over me more like," Vicky said, filling the kettle. "Her and Aunty Viv were round this morning to see the boys, then she's been calling me about catering arrangements — like I'm the fountain of all knowledge on this."

Kate smiled. "You did do Dad's."

"That's what she said! But it was five years ago." Vicky paused. "Besides, I don't think food is a top priority at funerals. People aren't turning up for a gastronomic feast, are they? It's not a bloody wedding." She grabbed two mugs from the mug tree and set them down on the counter-top. "And anyway, did Mike have any friends?"

"Oh, you're going to hell," Kate said, laughing. "Along with me, by the way. I just went to organise the flowers and my oh my, the florist is smokin' hot."

Vicky let out a hoot of delight as she made the tea.

"I mean, properly gorgeous. But straight too, obviously." Kate shrugged and took the biscuit tin from her sister.

Seconds later, Vicky plonked herself down opposite Kate at the kitchen table. "Why straight too, obviously?" Vicky swept some of her long hair out of her face and eyeballed her sister.

"You know," Kate replied. "She's a *florist*."

Vicky gave Kate a look. "And that means she's straight because?"

"How many lesbian florists do you know?"

"Seriously?" Vicky looked amused.

"Look, I know loads of lesbians and not *one* of them is a florist."

"So that means no other lesbians can be either? You're very close-minded sometimes." Vicky took a Jammy Dodger from the biscuit tin and took a bite. "I don't think being a florist is a barrier to being a lesbian."

"I think it might be," Kate replied, deadpan. "I'm just saying that lesbians tend to be in certain occupations. Teachers, nurses, designers, writers, mental health, that sort of thing. Florists aren't high on the list."

Vicky took another bite of her biscuit. "And you tell me I'm prejudiced."

Kate pouted. "I'm allowed to say these things, I'm a lesbian."

"If you say so." Vicky paused. "But more interesting than whether or not Ms Florist is gay is that you're interested in her. And you haven't been interested in anyone since Caroline. So I say a thumbs-up for Ms Florist." Vicky gave Kate a double thumbs-up. "Does she have a name?"

Kate fluttered her eyelids and smiled. "Meg."

Vicky snorted again. "Look at you, Ms Giggly! Did Meg have a wedding ring on?"

"She did not," Kate replied, then blushed. "But I imagine florists wouldn't wear them because they get their hands messy all the time." Kate shrugged. "Anyway, nothing's going to happen apart from Meg's going to give us some lovely flowers for Uncle Mike's funeral. And then I'll never see her again and she can go back to her boyfriend — let's call him Phil. The end."

Vicky stuck her bottom lip out. "You're so cute when you like someone," she said. "And can I just say again, I like this very much — the 'you liking someone' bit. You've been so down on relationships since Caroline cheated on you, but life goes on. It's high time you found somebody else."

Kate gave her a look. "Spoken like a happily married person."

Vicky just laughed. "I'm not apologising for my relationship status and my gorgeous husband." Pause. "And I'm serious. You've been all doom and gloom when it comes to love, so it's good to see you taking an interest." Vicky's smile grew wider. "Even if she is straight."

"She's bound to be, isn't she?" Kate said. "She's a *florist*."

"So you said." Vicky rolled her eyes again. "Anyway, are you staying for dinner?"

Kate thought about it. "What you having?"

"Probably a Chinese takeaway. Just don't report me as bad mother of the year, okay?"

"Guides' honour," Kate replied, holding up her three middle fingers.

"You weren't even in the Guides, you liar."

6

Meg closed up the florist and walked along Finchley High Street, thinking about Kate. Specifically about Kate's gorgeous blue eyes and endearing smile, but in her business brain working out what flowers she might need to buy for the funeral. And then which flowers would go best with Kate's eyes. Maybe irises? Or perhaps blue orchids? And also which flowers she could put on the table when she made Kate dinner. A bunch of baby blue eyes?

Stop it. For the rest of the afternoon, she'd had the song Blue Eyes in her head and it was playing again now. What if it got lodged there for good and she was doomed to spend the rest of her days with Elton John on repeat? It didn't bear thinking about.

Really, Meg had no idea what her brain was doing. I mean, first the song. And second, hadn't she learned? That women were to be avoided at all costs and that her life had been so much simpler since she'd thrown herself into work and avoided any issues — well, most of the issues anyhow. And then a woman walked into her shop one day and she was ready to throw all logic out the window and fling flowers in her direction. Meg shook her head as she arrived home 15 minutes later, letting herself in through the black front door, eyeing her reflection in the shiny chrome knocker.

Once inside, she heard Tanya in the kitchen, her laughter echoing down the hallway of their Victorian terrace. Meg's shackles went up immediately and she narrowed her eyes. Tanya was cooking again. Tanya was *entertaining* again.

In their four years together, Meg could count on her two hands how often Tanya had cooked for her. But now, Tanya couldn't seem to get out of their kitchen, which made it awkward for Meg to cook most days. Plus, Tanya seemed to have a never-ending stream of new friends to invite for dinner, which also set Meg's nerves on edge.

In the year since they'd split up and been trialling their new 'situation', Tanya seemed to have embraced London lesbian living, whereas Meg had retreated into her floristry world, happy to watch life pass by on the pavement outside rather than experience it first-hand.

And every time Tanya flaunted her new life in Meg's face, it hurt — physically hurt. In her bones and in her flesh. Like today.

Meg hung up her jacket on the bulging coat rack and was just about to take the stairs up to her room when Tanya appeared in the hallway. She was wearing her usual cocky smile and a black apron with 'Good Lookin' And Cookin'!' emblazoned on the front in red. Tanya licked the last remnants of tomato sauce off of a wooden spoon, pausing briefly to give Meg a satisfied glance.

"I thought I heard you sneak in — you're working late again." Meg looked at her watch: 7.15pm. Twelve-hour days weren't uncommon in her life and besides, it kept her mind off other things. Like the fact she was still living with her ex when they officially split up over a year ago.

"You look tired too." Tanya waved the wooden spoon in her direction. "And I bet you haven't eaten properly today."

Meg held up her hand. "I already have a mother to do this speech."

Tanya cocked her head in response. "I'm cooking a lasagne, it's just gone in the oven." She shrugged. "Imogen's over and we're having dinner in 45 minutes. Get washed and join us. There's plenty."

Meg gripped the stair banister. This arrangement wasn't working. She wanted to get on with her life, but she was stuck in a rut with no way out. When she'd mooted the idea of getting the house ready for sale, Tanya had been non-committal, claiming she had far too much to do at work to think about selling the house too. But that was nearly nine months ago. Now, it should be clear they needed their own space and to move on with their lives.

However, much to Meg's surprise and horror, Tanya appeared to be revelling in the new status. No upheaval to her life at all, and no Meg to deal with as a girlfriend, either. Tanya appeared to have just slipped effortlessly into friend mode without so much as a backward glance. And now here was Tanya, inviting Meg to dinner in her own house like she was a lodger, with Tanya's hippy friend Imogen along for company. How was it that Meg was so in charge of her business life, yet so ineffective in her personal life?

"Great," Tanya said, not waiting for a response. "And don't worry about wine — I already used the bottle you'd half drunk and you've got another couple in the rack anyway."

Meg stood on the second stair up for a few moments as she watched Tanya disappear and then heard laughter coming from the kitchen once more. Meg clutched the bannister even tighter, exhaled and took the rest of the stairs one by one, feeling the reassuring soft carpet cushion the soles of her feet.

Even if she did like Kate and got as far as bringing her back here, how was that going to work out with Tanya forever parading around like some sort of social house mascot? Every time Meg walked in the door, there was Tanya, asking about her day, cooking her dinner, arranging her time. Often, it felt as if Meg still had one leg in the relationship, the other dangling over some precipice she was too scared to look over.

Meg pushed open the door to her room and collapsed on her unmade bed, the sheets tangling uncomfortably beneath her. Her eyes flicked around her room — the room that used to be their room, but was now hers alone. She should get new bedding — Tanya had done so straight away. Maybe change the lampshade, hang some new curtains. Plus, the walls could do with a lick of paint too, the pale blue they'd chosen three years ago now seeming to represent a cold prison of her own making.

Meg had to talk to Tanya again; the situation had to change. She couldn't carry on like this and expect to move forward. Up until now, she'd been too lazy to push it, too scared to deal with the rest. Even her mum had stopped asking her when she was selling the house as often, with Meg having jumped down her throat about it one too many times.

And Meg knew nothing would ever happen with Kate. Of course it wouldn't. The woman had just come into her shop to get some flowers for her uncle's funeral; she hadn't come in for a date. Besides, someone like her was bound to have a girlfriend.

They usually did.

7

The next day at work, Kate managed to have a meeting with her publisher and sort out a magazine shoot before her finger clicked onto the Fabulous Flowers website. Once there, she again admired the design and kicked herself for not telling Meg that. She'd planned to, but after Meg revealed herself to be a florist goddess, all rational thought had flown from Kate's head. *Next time*.

Kate clicked on the About Us page and saw a photo of Meg and her mum, Olivia, grinning at the camera while holding some expensive-looking flowers. Apparently Olivia had opened the florist over 30 years ago and Meg had joined straight from school, learning the ropes on the job. Now that Olivia was nearing retirement, Meg was taking over the family business. No mention of Meg's husband working at the business or her children, which kept a faint glimmer of hope alive in Kate's chest.

However, she quickly brushed it away. *Florists are not known for being lesbians.* Or was Kate guilty of the sort of stereotyping she would baulk at? After all, it takes all sorts as her mum was constantly pointing out to her. Maureen was still getting over the fact that "that nice BBC newsreader is a lesbian, too." She always clicked her tongue when she said it.

Kate went back to the main page and opened up Meg's email outlining the popular funeral packages. She was deep into her task, so didn't hear Dawn creeping up behind her.

"Who's the lucky lady?" Dawn leaned on Kate's desk, as was her habit. She was sucking on a lollipop and slurping like a small child, which didn't endear her to Kate.

"Nobody — it's for my uncle's funeral, remember?"

Dawn looked suitably chastised. "Right, sorry." She paused. "Is this the place you went to yesterday?"

"Uh-huh."

"And how are florists in the suburbs these days?"

"They're okay," Kate smiled.

Dawn eyed her suspiciously. "That was a devilish smirk from you Ms Carter — what happened at the florist?"

Kate leaned back in her chair and stretched. "Let's just say, the flowers weren't the only pretty thing in the shop."

Dawn's face lit up, but Kate held up her hand.

"And before you get excited, the florist is not a lesbian. I didn't pick up *one* gay vibe from her. She was just a hot florist, that's all." Kate shrugged. "Clearly I should just steer clear of florists in future to avoid crushing disappointment."

"But you are going to see her again?" Dawn's face was still creased with excitement.

Kate rolled her eyes. "Were you listening to any of the words I just said?" she asked. "But the answer is, probably not. I just need to work out which flowers say 'happy dying' more than the others, give her a call and we're done. And the hot florist can go back to her loving boyfriend who is undoubtedly waiting in the wings. A crying shame, though."

Dawn patted Kate on the shoulder as she pushed herself up. "Perhaps she could be persuaded, you never know. Or perhaps you should just stick to more lesbian-friendly occupations. Truck drivers, gardeners, that sort of thing."

Kate ignored her. "Did you want something? Other than to ridicule my life?"

Dawn looked thoughtful, then clicked her fingers together. "Yes — you free at 3pm for a meeting? We need to come up with some good ideas for cover features for the next few issues."

Kate raised her eyebrows. "Forward planning — I'm impressed. You're like a Duracell bunny today."

Dawn winked. "That's me. I gotta hop to a meeting, but 3pm?"

Kate nodded.

"Excellent. I thought down The Grapes?"

"Oh, one of *those* meetings…"

* * *

Dawn had summoned the whole team to the features meeting, which was usual every few months. Even though Kate was responsible for the look and feel of the magazine and Dawn responsible for what went in it, she agreed with Dawn on the fact that everyone should have a say in how the magazine evolved. Dawn was keen on teamwork and brainstorming to get the best possible ideas.

This particular afternoon was a team meeting in a pub, which Dawn liked to do periodically. Both Kate and Dawn knew that this was often where the magic happened, where their eureka moments occurred. Getting people out of their normal environment and into a more relaxed frame of mind was on old-fashioned trick, but one that worked well.

There were seven of them in total, which was still a big team compared to some magazines. They sat with their drinks at a round table, most with tablets or laptops in front of them, Dawn with her pen poised over a crisp, white notepad.

"So, cover features for the next few months. What have you got bubbling, Hannah?" Dawn asked.

Features editor Hannah tapped some keys on her laptop and looked up. She was an ambitious, perky 28 year old who seemed to go through dates at a rate of knots — men and women, Hannah did both. If there had been a week when

Hannah hadn't had a new date, it'd passed Kate by.

Hannah had offered to set Kate up on the dating app of the moment so that Kate could share her love of meeting new people and sleeping with them, but Kate hadn't been so keen. For one thing, she wasn't sure the pool of available London lesbians was quite as large as Hannah thought. Plus, Kate had a six year head-start on Hannah, so her pool was dwindling, and she certainly didn't want their pools to mingle — that would be a step too far. Kate preferred to date the old-fashioned way — see someone in a bar, avoid talking to them, get drunk, end up in bed. It'd worked so far in her life. Up to a point.

Hannah trailed her conker-brown eyes around the group and pushed her glasses up her nose. Hannah always wore glasses when she was being uber-professional. "Right, next month I've finally snagged the Olympic gold medallist for the cover — can I have a whoop!?" She got the necessary response before she moved on.

"When's the interview happening?" Dawn asked, chewing the top of her pen.

"Next week with luck — should hear back from the PR this week," Hannah replied.

"Great. What else?"

Henry sat up in his chair. "Can I go with you on that?" He blushed slightly as all eyes turned to him.

"Aw, does Henry have a crush on the superstar?" production editor Casey said, twiddling her pen between her thumb and forefinger.

Henry pulled his face into a frown. "No, I just admire her." Henry paused. "Plus, I think it would be good to send me out on more photoshoots. You said so," he told Kate.

Kate grinned. "Funny you didn't fancy going out with that running club last issue, yet an Olympic gold medallist and you're all over it."

Henry exhaled. "I'm just trying to be proactive!"

Dawn held up her hand. "Children, please. Speak to Kate and Hannah afterwards, okay?"

Henry nodded, slumped down in his chair and took a swig of his pint.

Hannah checked she had everyone's attention, then continued. "After that, we've got a Christmas food special — how to eat right over the festive period — and I'm setting up interviews with key nutritionists and health experts."

"Can we get some celebs to talk about what they eat, too?" Kate asked.

Hannah nodded. "I'm working with a couple of PRs on that. Should hopefully have some news at some point soon."

"Great," Kate replied. "And if there's a hot woman among them, we're fighting for the photoshoot, Henry, got it?"

The whole table laughed.

"After that, we've got a New Year fitness special, how to shift those extra pounds, great healthy recipes and a free recipe booklet. Oh, and I forgot to say, we've got our calendar coming out next issue too." Hannah sat back. "I'm also thinking about a lead feature on pregnancy and fitness, and maybe get a pregnant celeb to talk, too."

"Great." Dawn took a sip of her white wine and looked around the table. "We'll talk about possible celeb cover stars another time. Anyone got anything pressing before we start on the sub-features?"

"Actually, I do." Kate sat up in her chair.

Dawn raised an eyebrow in her direction.

"I know I sound like a stuck record, and honestly, I'm boring myself, but what about a feature on a lesbian running club? Lesbians don't get enough coverage in a magazine devoted to women, and I think it would be an interesting angle. Plus, you'd snag a bunch more readers by covering it."

Kate sat back and looked around the table, where everyone but Dawn was wearing their positive faces.

Dawn sighed. "We can do a running club of the month feature in our regular section, but you know what Ben thinks about doing a cover feature on lesbian stuff. The advertisers don't like it; he's tried it before."

Now it was Kate's turn to sigh. "And that was years ago — things have changed, as I keep saying. Lesbians can get married now and lesbian families are everywhere — we need to start doing more positive promotion to make it more normal. And I really don't think readers would have any objection."

"I agree with Kate," Hannah said. "We should have more lesbian coverage in the magazine — famous and otherwise. My mate goes to a running club called Dashing Dykes. Meets in north London — I could ask her?"

Henry spat out his lager. "Dashing Dykes?!"

Hannah reached out and cuffed him round the ear, while five other pairs of eyes challenged him.

Henry shut up swiftly.

Dawn drummed her fingers on the table. "Like I said, *I would*, but Ben doesn't like it." She turned to Kate. "But let me talk to him again — we haven't brought it up in a while. I agree with you, but we've got to think about the advertisers and what they want too. It's the way of the world, I'm afraid."

"The world is stupid," Hannah said. "We're women too, you know." She drank her bottle of Heineken and raised an eyebrow at Dawn.

Dawn held up both hands, then sat up straighter in her chair. "Look, I'm on your side. I just need to clear it with the powers that be, okay? But like you say, things have moved on. Let's hope publishing has too." Dawn stood up and looked around the table. "Now everyone can have a bitch about me while I go to the loo, then we can go for round two."

8

Meg was just packing up at the florist after a particularly busy Wednesday — even after a lifetime in the business, customer habits still sometimes caught her off-guard. What started off as a run-of-the-mill day had quickly mushroomed into an all-out decimation of stock. An early morning dash to the flower market was needed tomorrow, which meant an equally early night. Still, she wasn't complaining.

She was out the back of the shop when she heard a rat-a-tat-tat on the front door. She poked her head out, just about to tell whoever it was that she wasn't open, but then she spotted her brother, Jamie. Who, like her, was also gay. There had never been a nature/nurture debate in her family.

Meg cracked a smile as she sauntered across the shop and unlocked the door. Her brother greeted her with a hug and a kiss, his newly grown designer stubble alien against her chin.

"I don't know how women put up with this." Meg pinched Jamie's cheek.

"I don't either, but the men love it." Jamie followed Meg into the shop and leaned against the counter as she went out back.

"What are you here for, anyway?" Meg shouted, before reappearing with her black tote bag. "If you wanted Mum, she left about an hour ago. And I'm just off."

"And that's the welcome I get? I hope you're nicer to your other customers."

"They're normally buying something, so of course I'm nice to them."

While Meg and Olivia were tall and blonde, Jamie was tall and ginger — just as their maternal grandfather had been. Meg had always loved Jamie's hair, a rich, deep copper colour. Jamie ran his own property developing business and, bucking perceived gay stereotypes, was also the handiest man Meg knew. In a DIY emergency, Jamie was her first port of call.

"So, by process of elimination — you're here to see me?" Meg flexed her neck as she asked.

Jamie nodded. "I was in the area sizing up a property for a client, so wondered if you fancied a drink, or can I tempt you for dinner? My treat, because if this property comes off, I'm going to be a happy and rich man. For at least two months."

Meg put her hand on her hip and smiled at her brother. "When you put it like that, how can a girl resist?"

* * *

Half an hour later they were sitting in the Chinese restaurant down the road, crunching on prawn crackers and sipping bottles of Tsingtao.

"So tell me again. A woman comes in wanting flowers for her dead uncle's funeral and you want to jump her bones?" Jamie grinned broadly.

"You make me sound awful — 'jumping her bones' isn't exactly how I'd describe it." Meg took a sip of her beer.

Jamie smirked. "No? Then how would you describe it?"

Meg thought about it for a moment. "I'd like to get to know her better, she seemed really lovely."

"And then jump her bones?"

Meg grinned. "Yeah, pretty much."

"And she's gay?"

Meg nodded. "I'd bet my house on it."

"And she's coming back in again?"

Meg nodded again.

"So what's the problem? Ask her out."

Meg rolled her eyes. "That might be the protocol in gayman world, but in lesbo-land we have to feel out the terrain, make sure there are no obstacles."

Jamie ran his hand over his stubble. "Like an assault course?" He didn't sound convinced.

"Obstacles as in girlfriends. And in my experience, where this sort of woman is concerned, there normally is."

"This sort of woman?"

"Stylish, good-looking, funny, smart. Probably also married with a baby." Meg paused. "It's still weird that we can get legally married now, isn't it? Weird in a good way."

"A very good way," Jamie said. "But back to the matter in hand — here's another thought. Possibly, just possibly, she might *not* be married. Have you thought about that?"

Meg sighed. "I know — but if that's true it's also too scary to contemplate. Because then I'd have to *do something*." Meg cupped her chin in her hand, elbows on the table. "So I'm sticking with my story and taking the path of least embarrassment."

Jamie laughed as the food arrived and was set down in front of them. "That's exactly the spirit that will get you laid after your year-long slump."

"Year and a half." Meg scooped some chicken and black bean sauce onto her plate, sat alongside her rice. "Remember, me and Tanya didn't have any sex for the final six months. We just slept on the outskirts of the bed and avoided each other as much as we could."

"Glad to see your life's moved on so dramatically, then." Jamie munched on a mouthful of noodles as he raised his eyebrows at Meg.

"Now you put it like that."

They were silent for a few seconds, both pouncing on the food after a hard day at work.

"How's Mum, anyway?"

"Fine. Loads better. Check-ups all came back okay and she's easing back into work." Meg paused. "That is to say, she's doing far too much still, but less than I anticipated she might, so that's good."

"Make sure she doesn't do too much."

"I'm trying." Meg shrugged. "But you know what she's like."

"I do." Jamie pursed his lips. "The type to run around till she's blue in the face and then have a minor heart attack." He shook his head. "Is she any closer to getting help with the deliveries?"

Jamie had been helping out at the florist with deliveries since their mum's heart attack, and was still doing so at the weekends. He'd been a massive help and Meg didn't know what they'd have done without him.

"I think she had a friend whose son was interested, but I'll follow up with her, promise."

"Cool. Only if this deal takes off, I might need my weekends back to work on that."

"I get it," Meg said. "I'll speak to her. You still okay for this month?"

"Course — me and Greg." Jamie paused. "I have something else to tell you." He winced as he spoke.

"Sounds ominous."

"Dad's been in touch."

Meg stopped chewing and put down her cutlery. "He's being persistent, isn't he? That's twice in a few months." She sighed. "What should we do?"

Jamie shrugged. "I don't know. Part of me wants to tell him to piss off. But then part of me wants to meet him, to see what he has to say. But with Mum how she is, I don't want to upset her."

Meg shook her head. "Mum has to be our priority. It's too soon after everything for unnecessary stress for her. So just tell him now's not a good time. Can you do that?"

Jamie nodded slowly. "It seems a bit mean, though. He really does want to be in our lives for good this time. He sounds like he's changed."

Meg furrowed her brow. "You always were the softer one. He's been out of our lives for this long, he can wait a bit longer. Agreed?"

"Agreed." Jamie pushed some food around his plate. "It's just, none of us are getting any younger, are we? Mum's heart attack put that into clear perspective."

"I know. But he can wait — he's made us wait a lifetime." Meg's tone held steely finality. "Anyway, let's change the subject — how are Greg and Jupiter?"

Greg was Jamie's boyfriend and they'd been living together for two years. Jupiter was their cat, and every time Meg went round there, she swore she wanted to come back as Jupiter. A more spoilt and loved animal Meg had yet to meet.

A slow smile spread across Jamie's face as Meg knew it would. It always did when he spoke about Greg — and that was exactly what Meg wanted. Someone who made her light up just like Jamie was doing right now.

9

The next morning, Kate knew she could postpone it no longer. Once she'd made it to work and sorted through her morning emails, she snuck off into one of the smaller meeting rooms in the office and closed the door quietly. She plugged her laptop into the network, called up the Fabulous Flowers website, took a deep breath and dialled their number. Her knee jigged up and down under the table and her blood began to tumble around her body, as if competing in some amateur gymnastic event.

"Hello, Fabulous Flowers."

It was her. Kate gulped. "Hi Meg — it's Kate, we met earlier in the week. You're doing the flowers for my uncle's funeral."

Meg cleared her throat before replying. "Of course — how are the arrangements going?"

The arrangements. Not asking how Kate was, but how the arrangements were going.

"It's set for Monday, if that's good for you?"

"Fine for us. Did you get a chance to look at the options I sent over?"

"I did — I like option two. The wreath for the coffin, some posies and other bits too."

"Excellent choice." Meg paused. "You can pay now if you like — or if you have time, you can come in and sort the tribute and the payment on Saturday?"

Kate stalled. Did she want to go in again? Of course she did, even though she knew it was probably pointless.

"Saturday's fine. I'm over at my mum's anyway, so I could pop in then."

Meg cleared her throat again. "Best time would be around midday, when all the wedding flowers have gone out."

"Right — busy day for you?"

"Yep, but at least it's September, the wedding season's nearly over." Meg let out a low chuckle. "Come at midday and we can have a coffee and a chat."

"Great — it's a date," Kate said. And then smacked her forehead with her free hand. *A date? What a moron.*

"A date." Meg let out a nervous laugh. "And don't forget to think about what you might want to write on the tribute."

"Tribute, got it."

"I'll look forward to it — see you Saturday." And with that, Meg hung up, leaving Kate staring at her phone.

Kate's face was glowing red — she couldn't believe what had just come out of her mouth. On the plus side, though, Meg was looking forward to it, so it wasn't the worst idea in the world for her.

For Kate, this funeral-flower appointment sounded just about perfect.

* * *

A few hours later, Kate was laying out the readers' letters page and staring at a stock photo of a runner. Was the runner attractive? Kate couldn't quite decide. Her phone ringing interrupted her thoughts. It was Jess.

"Hello, dearest." Kate settled the phone to rest at an awkward angle between her neck and ear — the sort of position that keeps physios in business.

"Hello yourself," Jess said. "I'm calling with a question."

Kate smiled. "Shoot."

"On a scale of one to ten, how lovely am I?"

Kate's smile got wider. "Depends on the day."

"Let me tell you, today I'm a ten."

"Really?" Kate moved an image box on screen while she spoke.

"Really," Jess replied. "Because today, as well as being your lovely flatmate, I also come bearing a hot lady for you."

Kate sighed. This was a road they'd been down a few times since Kate's last relationship, which ended badly. Since then, Kate had been wary about dipping her toe back in the dating pool. Actually, scrap wary, she'd been actively avoiding it, declaring women toxic. In fact, the only woman Kate had laid eyes on and immediately felt something for was Meg. Her straight florist.

So on second thoughts, perhaps Kate *should* listen to Jess.

"How hot?" Kate asked.

"Sizzling. George Foreman-grill hot. Smokin'."

"That is a weird way to describe a woman," Kate said. "George Foreman-grill hot? My George Foreman grill had faulty wiring and I had to send it back. Not a good analogy."

Jess laughed. "You get the idea."

"So where did you pick up said smokin', presumably char-grilled lady?"

"Friend of Lucy. Well, not strictly a friend of Lucy…"

Kate sighed. "I'm going to stop you there. Does this have anything to do with Julia?" Julia was Jess's oldest friend from school who delighted in matchmaking all around her — and now that Jess was happily coupled, she'd turned her attention to Kate.

"Negative — nothing to do with Julia."

"Okay, continue."

"She's a friend of a friend of Lucy's."

Kate surveyed her nails. "The link sounds tenuous. I think I preferred her as a George Foreman grill."

"Anyway, I've got to get back to work." Jess cleared her throat. "We're going out on Friday, you're coming and so is she. I'm staying at Lucy's tonight so I won't see you till tomorrow, so this is your early warning."

"I can't do tomorrow."

Kate was lying and Jess knew it.

"There's a difference between can't and won't. I'll see you at home after work tomorrow," Jess said. "It's going to be great."

The line went dead as Jess hung up and Kate was left staring at her phone. She wasn't sure 'great' covered it, but she had little choice. When you arrived in your mid-30s, it seemed the whole world was coupled up and you're the odd one out.

Plus, her uncle's death had made Kate think. If she died at his age, she might only have another 30 years on the clock. If she died at her dad's age, she only had another 21 years left. Now that was a sobering thought. Preferably, she would like some of those years to be with someone she loved, in a meaningful relationship. Not too much to ask, was it?

So perhaps Friday should be the date Kate concentrated on. Not Saturday, with the hot-but-straight florist. Yes, the hot-George-Foreman-like lesbian should be her focus. Which didn't really conjure up a great image, if Kate was honest.

10

Friday duly followed Thursday, and after work, Kate found herself being nudged by Jess in their kitchen, a grin playing on her features.

"It's like the tables have turned, isn't it?" Jess looked terribly pleased with herself.

"How so?"

"Not so long ago, you were in a relationship, I was single and you were pushing me into the dating game. Now I'm doing the same for you."

"You are so giving," Kate said.

"I know."

Kate took two beers from the fridge and Jess walked ahead of her through to the lounge. Kate moved a couple of cushions from the sofa onto the floor. She knew she had too many, but cushions were her weakness. Particularly fluffy ones. The brown leather couch creaked as Kate sat down, and she breathed in the smell of freshly polished leather.

"You excited about later?" Jess asked.

The plan was to meet Lucy and three of her friends in the Data Club, a new bar in Dalston. Kate's mood could best be described as nonplussed, which even she knew was not what Jess wanted to hear. Somewhere in the back of her mind, she was willing this new, apparently perfect, woman to be a florist called Meg.

"Beside myself. Cannot wait. Literally chomping at the

49

bit to meet the woman who resembles a boxing legend." Kate took a swig of her beer and stared evenly at Jess.

"George Foreman was a very handsome boxer," Jess replied.

"Is there such a thing? Don't all boxers look a bit, well, battered?"

"She's not battered — she's grilled." Jess sat back, her features creased with the enormity of her joke.

Kate gave her a minute to recover. "What's she called anyway?" Kate paused. "And don't say Georgina."

"Wouldn't that be great?" Jess's sides were, literally, shaking. "But she's actually called Tanya — I think. Check with Lucy on the details. Kate and Tanya. Tanya and Kate. 'Where's Kate? Oh, she's out with Tanya'." Jess's voice was sing-song.

Kate couldn't help but smile at her friend. "She sounds like a school prefect. Or somebody who owns a horse."

"Let's not start Tanya-bashing before you've met her. And Clare Balding owns a horse — you like her."

"I'm not sure I'd want to *date* her, though. Clare's not really my type."

"Do you have a type?" Jess asked.

An image of Meg popped into Kate's mind. "I do when I see it." Kate shifted on the sofa, grabbed another cushion and leaned back. "And will she be wearing a badge too? What if I hit on the wrong friend and I accidentally split up a couple? That would be a bad night."

Jess smiled. "Lucy told me about this custom — it's called introductions. Never heard of it myself, but apparently it sorts out any potential problems like that." Jess took a glug of her beer before continuing. "Look, I know this is another set-up, but if this doesn't work, I promise I'll leave you alone. It's just that Lucy thinks this has potential and I trust her judgement. My girlfriend is a trustworthy woman. Are we agreed?"

Kate grudgingly nodded. "We're agreed, she is."

Jess leaned forward and held up her beer bottle for Kate to clink. "So here's to a Friday of adventure. And if nothing else, we get to have another night in Dalston where we can laugh at all the hipsters and their funny hair."

* * *

A little over two hours later, Kate and Jess arrived at the Data Club, a cool Dalston hangout with the requisite low lighting, scuffed chairs and dusty flooring. Outside, the main road was just warming up for the Friday night ahead, with neon lighting coming to life and traffic fumes choking the air. Inside, a tall, skinny man with a concentrated expression was filling tall glasses with ice, ready to shake up the bar's signature cocktail, the DillyDally.

"Didn't this used to be an estate agents?" Kate and Jess edged their way through the crowds of people, shoulders bumping.

"Yeah — they've still got the sales board up at the back of the bar — Lucy and I were here last week," Jess replied. "Achingly hip."

Kate grinned — she had a soft spot for uber-cool bars. She knew they overcharged for sub-standard drinks and yes, she knew the furnishings were sometimes not so comfortable, but look at the ladder on the wall, hung sideways and adorned with plants! Look at the array of bicycle parts hanging from the ceiling! Listen to the DJ pumping out pulsing beats that would never be played if these bars didn't exist!

Jess made it to the bar and ordered them both beers. She gestured with her hand for Kate to follow her, and they made it through the crowd to the back of the bar. Kate took in Jess's new grey shirt that she'd been inordinately proud of before coming out, sashaying up and down the hallway of their flat like a catwalk model.

"Told you it was less crowded at the back," Jess said.

"You did, oh wise one." Kate was just about to start talking about the weekend's football matches when she saw the smile on Jess's face increase, which meant Lucy had to be near — accompanied by her date. Kate straightened up, loosened her hips and turned her head.

She saw Lucy first, her dark hair artfully styled, her leathers exchanged for heels. Lucy was the only person Kate knew who flew around the city on a bike during the week, then traded them in for lady attire at the weekend.

"Hello, gorgeous," Lucy said, breaking Kate's thoughts. She brushed Kate's cheek with her lips, but Kate's gaze was already dancing over Lucy's shoulder, looking at the women she had in tow. Lucy spotted her stare and was quick to act.

"So this is Belinda." Lucy indicated the woman beside her, who Kate would guess to be Chinese.

Kate shook her hand enthusiastically, eyes darting left.

"And this is Belinda's friend, Tanya. Tanya, Belinda, this is Kate."

"Hi Kate, nice to meet you," Tanya said, offering her hand.

The bar noise dimmed as Kate assessed her catch for the evening. Slim and poised, Tanya had an unusually long neck, chiselled cheekbones and an easy confidence that radiated from her smile. It didn't hurt that she was attractive, too. Kate's shoulders relaxed. Maybe this date wouldn't be quite so bad as Kate had imagined — heck, they might even get on. Kate also noted a home counties accent — she'd lay bets Tanya was from Surrey. Perhaps she *did* own a horse.

"So have you been here before?" Tanya asked, getting right into Kate's personal space.

Kate shook her head, holding her ground even if she was slightly unnerved. "First time, but Jess and Lucy have."

Tanya nodded her head slowly. "Right. I haven't, but it seems cool." She paused. "Lucy tells me you work in magazines?"

Was it Kate's imagination, or did Tanya have her hand on Kate's hip? Kate tried to move backwards, but was hemmed in by the crowd.

"Yeah, I'm the art editor. Pays the bills." Kate smiled with her mouth, even though her mind was frowning. "How about you, what do you do?"

Tanya rubbed Kate's hip, her fingers firm on Kate's body.

Kate held her breath. She'd known the woman five minutes and she was already touching her. Tanya was either highly confident, used to getting her own way or a complete loon. Or possibly, a mix of all three.

"I'm a barrister." Tanya looked terribly pleased about that. She dropped her contact with Kate and winked. "So if you ever get into any trouble, you know who to call."

Kate was pretty sure Tanya would be the last person she'd call in a bind. She willed Jess to come to her rescue, but Jess was in animated conversation with Belinda. She glanced over to the bar, but Lucy was still waving a £20 note in the air.

"Barrister — quite impressive," Kate said. She was going to be open-minded about this and give Tanya another chance.

"Yeah, it tends to be. Opens up doors and women seem to like it." Tanya smiled broadly, before moving back into Kate's personal space. And there was the wink again. *Did she practise that in the mirror before she left the house?* Kate would not be surprised.

Kate assessed the facts. One socially inept barrister, one bottle of beer she was gulping at a rate of knots. This was going nowhere, but even Kate wasn't impolite enough to bolt after barely five minutes. She just had to hold on until Lucy or Jess saved her, which would be any minute now. *Surely.*

"What kind of magazine do you work for?"

Tanya's voice jolted Kate, and she let the words soak into her brain before answering. "Female Health & Fitness — health, wellbeing, that sort of thing."

"Lucky you." Tanya nudged Kate with her elbow.

"Lucky me?"

"You know." *Another wink.* "Looking at all those semi-naked women all day long. That's every lesbian's dream job, surely?"

Kate snorted. "I thought every lesbian's dream job was to be Angelina Jolie's PA."

"Good one," Tanya said, touching Kate's arm. She was clearly a lover of physical contact.

"Do you work out? You look like you do," Tanya asked. But before Kate could respond, Tanya was off again. "I do, but I try not to be a gym bore. You know what those people are like. But I do like to keep in shape." Tanya felt her own biceps and nodded. "A firm body is a firm mind."

"Right," Kate said. "I'm not really the gym sort, but I do like riding my bike — beats taking the tube hands-down. Keeps me fit and gives me a real feeling of freedom."

Tanya screwed up her face. "I think bike-riders have a death-wish. You wouldn't catch me cycling round this city with its clogged up roads, just waiting to be killed. It's hardly Amsterdam, is it?"

Kate knew this argument well, she'd heard it many times. "You've just got to be determined — give the drivers back the attitude they give you." She ran a hand over her leg. "Plus, it gives you thighs of steel."

"Really?" Tanya said, a sly smile taking over her face.

As soon as the words flew out of Kate's mouth, she knew they were a mistake. She stepped sideways, just too late as Tanya's hand snaked onto her thigh. Kate jumped as if she'd just sat on a lightning bolt.

"Excuse me a minute, I'm just nipping to the bar." On the way past Jess, Kate snagged her arm, apologising to Belinda.

Kate didn't stop till she made it to the bar, then turned to face Jess. "So do tell me," Kate said. "Where exactly did Lucy find Tanya?"

Jess smiled. "Pretty hot, isn't she? And that hair — I really want to touch her hair."

Kate narrowed her eyes.

Jess raised an eyebrow. "Not that hot?"

"Try a bit full of herself. She was stroking my hip within five minutes like we were bosom buddies. And she clearly has her own stash of cheesy one-liners. Can I go home now?"

Jess turned and sneaked a glance back to their group. "Are you sure?"

"Yes, I'm sure! The woman thinks she's God's gift."

The bartender arrived and Kate ordered two beers, with a spiced rum chaser.

"Shots already?" Jess said.

"Yes. I'm not going back over there without more alcohol in my system."

Kate grimaced as the bartender set their drinks down in front of them. She handed Jess her shot and held up her own. "And by the way, you owe me big time — and remind me never to come on another set-up with you again, okay?"

The pair downed their shots, then strode back to the group. Kate made Jess stand next to Tanya while she stood in between Lucy and Belinda, which certainly kept any wandering hands at bay. Kate learned that Belinda was in online marketing and had met Lucy at a networking evening.

"And how do you know Tanya?" Kate was intrigued.

"I worked on some stuff for her law courts. She's an absolute scream!" Belinda said. "I mean, a bit out there and socially free, but she totally blew my concept of what a barrister was out of the water. I mean, she *seriously* is not the norm." Belinda broke into a wide grin as they both looked over at Tanya.

"Nope, definitely not your average barrister," Kate agreed, before excusing herself to go to the loo.

A quick wee, finish her beer and she was out of here. Perhaps she could make it home in time for some trashy reality show on Channel 4? That sounded like her kind of Friday night. Besides, she didn't want to be too late tonight, as tomorrow she had the lure of a flower date with her newly installed favourite florist.

Kate was just washing her hands a few minutes later when the door opened and in walked Tanya. Kate saw her in the mirror and gave Tanya her best fake smile.

"So this is where you've been hiding!" Tanya said.

Kate braced herself, almost ready for Tanya to grab her round the waist from behind and nuzzle her neck. Instead, Tanya simply propped herself up against the row of sinks in the toilet and leaned back, extending her long neck and shaking her glossy hair. It was another well-rehearsed move.

"We missed you back in the bar." She fixed Kate with a steely gaze.

Kate was flummoxed. Tanya did not behave like anybody she'd ever met before. Like Belinda said, she was socially free. And this socially free one-woman tour de force was soon on the move, edging towards Kate. Even though she was a bit shorter, Tanya oozed presence and power, something Kate was all too aware of.

Kate shuffled sideways to the hand-drier and Tanya stopped just short of her.

"I know you might think I'm forward, but I like to get the ball rolling early, leave nothing in doubt. I'd love to go on somewhere later, just the two of us and get to know you better. What do you say?"

Kate could think of nothing to say and was short of breath. She exhaled, her eyes darting round the bathroom like a pinball — anywhere but Tanya. Where had she come from?

"Erm... I don't think that's going to work tonight."

Tanya's face dropped slightly, but then she recovered, instead fixing Kate with a concerned face. "You're not going, are you?"

Kate shook her head. "No, it's just I'm not up for a late one tonight — got things to do tomorrow — family things."

Tanya moved to within inches of her, face like a trained weapon, her mouth the glinting blade. "That's a shame — perhaps another time?"

Kate leaned to the side and hit her head against the wall. "Perhaps." She winced and held her head. "I should get back — the toilets are that way," Kate said, pointing. She slipped away before Tanya had time to react. Once back in the bar, Kate walked up to the group and peeled Jess away from Lucy.

Jess had the good grace to be concerned. "You okay?"

Kate gave Jess an 'I-told-you-so' look. "Well, if you call okay being cornered in the toilet by Tanya who 'wants to get to know me better', then yes, I'm brilliant." Kate's cheeks were aflame. "I'm almost impressed with her utter persistence. Notice I said *almost*."

Jess grimaced, then laughed. "Perhaps the George Foreman nickname wasn't so far off the mark."

"Perhaps not. If this was a boxing match, I'd fear for my life."

Jess let out a bark of laughter. "She's not *that* bad."

Kate raised an eyebrow. "She's not trying to chat you up though, is she?"

Kate managed to navigate the next half an hour without having a one-on-one with Tanya, although Tanya did keep catching her eye and attempting to make 'meaningful contact'.

Kate was having none of it.

When it looked like Tanya might be making a beeline for her once more, Kate checked her watch and made her excuses.

After 34 years in the game, she knew when to call it a night.

11

Saturday morning and Meg had been in the shop since 6.30am. Saturdays were always her busiest day, and today had been no exception. She'd had three weddings to sort, as well as the steady footfall of passing trade once the doors opened at 9am.

Now, at 11am, she could finally afford to take a break and enjoy the cup of coffee and croissant her brother had brought in for her when he came to pick up the last delivery 15 minutes ago. Meg and Jamie hadn't always loved each other growing up, but right at this second, Meg thought she loved him more than anybody else in the whole world. The coffee slipped down a treat and the almond croissant she'd just posted into her mouth was buttery heaven. Sometimes, food didn't need to be fancy, it just needed to be exactly what you wanted.

Meg surveyed the store — it would have to be a quick break. The place was in desperate need of a tidy-up after her mammoth schedule this morning. Plus, Kate was due to arrive in an hour and she wanted the shop — and herself — to look presentable.

Kate. Who Meg had definitely picked up gay vibes from, but then really, what did Meg know about gaydar? Nothing. She swore she was born with a faulty one. She quite often picked out women who she'd swear were gay, right up until the moment their husband and four children pitched up and she rolled her eyes at her inability to pick another lesbian. But if Meg were asked to lay a bet on Kate, she was fairly sure it was a bet she'd win. Or perhaps that was just wishful thinking on her part.

Half an hour later, things were as ship-shape as she was going to get them, and she'd just sold a dozen red roses to an endearingly nervous twenty-something whose hands had shaken while he was paying her. When Meg had asked him if the roses were for any particular occasion, he'd told her he was planning to propose to his girlfriend that night. One knee, diamond ring, the works. Meg had wished him luck and smiled as he left the shop. She worked in a world swathed in romance, yet her life appeared insulated from it.

She walked through to the back kitchen and grabbed a glass of water, picking up the order book she'd left out the back too. There was a stray red rose left over from one of her wedding orders too, so with hands full, she gripped it between her teeth and strode back into the shop.

And that was where she came across Kate, looking breathtakingly cool in a long blue T-shirt, skinny jeans and brogues, with sunglasses on top of her head. She looked like she'd just walked off an advert for a better you, and Kate was the poster girl.

Meanwhile, Meg was standing with a rose between her teeth.

Kate's face broke into a grin. "Is this how we were supposed to meet? With a red rose between our teeth? Only, I think you should have warned me. Plus, you're a florist, so I'd say you have an unfair advantage."

Meg quickly put down her order book and water, then removed the rose from her mouth, wiping across her mouth to check she had no greenery protruding. Her cheeks reddened as she looked back up to Kate, who was still smiling.

"Extra rose — from one of the wedding orders this morning," Meg explained. "I short-changed them, but don't go telling anyone."

"Florist Ruins Wedding Day, Bride In Tears'…" Kate said, writing the headline with her hand in the air in front of her. "I can just see the scandal now."

"You'd be surprised." Meg's heartbeat was slowing down. She might get over the embarrassment soon.

"Anyway, I know I'm early," Kate began, looking at her watch. "And clearly I caught you on the hop. But I just came in to see what coffee you wanted — I'll go and grab some from the Pret over the road." Kate let her eyes roam up and down Meg's body once, twice, before they settled on her face. "I'd say you're a latte kind of girl. Or perhaps a flat white. Am I close?"

Meg scratched her ear and tilted her head to one side. "Latte? *Way* too milky. I'm a black coffee. Straight up, no messing."

"I'll remember that." Kate didn't miss a beat. "Black coffee. Back in a minute." She strode out of the shop.

Meg covered her mouth with her hand. *Sweet baby Jesus.* But somehow she didn't think even he could help her out of this one. Okay, so Meg had thought Kate was easy on the eye the first time she'd seen her. But this morning? She seemed to have ratcheted up her charm offensive. Television teeth, just-so hair, stylist wardrobe and an assured air.

And her butt as she'd walked out of the shop…

Meg exhaled. Okay, this was her libido talking. She'd had no action in over 18 months. *Nada.* She'd pulled herself out of the game, shut off that part of her life because she didn't need the hassle.

Unless that hassle came wrapped in the guise of someone like Kate, apparently. Her body was not one to lie and her body was telling her, 'I want this woman!' Her body might be disappointed.

Meg put all other thoughts out of her mind and got out the funeral brochures. If that didn't douse her libido, nothing would. She set two chairs around the end of the counter and concentrated on being composed. She could do that, no problem.

A few minutes later, Kate swept back into the shop with coffees and two popcorn bars. She set the drinks on the table and handed a bar to Meg, who was smiling inanely and trying to keep her emotions under control. An image of pushing Kate onto the long counter-top and kissing her slow and hard flashed into Meg's mind and her cheeks coloured even more. And she hadn't actually thought that was physically possible.

"Have a seat," Meg said, indicating the chair next to her. "Now, option two, wasn't it?" Meg switched on her professional mode as she sat too, turning to Kate, who had icy cool, clear blue eyes. Did Meg's heart just skip a beat? Good grief, her thoughts were beginning to sound like cheesy pop songs. Meg quickly stared back down into the brochures and hoped Kate would have looked away by the time she flicked her head back up.

She had.

"Yeah — option two." Kate took a sip of her coffee.

"So a coffin spray..."

"Is it just me or is that weird?"

"Weird?"

Kate nodded. "Sounds like you're going to graffiti the coffin."

"I suppose it does." Meg grinned. "We can do that if you like?"

"Don't think my Uncle Mike was into modern art much." Kate smiled. "Is it bad to be laughing about this?"

Meg shook her head. "Not really — death's a part of life, and life is better with humour in it."

"Very true."

"So the usual flowers we go for are lilies and roses, with some chrysanthemums and berries for an autumnal feel. Mainly creams and whites, and perhaps some pale green — does that sound okay?"

Kate nodded. "Sounds perfect. And then my mum will stop moaning at me. Maybe."

Meg took the lid off her coffee and blew on it before taking a sip. "If you could ask my mum to do the same, that would be great."

* * *

They shared a conspiratorial smile about parental woes, and Kate held Meg's gaze for way longer than was necessary for a flower consultation. But Kate couldn't take her eyes off of Meg. No matter what she did, her vision was always drawn back, her eyes not satisfied until they'd soaked up a little bit more. She could stare at this view for hours.

Kate snapped out of her reverie as Meg opened her popcorn bar. "Thanks for the food, too — my brother brought me a croissant earlier but I'm still starving. It's been a long day already."

Kate opened her bar. "You put me to shame. I've only been up an hour and a half. And even then, I woke up with the crushing realisation I'm going to be single forever."

Oh, hello — where had that comment come from?

Meg sat back in her chair and moved the brochures to one side, giving Kate the once over. "Why's that then?" she asked. "I mean, I've only met you twice, but you seem presentable and sane. You should have a list of suitors at your door."

Kate snorted. "Maybe they got the wrong address." She paused. "It's just on my mind right now because I've been single for a while and oh my god, I'm really over-sharing again, aren't I? I'm not normally like this, honest. There's clearly something about this place that brings it out of me." Which was mildly disconcerting, to say the least.

Meg waved her hand, telling Kate it was fine. "I'm right there with you, so I get it."

Kate sat up. *Right there with you.* What did that mean?

That Meg was single? That she was gay? What did it mean?

Kate took another sip of her coffee. "I was set up last night with a friend of a friend." How should Kate tell the rest of the story? In gender-neutral pronoun form, or should she out herself straight away? She had to decide, there was no time to formulate a plan.

"So yeah, I was set up for drinks last night — I took my friend and they took theirs." Kate wasn't feeling brave enough yet. "And while my date was attractive and had a good job, they just weren't my type, you know?"

Kate's cheeks hissed red as she scanned Meg's face for any sign of reaction to the use of 'they' rather than 'he' or 'she'. She couldn't detect one. She ploughed on. "But the end result — another failed date." Kate ran her finger up and down the side of her cardboard cup.

"Sometimes I think I should just give up and stay in. Take up knitting. But then something like this happens to my uncle and it makes me think I need to start getting out and living a bit more. And clearly part of that remit is to get way too personal on the second meeting with my florist." Kate held up both palms and flashed Meg an apologetic smile. "I really am sorry for blurting out my life story to you. I'm going to drink some coffee now so my mouth can't talk anymore."

Kate sat back with her cup, staring at the table. So she'd come into the florist with the intention of ordering flowers while giving off an air of self-assurance. And within 15 minutes she'd blurted out she was single and doomed to a life of spinsterhood. *Genius*.

But when Kate looked back up at Meg, all she saw was warmth, along with a beautiful smile.

"So what exactly is your type?" Meg wasn't laughing at Kate, she seemed genuinely interested. "Just so I know what to look out for on your behalf." Meg shuffled some papers on the table that didn't need shuffling.

Kate smiled back shyly. "Warm, friendly, two eyes, nose, mouth."

"Fussy," Meg said.

Kate let out a bark of laughter. "So my sister would say. And my flatmate. And my boss."

"That's a lot of fussy." Meg sipped her coffee and contemplated. "You know what I think?"

Kate sucked on the inside of her cheek. "No, but I think you're about to tell me."

"I think you don't need to worry. You're good-looking, intelligent and have good taste in flowers. When it's meant to happen, it'll happen. So stop stressing. And you owe me £20 for this mini-counselling session." Meg let a grin spread across her face.

"Well worth it. I might make it a regular feature of my Saturday morning routine." Kate locked eyes with Meg and her stomach fell. Hang on, had Meg just called her good-looking?

"I wouldn't mind one bit."

Another wave of longing rumbled through Kate. Good grief, Meg was one hot florist.

"Can I use your loo?" Kate asked, getting up.

Meg showed her through to the back and Kate gratefully disappeared into the bathroom, turning the lock and closing her eyes. This meeting was a straight-up mixture of disaster and farce in equal measure. Why had she rambled on about her love life when she'd met this woman only once before? She needed to brush up her flirting skills. But being around Meg appeared to render Kate incapable of logical thought.

Kate flushed the toilet and ran the tap, eyeballing herself in the mirror. Okay, calm. She could do this. Go out, settle up and walk out of the shop without tripping over any flowers or her laces. *Piece of cake.*

When Kate walked back through, Meg was tidying up the brochures, looking gorgeous against the backdrop of flowers all around. Her hair was artfully messy, her Camper shoes adding the necessary dash of funk.

When she heard Kate, Meg looked up and flashed her an all-conquering smile.

Kate was rendered incapable once more.

She just managed to make it through payment, and then they stared at one another, in the manner of what Kate assumed happened in Hollywood films. Kate didn't want this to be there final meeting, but did Meg feel the same? There was definite hesitation in her words and movement.

"So, I hope the funeral goes well on Monday." Meg held Kate's gaze once more.

Kate simply gulped. "Will we see you there?" *Say we will.*

But Meg shook her head. "No — we deliver the flowers to the funeral home and they take it from there." She paused, looking pained. "So I guess this is goodbye."

Kate stood rooted to the spot. How could she be feeling like this after less than an hour in this woman's company? "I suppose so."

"But you know, if you need any more flowers, you know where I am," Meg said.

A lifeline. Kate was drowning, and Meg had just thrown her a rubber ring.

"I do. And I will." This was the upbeat ending Kate was after. She smiled broadly at Meg and held out her right hand. Meg's handshake was firm yet soft, and Kate imagined what it might be like to be caressed by those hands, held by those hands.

And then she bit her lip so hard, she tasted blood. "Until my next flower emergency, it was lovely to see you again."

Meg smiled. "You too. Take care."

Kate turned and walked towards the door.

"Oh, and Kate?"

Kate turned back, her shoes squeaking as she did.

"Thanks for the coffee."

12

Uncle Mike's funeral went off without a hitch and the flowers were beautiful — just like the woman who put them together. The funeral wake was at the local golf club, and Vicky was dressed in red, holding no truck with funeral traditions. As Vicky had decided at Dad's funeral, these occasions were a celebration of someone's life, not a day of compound misery. And true to her word, Vicky had held it together that day, while Mum and Kate had fallen to pieces.

"I thought Mum told us Mike had no mates?" Vicky raised an eyebrow as she surveyed the packed club.

"Apparently, Mum didn't know him very well," Kate replied.

Vicky's husband Jack put an arm around his wife's shoulder. Despite being clean-shaven, his five o'clock shadow was still pronounced. "If this is what no mates looks like, make sure you rent some for mine." Jack loosened his black tie and nodded his head towards the bar. "Drinks, ladies?"

Vicky stroked the side of his face and then headed south to pat his bum. "Two wines would be delightful, husband." She looked at Kate. "White wine okay?"

"Fine," Kate said.

While Jack brushed past her, his Ralph Lauren cologne coating her nostrils, Kate scanned the room and was again impressed with the turnout — there were at least 80 guests present. Laughter reverberated off the walls as sausage rolls were munched, tea poured and beers uncapped. Kate counted three different types of quiches dotted along the spread, along with cold meats, bread, cheese and four types of salad.

Kate nudged Vicky with her elbow. "I'm starving — you want some food?"

But Vicky was barely paying attention, resting her hand on Kate's arm as she studied something intently. Kate followed her line of vision and saw it honed on their mum, who was talking to a tall man in a fawn jacket. Mum was listening to him intently, every now and again smiling, laughing and throwing her head back, enthralled. Kate had watched enough rom-coms to know that hair swishing and elbow touching (their mum was doing that *right now*) were clear signs of flirtation.

"Is that what I think it is?" But even as she said it, Kate knew the answer. Plus, the flirting wasn't one-way — for every hair swish and head flick her mum pushed out, Mr Silver Fox was giving her back his best too, with arm rubs, lean-ins and shy smiles.

Vicky nodded, without taking her eyes off the scene. "I believe it is. I believe our mother is at a funeral and is brazenly flirting with that man." A few moments later, Vicky turned to face the Kate. "Do we know who the hell he is?"

Kate shook her head. "No idea."

Vicky frowned. "He might be some kind of money-sucking lothario, right now laying the groundwork to swindle Mum out of her house and life savings."

"Or he could just be a friend of Mike's, perhaps?"

Vicky ignored Kate. "She's still at it, look," she said. "Laughing, flirting and joking at her *only brother's funeral*." Vicky shook her head and sucked through her teeth. "Don't you dare do that at mine."

Kate raised both eyebrows at her sister. "Seriously? Miss 'funerals should be happy occasions rather than sad ones'? You're going to play that card?"

At that moment, Jack arrived back with two glasses of white wine and a pint of Guinness on a tray, which he placed on a nearby table. Handing out the wine to Kate and Vicky, he narrowed his eyes before taking a sip of his Guinness.

"I know that scowl," he said. "What did I miss? Who's in trouble?"

Vicky ignored him and continued to stare.

"Mum." Kate nodded towards her.

Jack followed Kate's gaze.

"She's been talking to that man for ages and *flirting* with him." Vicky spat the word 'flirting'.

Jack grinned. "Good for Maureen! Life in the old dog yet."

Vicky slugged him in the arm. "It's only been five years," she whined, before sticking out her bottom lip. "I want to know who he is." She looked at Jack. "Will you go and find out?" Her face resembled that of her four-year-old son, Luke.

Jack put his arm around his wife. "Sweetheart, your mum is allowed to talk to whoever she likes. And besides, he might be an old friend — you don't know everything about her."

"But I want to know who he is," Vicky mumbled.

"And you can ask her later. But for now, let's have a drink, get some food and socialise. Stop obsessing." Jack took another sip of his beer. "And if your mum is flirting, I say good for her."

"I do, too," Kate said.

Vicky pulled away from Jack and glared at them both. "You two are impossible. I'm going to talk to Aunty Viv." And with that, she flounced off, leaving Jack and Kate grinning at each other.

"Isn't she adorable when she's angry?" Jack said.

* * *

Later that day, back at their mum's house, Vicky and Kate were dividing up the flowers to give to various friends and family.

"You want this one?" Mum said, holding up a bunch of lilies to Vicky.

Kate could tell Vicky was still sulking, but Mum was either ignoring it or was oblivious. After a lifetime of Vicky's sulks, her mum had probably learned how to tune them out.

Vicky shrugged. "Sure, I'll take it. And I've got to go soon, the boys need picking up." Only she didn't move. Instead, Vicky sighed and turned to Maureen. "So, Mum."

Maureen turned to her daughter.

"That man you were talking to today — who was he, an old friend?" Vicky really tried to keep the edge out of her voice, but didn't quite manage it.

There was a definite twinkle in Maureen's eye as she replied. "Which man?" she asked. "I spoke to a lot of men today. Was it Uncle Derek?"

"I *know* what Uncle Derek looks like." Vicky paused. "No, the one I mean had silver hair, beige jacket — you were talking to him for quite a while." Vicky was staring at their mum and holding her breath.

Kate had to admit she was, too.

Maureen waved a hand through the air. "Oh, him. Yes, I had a lovely chat with him — Lawrence was his name. He's a colleague of Mike's, worked at the same place for years. Had so many lovely things to say about your uncle." Maureen stuttered. "He was a true gentleman." And then her cheeks coloured crimson and she was rumbled. "I'm actually seeing him again next week. He's asked me to go with him to see that exhibit at the Tate, and then dinner afterwards. Gave me his card and everything." Maureen looked down at her kitchen table then back up. "So I'm... I'm going. On a date. With Lawrence. What do you think?"

Maureen's face lit up as she told them the news and Kate couldn't help but reflect that happiness right back. She risked a sideways glance at Vicky, but couldn't quite make out her response. Kate walked around the table and embraced her mum in a tight hug, feeling her warmth and familiar smell as she did so.

"I think that's brilliant, Mum — I really do. Pulling at a funeral is quite some feat." Kate smiled as she stepped back.

Maureen reached up and kissed Kate on the cheek, brushing a thumb across the spot straight afterwards as she always did.

They both turned to Vicky, whose face was blank, her eyes giving nothing away.

"And what do you think?" Maureen asked finally, tired of waiting for a response.

Kate could see Vicky weighing up her options, but she wasn't sure which one her sister was going to plump for.

They didn't have to wait long.

"Terrific." Vicky's voice was flat, her words hollow. She whipped her head round, picked up the nearest bunch of flowers and walked round to kiss her mum, then Kate. "Gotta dash. Say bye to Viv and Derek for me."

And with that, Vicky and her red dress walked out of the kitchen. Moments later, Kate and her mum heard the front door slam.

Maureen gave an audible sigh.

Kate put an arm around her. "I wouldn't worry — Vicky's not good with change, she needs time to process." She squeezed her mum's shoulder and kissed the top of her head.

"I'm not marrying him," Maureen replied. "I'm just going on a date." She shook her head. "She's always been a drama queen, that one."

"True enough."

"And it wasn't what I expected to happen today. I mean, who gets a date at a funeral?" Maureen laughed as she said it. "But Mike's death has made me think that it might be nice to find someone to share things with. Is that so bad?"

Kate shook her head. "No, it's not bad at all."

13

Tuesday morning and Dawn met Kate at the coffee machine.

"Can you believe we drink this stuff every day? I dread to think what it's doing to our insides."

"Best not to think about it," Kate said.

"Can you follow me for a chat?" Dawn didn't wait for an answer. She was wearing a smart blue dress today with blue heels, looking every bit the publisher rather than an editor. She waited for Kate to come through the meeting room door, before shutting it and sitting down in one of the chairs.

"Have you got a job interview or something?" Kate said.

Dawn gave her a puzzled look.

"The dress, the make-up." Kate wafted her hand up and down in front of Dawn's body.

"Oh, that." Dawn rolled her eyes. "Had a breakfast meeting this morning, so I thought I'd wow them. You know what marketing people are like."

"And did it work?"

"I think it did. We've got some fabulous cover gifts all signed, so 'operation dress' was a success." Dawn sat back.

Kate gave her a high five. "Good work."

"Thanks." Dawn paused. "But anyway, that's not what I wanted to talk to you about."

Kate sat up in her chair.

"I spoke to Ben yesterday about putting the lesbian runners

on the cover. I explained the feeling in the team, that we'd got a potential group in mind and that things have moved on since they tried it last time, which they have."

"And?" Kate's interest was piqued.

"And he agreed. So long as we partner it with something strong to appeal to our core readers, too — and believe me, the cover gift I've just secured is just that. So it's all systems go. I'll tell Hannah to get in touch with her mate and you can both go and flirt with the runners. Aren't I lovely to you?" Dawn sat back, grinning some more.

Kate chuckled. "You are the loveliest boss in the world. Shall we go and tell the troops?"

They both got up. "After you," Dawn said, rolling her hand in a royal wave.

14

Wednesday morning. Hump day. Meg was slouched behind the counter in the florist's kneading her temples in a bid to stave off an impending headache. In truth, the headache had been lingering for around a year, but at least she had the shop as her refuge from her home life, her place to get some peace and boost her sanity levels.

Not that she'd had a whole lot of peace today. Outside, the September weather was doing its usual unseasonal thing, but the sun searing the pavements was doing wonders for walk-in trade. People always bought more flowers in the sunshine; it was just the way of the world.

"You want a cup of tea?" Meg's mum appeared from the back of the shop where she'd spent the morning poring over spreadsheets and ordering paper and ribbon. Olivia's cream blouse clung to her slender frame perfectly and she had a spring in her step, which fairly represented her attitude towards life: grab it, live it. And that attitude had only increased after her dicing with the grim reaper.

"Go on, then. Couple of those biscuits wouldn't go amiss either," Meg said, through a yawn. She was still at a loss as to quite how her mum qualified as a heart attack sufferer — she was slim, walked everywhere and did yoga twice a week. But a heart attack she'd had.

The doctors had informed them it was a hereditary heart defect, which had filled her and Jamie with no end of joy. Still, it was apparently controllable with some lifestyle changes and some clever white pills. Olivia took them grudgingly. Plus, she only worked two to three days a week now, and Meg was looking forward to the time when Olivia gave it up altogether — for Olivia's health and Meg's sanity. It wasn't that she didn't like working with her mum — but, having run the show in her mum's absence, allowing her back was proving more painful than Meg had imagined.

A few minutes later, Olivia walked back through carrying two mugs of tea. She put them down on the counter, then went to retrieve the biscuits.

"So any big plans for the weekend?" Olivia's eyelids were painted with smoky colours, her favourite for autumn. Whereas Meg's make-up routine had been stuck at the same level for a fair few years now, her mum was into seasonal colours and could often be seen flicking the pages of Cosmopolitan to get the latest beauty tips.

Meg shook her head. "Nothing yet. I'm doing a run on Saturday and seeing Nathan in the evening, but apart from that, no." She bit into her custard cream and it took her right back to her childhood. Summers in the back garden playing Swingball with her brother Jamie, and splashing about in the paddling pool. Funny how tastes and smells could evoke so much emotion — Meg could almost taste the summer air, even now.

"And how is wonder boy?"

Meg smiled at her mum's nickname for her best friend. "He's good, you know Nathan. Nothing fazes him, nothing changes. He wants to drag me out into town at the weekend, but I'm not sure I'm up for it." Meg paused. "But Nathan says we both need an injection of excitement in our lives, so he's determined."

Olivia took a sip of her tea. "I'm with Nathan on this one. And don't even get me started on the fact you're still living with Tanya The Terrible."

"Mum…"

"I've been very good at not saying anything lately, haven't I?"

Meg nodded her head slowly. She had to admit her mum had known when to shut up of late when it came to Tanya, which was very unlike her. Olivia was usually one to get her opinions heard. From being a daily record, she was now down to once a week with her rant, perhaps once a fortnight.

"But really, that is one situation you need to sort out. Put the house on the market and move on with your life. She's going to have to accept you're over eventually." Olivia's face hardened at the mention of her daughter's ex.

"Oh, she's accepted it alright, she's got plenty of new friends and admirers." Meg couldn't stop the bitterness creeping into her voice.

"You see!" Olivia said. "She's over it, she's happy as a lark living the life she wants — and what are you doing? Getting in late, avoiding her, shuffling up to your room and then spending all the hours here."

Meg stared at the floor, not daring to look up into her mother's eyes, because she knew what look would greet her. Concern. Pity. Disappointment. And they were the things she really couldn't bear. And it was at times like this Meg wished she worked in a normal workplace and didn't have to listen to her mother during the day. And of course, the worse thing about the whole sorry debacle was that her mum was 100 per cent correct.

"I know, you don't have to keep telling me." Meg's cheeks were burning now. "And stop getting so worked up — it's not good for your heart."

"Don't worry about my damn heart!" Olivia said.

"But I do worry." Meg twisted her hands together.

There was silence for a couple of moments.

Then Olivia's shoulders dropped and she sagged slightly. "Okay, you're allowed to worry about my heart, but I'm also allowed to worry about what you're doing with your life. So I'm saying this as your mother but also as your friend. Put the house on the market. Move in with me or Jamie or Nathan for a bit — whoever you like. But just get out of there, get your money and start again. It's time."

Meg looked up at her mum and knew she was right. She would. She would make the decision and move out. And whatever Tanya said, whatever obstacles she threw in her way, she would deal with them. A brief image of a new flat with brand new stainless steel appliances popped into Meg's head and she allowed herself a fleeting smile, closely followed by a puzzled look. Because leaning up against the cooker, with a smile on her face, was Kate.

Interesting.

15

"Any news, Hannah?" Dawn was standing with a biro poised between her thumb and index finger.

Hannah swivelled in her chair. "For?"

"Any of it — the interviews, the runners, the baby feature?"

Hannah nodded. "The Olympian is in…"

"Yes!" Dawn said, emphasising her delight with a fist pump.

"…and we're getting some traction with the baby stuff. We've got a few leads on people to chase up with it. And the Christmas feature is coming along really well. Pippa Gould has agreed to be featured — and you might want to sit down." Hannah gestured for Dawn to take the empty chair beside her.

Dawn did as she was told. "I've gone all tingly. Is it Carrie Branch?"

Hannah laughed. "Now I'm really going to disappoint you because, strangely enough, Carrie Branch is not chomping at the bit to share her fitness secrets with us."

"Shame, she'd be good."

Kate saved her current open spread and swung round into the conversation.

"No promises yet and nothing definite," Hannah said. "But I've been speaking to her PR today and we might be able to get some fitness tips and tricks from Princess Emily." Hannah sat back in her chair, a smile so big slapped across her face that Kate thought it might fall off.

"Princess Emily!?" Dawn's excitability levels were legendary at the best of times, but Kate thought she might be about to blow a gasket. Her mouth had dropped wide open and now she began spinning on her chair like a sugar-crazed five year old.

"I love it! Yoga confessions of a royal. Just think of the front-cover splash we can put on that one." Dawn finished spinning, had the good grace to look a bit dizzy and then snapped her fingers in front of Hannah. "But hang on — is she doing interviews again? She's been underground for a very long time."

"Perhaps that's her fitness routine — stay underground where there are no shops to buy chocolate?" Kate said.

Hannah laughed. "She hasn't done a lot of press recently, but she looks amazing and she attributes it all to her new regime — and she's happy to share it. Plus, she's got a new book coming out." The features editor sat back in her chair, a satisfied smile on her face.

"Good work, really good," Dawn told Hannah. "And the running club feature's all set?"

Hannah nodded again. "Yup. Me and Kate are going over there on Monday night. See if we can't snag a fit runner for our esteemed art editor." Hannah moved back in her chair, just out of Kate's immediate range.

"You two are incorrigible. We're going to turn up, do our work and go home. End of." Kate shot them both a stern look, which Dawn and Hannah ignored.

"Yeah, yeah, whatever." Dawn placed both hands on her trim thighs and pushed herself upright with a groan. "Great work, team! Now the next step of our plan will obviously be to put royalty next to a bunch of lesbians on the front cover, and then my work here is done."

* * *

Kate had laid out six pages of this month's magazine when her finger idly clicked onto the Fabulous Flowers website. It had been almost a week since she'd seen Meg and she couldn't quite get her image out of her head, no matter how hard she tried. Which admittedly hadn't been *very* hard. Kate's fingers drummed on the desk as the website eased onto her screen. She automatically clicked onto the About Us page and saw an image of Meg and her mum smiling back at her. Meg had her mum's eyes and mouth, and her mum was an extremely attractive woman.

Just laying eyes on Meg had Kate's stomach dropping — she had to visit the florist's again, it seemed ridiculous not to. Seize the day and all of that. Yes, she didn't know yet whether or not Meg was a lesbian, but she was never going to know unless she… What exactly? Stalked her? Pestered her? Went into the shop wearing her rainbow scarf and her 'This Is What A Lesbian Looks Like' T-shirt?

Slightly over the top. Perhaps just the scarf.

Sunflowers. Kate loved sunflowers, loved the way they drooped and then sprang to life as if they'd been playing you all along. So maybe she could show up with a sunflower urge and Meg would be none the wiser. She could even stop off and see her mum later, take her some of the sunflowers — she knew her mum would like that. Kate could ask how things were progressing with Lawrence, if they were at all. Talking of which, she really must speak to Vicky — her reaction to their mum's date had been bordering on absurd.

But back to Meg. Seemingly, Kate had made a decision. With no firm plans of her own this Friday night, Kate was going to go round to her mum's for dinner and stop in on the way to say hi to Meg. See how her week had been, like any normal friend would.

Out of the corner of her eye, she saw fingers clicking. Kate snapped out of her daze to see Henry trying to get her attention. He'd been to the barbers that morning and his beard was closely trimmed and softened to perfection. It was a magazine tradition now to stroke Henry's beard daily. Kate swore she'd never felt hair so soft.

"You coming to the pub later?" Henry asked.

"Pub?"

Henry rolled his eyes. "You know — big building, serves beer."

Kate shook her head. "Don't think so. Otherwise engaged."

Henry nodded towards his screen. "Buying flowers again?" He curled up one side of his mouth.

"Going to see my mum — can't turn up empty-handed, can I?" Kate nudged Henry gently on the arm. "Anyhow, stop being so nosey, Mr Beard."

"You wanna touch?" Henry leaned forward and jutted his chin towards Kate.

She stroked and let out a satisfied purr. "You could honestly sell that to insomniacs. Or maybe even market it as a pet substitute — for people who want the soothing aspects of our furry friends without the hassle of walking or feeding them. You'd make a killing."

Henry twirled in his seat, letting his head fall back as the seat spun around. "You might be onto something there."

* * *

Kate's breathing was heavy as she exited Finchley tube — she'd decided against her bike tonight to ensure she wasn't too sweaty on arrival. This kind of behaviour was completely out of character for her — she was used to being chased rather than being the chaser. She wasn't one to blow her own trumpet, but she was rarely short of female attention. So long as you didn't count the past year and a bit. Which Kate definitely didn't.

Her last girlfriend had seemed exactly what Kate was looking for: Caroline had been edgy, gorgeous and a nurse.

And nothing to do with the media industry, which Kate had warmed to. Kate had slept with too many media types in her time and she knew them back to front before they even opened their mouths.

With Caroline, it was different. She was a couple of years older, definitely wiser and not at all star-struck by what Kate did for a living. Plus, she was a nurse, which as everyone knew was a proper job. However, somewhere along the line, Caroline had deviated from their agreed path, met someone else and their relationship was brutally killed. Kate had been devastated and it'd taken this long to get over it. But now, here she was, ready to lay the curse of the past once and for all. With a woman who might not even be gay. A bold and somewhat dicey move.

Kate's feet moved along the cracked pavement, the September air still around her. It had that clammy feel to it, almost like you could squeeze it and shape it. The air was light on her skin, and at 5pm, it held the promise of a glittering Friday night to come.

However, having willingly travelled the distance between the tube and the estate agent next to Meg's shop, Kate panicked. What was she doing? What if Meg wasn't even there? What if her make-believe boyfriend Phil was coming in to sweep her off her feet with chocolates and flowers? Could florists be swept off their feet with flowers, even?

Kate swallowed hard. Her nerve was leaving her, running off down the street. She stopped, stuck to the pavement, now completely focused on the estate agent's window display. She could buy a nice flat up here if she sold hers. Perhaps even stretch to three bedrooms. But then she'd be living far too close to her mum and Kate liked a bit of distance between them; it stopped any unannounced popping in, which was a favourite pastime of Jess's mum.

Kate moved to the left of the estate agent's window and craned her neck to check if Meg was in the florist. She couldn't quite see. She shuffled a bit further left. Then she tried to poke her head around the window frame, but only succeeded in banging her nose. Damn it. Kate recoiled, cursing.

She looked at another flat she would never buy, before trying to see into the florist again, but she couldn't see past an enormous plant in the window. She stood on tip-toes — still nothing. Kate moved as far left as she dared without giving herself away, craned her neck again, but couldn't see anyone. She was straining every muscle in her body to see something — and then, jackpot! Meg walked in from the back of the shop looking radiant, carrying a white mug.

Kate beamed — it was an involuntary response. However, distracted by Meg's sudden appearance, Kate's body forgot it was in a precarious position. She was straining too far left, her weight too focused on one side. In an instant, her pulse quickened as gravity took over and she fell sideways, crashing down on the pavement with a resounding thud, only just managing to stick out her arm to break her fall. She lay on the ground, not quite believing what had just happened. Her left arm was throbbing, but it wasn't quite as bruised as her pride.

She heard the bell of the flower shop jangle and then Meg was standing over her, concern etched on her face.

Perfect. So much for Kate's cool, calm and collected entrance.

"Are you okay?" Meg crouched down and put her hand on Kate's shoulder. "What happened? I just looked up and saw you kinda falling in front of the window." She searched the pavement for an offending item. "Did you trip on something? Or faint?"

Kate's face was flushed with embarrassment and it was oozing down her neck, her chest, her entire body. She sat up, trying to get her breathing under control, then pushed herself up to a standing position. She winced and clutched her arm, but still managed a half-smile for Meg.

"I'm okay — my arm and hand hurt, but I'll live." Kate avoided meeting Meg's concerned gaze. She might as well have the word 'idiot' tattooed on her forehead.

"You're bleeding," Meg said.

Kate lifted her hand and sure enough, the skin on her palm was cut and grazed, blood pooling at the surface. Nausea rose in Kate's throat and she felt faint.

"Come into the shop and grab a seat — you must be in shock. The council only redid these pavements recently, too." Meg put an arm around Kate and guided her into the shop.

"Probably my fault, not picking up my feet," Kate said. Her grand plan of action was now out the window, but she already had Meg's arm around her, so she wasn't doing *too* bad. As Meg tightened her grip and led her to one of the shop's chairs, Kate's legs faltered. Did she just wobble? Embarrassingly, Meg felt it too and gripped her shoulder tighter — it hurt like hell, but Kate said nothing.

Meg sat her down and waited, crouching beside her. Was she worried Kate was about to fall sideways to the ground?

"I'm okay, really. You don't have to look so concerned." Kate tried to deflect her attention.

"I am worried, though — my cousin had this thing where she kept fainting for no reason. Do you think you fainted? Perhaps you should see a doctor." Meg sized Kate up, but didn't wait for an answer. "Wait there — I'll go and get the first aid kit."

Kate watched Meg go and hung her head. She didn't think this casual visit could have gone much worse, but at least Meg seemed worried about her, so she'd take that. The doctor thing was going a bit too far, but she wasn't about to tell her the truth.

Meg reappeared with some antiseptic wipes which she applied to Kate's hand, making her wince.

"Sorry, I know this must hurt," Meg said.

"S'fine," Kate lied.

When the wound was clean, Meg carefully applied a thick plaster over the top, pressing down gently.

Kate tried to steady her airflow as she breathed in Meg's musky perfume, studied the top of her head, then smiled into her eyes as Meg looked up into hers. Yep, she had it bad.

When Kate was all cleaned up, Meg rose to her feet and threw the debris in the bin.

"What were you doing round here, anyway? You don't work nearby, do you?"

Kate shook her head and flexed her injured hand. "No — I'm just going to see my mum, so thought I'd stop by to say hi and get some flowers for her." Kate smiled. "So then I thought, why not throw some amateur dramatics in for good measure?"

Just at that moment, a woman stepped out from the back of the shop, and that woman could only be Meg's mum. Slim, tall and with what Kate presumed was dyed golden blonde hair, she oozed sophistication and glamour. She was looking down, pulling her pink shirt out of the sleeves of her navy blazer as she spoke. She also had long, slender hands, just like her daughter.

"Did you say you were doing anything tonight? If you're not, come round to mine — better than hiding in your room like I know you will." Meg's mum looked up and was startled by Kate's presence. "Oh I'm sorry, I didn't realise we had a customer." She squinted at Kate. "Are you injured?"

Kate held up her hand. "Just fell over outside." She wiggled her fingers. "My hand hurts, but my pride is more bruised."

"This is Kate — we did the flowers for her uncle's funeral earlier in the week," Meg said. "She was just coming in to get some flowers for her mum, before she collapsed dramatically in front of the shop." A smile was playing on Meg's lips. "This is my mum, by the way," she told Kate.

Kate got up and shook Olivia's hand. Kate's knee hurt too, as did her hip. She glanced down, but her jeans were still intact.

"Nice to meet you," Kate said.

"You too," Olivia replied, giving Kate the once over. "Does your mum have any favourite flowers?" Olivia's eyes were the colour of Meg's.

Kate cleared her throat and sat back down. "She likes sunflowers. And lilies."

"Loads more to choose from — have a look around, see what you fancy." Meg's mum doubled back round the counter and gave Meg a kiss on the cheek.

"Lovely to meet you briefly, Kate, and I'm sure Meg can handle things from here." Olivia raised an eyebrow at her daughter. "And remember what I said about later — I'm in if you're free. Or else we'll go for a roast on Sunday. Invite Jamie, too. Okay?"

Meg nodded. "Okay."

Olivia smiled, her work here done, turned on her heel and left the shop, the door rattling in its frame.

Meg turned her gaze back to Kate. "And that's my mum." Meg rubbed her cheek nervously. "Are you sure you're okay?"

Kate shook her head. "I'm fine, honestly." But Kate was far from fine, not after what Meg's mum had just said. More specifically, one word she'd just said. *Jamie.* Was he the deal-breaker? Was he Meg's boyfriend? She hoped beyond hope he wasn't. In fact, she didn't think she'd ever wished anything quite so much.

Kate searched her brain for something to say other than "Who's Jamie?" It took her a moment.

"Your mum seems great — and very stylish, too." Kate got up and walked towards the counter, trying to ignore her heartbeat racing in her chest. Being this close to Meg did strange things to her.

"Yeah, she's pretty cool most of the time," Meg said. "Anyway, enough of my mum — let's focus on yours. Sunflowers, right?" Meg walked over to a chrome vase of sunflowers on the right of the shop.

Kate followed her. "She likes them and they're a classic, aren't they?" Kate had forgotten what piercing turquoise eyes Meg had as they stood next to each other. Kate flicked her gaze away from Meg to stop herself staring, but when she looked back, Meg was staring directly at her, her gaze lowering briefly to Kate's lips, back up to Kate's eyes and then down to the sunflowers.

It's safe to say that flowers were the furthest thing from Kate's mind. In fact, standing here with Meg was a painkiller for her hand too. All Kate could feel was Meg's proximity and presence. *Man, did she have presence.*

Meg nodded, but she seemed distracted. "An absolute classic," she said. "Nobody turns their nose up at sunflowers." Meg grabbed a handful from the vase and turned back towards the counter without looking at Kate. She plucked two sheets of pink tissue paper and placed the flowers neatly on top. Kate watched as Meg's strong, skilled fingers wrapped the flowers expertly. When she was done, they both looked up at each other and there was another, weighted pause.

"So you're not doing anything tonight?" Kate's mind was screaming the word 'Jamie!', but she seemed to have lost control of her mouth.

Meg shook her head. "Weddings tomorrow, so an early night for me. It's been a long week." She paused, glancing at Kate. "But it's great to see you again." Another pause. "How did the funeral go by the way? Were the flowers okay?"

Kate nodded briskly. "Went well — and the flowers were a hit. In fact, I still have some at home."

Their eyes locked again, but this time, neither looked away.

"I'm pleased," Meg said.

Kate swallowed as Meg walked slowly around the counter

and stood next to her again. She was far closer than she needed to be and Kate's body whooshed to life.

Meg reached over and picked up the sunflowers. "The flowers are on me — a gift to your mum and a thanks for your custom."

But the words swam past Kate's ears. She was now firmly in Megzone, where all rational thought flew out the window. As their gazes locked once more, Kate had never felt more sure. She wasn't misreading the signals, was she? She was sure the heat in her gaze was reflected back in Meg's eyes. Or maybe she was wrong — where Meg was concerned, Kate's circuits were shorting.

The word 'Jamie' was still a flashing neon sign in Kate's mind, but right in front of her was Meg's perfect face, Meg's rouged lips, Meg's searching gaze. Meg. The air around them was hot with intent as Kate made a decision to throw her cards in the air. Right now, she didn't care a jot if there was a Jamie — that particular fallout could wait for another day.

Kate's blood roared in her ears as she leaned forward to press her lips to Meg's. Kate closed her eyes, steadied her hand on the counter and then opened her eyes wide and let out a high-pitched scream as pain shot up her left side. Kate jumped up and clutched her injured hand, eyes scrunched up.

Meg's eyes shot open too at the piercing sound, and just at that moment, the florist bell rang.

Both Meg and Kate turned their heads as a woman walked through the door, giving the pair a puzzled look.

"You okay?" Meg whispered to Kate.

Kate shook her head and waved Meg away. "I'm fine — go see to your customer."

Meg gave Kate a pained look, before turning to greet the woman.

Kate was left leaning against the counter, her heartbeat still thudding in her chest, pain still catching in her throat as she cursed her luck. She heard the word 'wedding' fall from the woman's lips and knew instantly the moment had passed and that Meg was now back to work, a world away from kissing Kate. If that's what *had* been about to happen?

As the woman and Meg approached the counter, Kate picked up her sunflowers and slung her bag over her good shoulder. Kate couldn't quite read Meg's face as she tapped her on the shoulder.

"Sorry to interrupt, but I'm gonna shoot off."

Meg's eyebrows shot up. "Are you?"

Did Kate detect resignation on Meg's face?

"Thanks for these." Kate picked up the sunflowers and cradled them to her chest. "Mum's going to love them." There was another pregnant pause.

Meg shot Kate an apologetic look, the corners of her mouth moving up slowly. "It was lovely to see you — and I'm always here if you need more flowers."

Meg winced as she spoke, which only left Kate more confused. Would the kiss have been a mistake? Would Meg have kissed her back? Was Kate going to drive herself mad thinking about a bunch of 'what ifs' for the rest of the evening? Probably.

"If I do, you're my first port of call," Kate said. "I'll see you around."

Meg nodded slowly. "Hope your hand heals soon."

Kate gave Meg a final stare, one she hoped was loaded with intent or could just possibly have made her look like a gurning fool. But there was no time to check as Meg had now turned her attention back to her customer, leaving Kate to slope out of the florist feeling more pained than ever.

16

Two days later and Kate pulled on her black bomber jacket, ready to head up to north London and have Sunday lunch with her family. Maureen hated cooking roasts, so the pub was their destination.

When Kate arrived at the Walrus & Carpenter, the troops were already there. Her sister Vicky was looking far more relaxed than the last time she'd seen her, chatting with Mum at one end of the table, while Jack was at the other end, playing cards with Luke and Freddie. The pub was spacious and inviting, with sleek wood, smartly varnished floorboards, crisp curtains and stylishly upholstered seating. Flowers adorned every table and it was Sunday-lunchtime packed.

Kate swept in and hung her jacket on the back of the spare chair next to her mum.

Her oldest nephew, Luke, turned and studied her for a moment. "You look nice, Aunty Kate," he said.

Kate grinned. "Thanks, Luke — you look gorgeous, too."

Luke grinned right back.

Kate ruffled Freddie's hair. "Alright, Fred — how are your crisps?"

"Very tasty, thank you," Freddie told her, smacking his lips together.

Kate greeted everyone else, before propping up the bar and surveying the family scene. Vicky had been lucky meeting Jack at university and marrying him — he was one of the good guys. Similarly, her mum had been lucky to meet Dad in her late teens — they'd had a great life together until the accident. It was only Kate who couldn't seem to get coupled up and settle down. Hell, even Jess, the walking book of heartbreak, had met Lucy and managed not to fuck it up just yet. Kate would love to bring a girlfriend into this family portrait. She was sure Meg would fit right in, chatting with her family, playing with her nephews.

Meg. The only problem with that was Meg was very clearly *not* her girlfriend. Kate shook her head. Two days on and she was still kicking herself.

She was just getting her change from the bartender when a man walked over to their table. Kate recognised him, but couldn't quite place him. However, when the man turned around to face her, an amused smile played on Kate's lips.

Lawrence. She looked over at her mum, who suddenly looked a bit giddy — she'd set them up. Now Jack was standing, shaking Lawrence's hand, Vicky had a strained smile on her face, and now he was walking towards Kate.

"You must be Kate." He held out a spade-sized hand.

Kate shook it with gusto. "Guilty as charged," she replied. "And you must be Lawrence."

He nodded and Kate noted the healthy glow of his skin — he clearly took care of himself.

"Can I get you a drink?"

"Gin and tonic would be lovely, thanks," Lawrence said.

"I'll bring it over if you take this to Jack."

Lawrence dutifully took the pint of Guinness in one hand, a white wine for Maureen in the other and went back to the table.

Vicky's face was now in glare mode.

This was going to be interesting.

* * *

Two hours later and Lawrence had bid his farewells. Kate had hugged him warmly and was more than pleased with her mum's choice — he seemed like a perfect gentleman. Yes, it was strange seeing Mum with another man, but she could do with a bit companionship — just like Kate could.

Jack and Vicky dropped Mum at home while Kate cycled back to theirs. They were heading home for a debrief — this hadn't been verbally agreed but they all knew it was going to happen.

Jack hung up Kate's coat in their hallway as she followed Vicky through to their spacious kitchen. Vicky filled the kettle, went to flick its switch, then decided against it. Instead, she opened the fridge and grabbed a bottle of white wine, plucking two glasses from the cupboard and setting them down on the table.

"What if I'd wanted a cup of tea?" Kate scraped back her chair before sitting down.

Vicky raised her eyebrows. "I've known you your whole life, remember?"

Jack walked into the kitchen and instantly recoiled. "Whoa," he said. "White wine. Serious stuff. Am I invited?"

Vicky shook her head. "You're the childminder for the next hour while we talk about this gold-digger who's trying to steal mum's pension." She walked over and kissed her husband on the lips. "You can take a glass with you, though."

"Too kind." Jack grabbed himself a glass from the cupboard, filled it, then gave them both a wink. "Happy bitching, ladies. I'll be in the lounge with the football on, trying to convert my sons to a love of Arsenal if you need me."

Vicky sat down opposite Kate and shook her head. There were bags under her eyes and her mascara had smudged, giving her a slight shadow across one cheek. But her hair was radiant as it always was — Vicky was a stickler for hair health.

"So what are we going to do?" Vicky asked.

"Do?"

"Yes, do. He was a bit weird with us, didn't you think? Asking too many personal questions? What does it matter to him where I work and if I like watching MasterChef?"

If there was anyone acting weird in this scenario, Kate was pretty sure it wasn't Lawrence. "It's called conversation — I'm sure you've heard of it. It's hardly the crime of the century wanting to know if you watch a cookery show."

Vicky screwed up her face. "But it was *the way* he said it — like he wasn't really interested, he was just doing it to please Mum." Vicky paused. "I got a very fake vibe — I didn't warm to him."

Kate rubbed the back of her neck and leaned back in her white wooden dining chair, surveying the kitchen. The fridge door was covered in Luke and Freddie's artwork, party invites and shopping vouchers. The work surfaces hosted jauntily coloured accessories and the debris of family life. It was all immaculately clean, though — Jack was hot on kitchen cleanliness, which Vicky often said was the main reason she'd married him. That, and his ability to cook a Beef Wellington without a soggy bottom.

"I think you're just pissed off that mum has a new boyfriend," Kate said. "He seems like a lovely guy and he has his own kids too, so he knows family dynamics." She paused. "I'm pleased for her."

"But we don't know anything about him." Vicky took a swig of her wine, then her eyes lit up and she clicked her fingers together. "We should Google him, see if he's really who he says he is." She looked at Kate for confirmation, but her sister just gave her a blank stare.

"I'm right though, aren't I?" Vicky got up and plucked her iPad from the top of the microwave. "I mean, you hear about this sort of thing all the time. Lonely widow conned out of her life savings by some charmer. Wasn't that a storyline on Coronation Street a while back?"

Kate could see that Vicky was already on Google's homepage and was typing in Lawrence's name. However, she stopped after Lawrence.

"Do you remember his last name?"

"I forgot to ask him when we were chatting about football." Kate rolled her eyes. "You're over-thinking this. Yes, there are conmen, but they're normally on dating sites or something like that. They don't tend to crash funerals to pick up women."

Vicky pointed her index finger at Kate. "But that would be the perfect place to meet women of a certain age, you have to admit."

Kate put her head in her hands. "You're deluded. He's a nice bloke. Mum's happy and you're going to have to get used to it. And anyway, they're hardly married yet."

Vicky threw up her hands. "But if they sleep together — and who says they haven't already? — then surely it's only a matter of time. And then Mum might even change her name. We might have to call him Dad. And then he'll run off with her pension." She shuddered.

Kate tried to suppress her smile. "Look at it this way. Mum might have met someone to make her happy. To keep her company. To look after her in her old age. How about that?" She raised her glass. "I say three cheers for Lawrence. Come on, he watches MasterChef. Conmen don't watch that — they watch Top Gear."

Vicky couldn't help but laugh. "Don't come running to me when we have to take him to court and he's all over the front pages."

Kate sipped her wine. "I won't." She paused. "Anyway, I have something else to tell you."

Vicky was still typing.

"I said, I have something else to tell you," Kate repeated.

"I'm listening." Vicky didn't take her eyes from the screen.

"I nearly kissed the florist."

Vicky stopped typing and looked up. "What do you mean, nearly?" She clapped her hands together, all thoughts of Lawrence temporarily suspended.

"Well, we were kinda close, exchanging looks and there was chemistry, *I think*. But then a customer came in just at the crucial moment."

"So you didn't actually lock lips?"

Kate shook her head. "Nope."

"And what happened when the customer came in?"

Kate shrugged. "Meg served her."

"And what did you do?"

"I left — she was busy."

Vicky let out a howl of laughter. "Can you see what might have gone wrong there? You really need to work on your flirting tactics, little sis." Vicky leaned her chin in the palm of her right hand. "When was this?"

"Friday."

"And have you heard from her since?"

Kate shook her head.

"But you think she's a lesbian now, even though she's a florist?" There was a smirk in Vicky' voice as she asked.

"I don't know. I mean, I think there was definitely something there, but there was mention of a Jamie, and her mum invited him to lunch with them today."

Vicky waved her hand in the air. "Back up. Her mum was there too?"

Kate nodded. "At the beginning, then she left. But she invited Meg to Sunday lunch — and told her to bring Jamie." Kate sighed. "Do you think Jamie is her boyfriend?"

Vicky chuckled, before rubbing Kate's hand across the table. "He could be — or he could be her friend, her brother, her cousin — you don't know. But you know how you find out?"

Kate sat up. "No — how?"

"Go back to the florist and ask her out. If she says yes, she's gay. If she says 'I'm sorry, I'm happily married to Jamie', then you can move on. It's very simple really."

Kate took a minute before replying. "You're annoyingly logical, you know that, right?"

17

Meg had never much cared for Mondays and today had been no exception. Today had dragged due to the almost biblical rain that had poured down since 10am which had meant virtually zero passing trade. Such days were made for sorting paperwork. But Meg was on a go-slow, her concentration levels running low.

She was due to go to her running club after work, but she was finding it hard to gee herself up to attend. She'd joined the group at the insistence of her friend Adele and her mum. Adele had told her she should channel her running because she was good at it; her mum had told her she should go because she might meet someone. On arrival at the running club, however, all Meg had found were a bunch of sprightly, coupled-up lesbians who were far keener on running than on finding her a girlfriend.

Now, after the sluggish day she'd had, Meg was entertaining visions of going home, eating pizza and settling down with a boxset. Perhaps the first season of The L Word, which everyone knew was the best. She could throw herself into the love lives of Bette, Tina, Shane and Alice and then she wouldn't have to worry about her startling lack of one.

What's more, she kept running the scene from Friday night through her head. Had Kate been about to kiss her when that woman walked in? Meg might never know. She shook her head thinking about it. Maybe she should take the bull by the horns and call Kate — she did have her number, after all.

Perhaps the run *would* do her good — run off her sexual frustration. At this rate, she might be running for miles.

The phone rang, breaking her thoughts.

"Hello, Fabulous Flowers."

"Hello you." It was Adele.

"Hey — how are you?"

"Very well. I'm having a particularly good Monday and I'm just phoning to check you haven't been sitting in your shop, looking at the rain teeming down outside and thinking about bailing on tonight."

Meg studied her fingernails. "The thought never even crossed my mind."

"Sure it didn't." Adele paused. "We're meeting at seven, usual place, so make sure you're there. You got it, Harding?"

Meg smiled. "Yes, corporal. Since when did you go all army film on me?"

"Since I know how you get sad in the rain. But running will make you feel better, mark my words. Come running, get wet, feel invincible!"

Yep, Adele was certainly more into running than Meg. "Aye aye, captain. See you at seven."

* * *

The rain had mercifully stopped by the time Meg arrived at Dashing Dykes, and the usual cluster of around ten women in brightly coloured Lycra were chatting prior to their warm-up run. Meg looked for Adele, who had recently taken over the admin for the club after the group's original leader fell pregnant with triplets and had to stop running when her bump became too large.

Meg spotted Adele in conversation with two women she didn't recognise from the back. She doubted they were new members, though, due to them being dressed in jeans and Converse. People who joined running clubs tended to have serious running shoes.

Meg strolled over to Adele and was just about to say something when she recognised the woman Adele was talking to. Meg did a double-take. It couldn't be, could it? But Meg was pretty sure it was.

"Cutting it fine!" Adele told Meg as she ushered her into her circle before resting an arm on her shoulder. "I was just telling Kate and Hannah about the group — they're from Female Health & Fitness magazine. Did I tell you they were doing an article on us?"

Meg shook her head mutely. She was still staring at Kate, who had a bemused smile on her face. Kate still looked totally edible, but it was odd seeing her in these surroundings and Meg was suddenly aware she was dressed in far less clothing than usual, with no make-up at all. She saw Kate's eyes flick up and down her body, before returning to Adele.

"Didn't I? I was sure I did. Well anyway, Hannah's a mate of Laura." Adele pointed over at Laura who was warming up with her partner Debra.

Hannah smiled at Meg and offered a hand. "Hannah, good to meet you."

Meg shook the offered hand. "Meg." Then she paused, before smiling at Kate. "And you must be Kate," Meg said, playing it cool.

"Good to see you again." Kate shook Meg's hand warmly and held her gaze invitingly.

Meg resisted the urge to flip Kate into a Hollywood-style embrace and silver-screen kiss her in the evening gloom. "You too," she replied.

"You two know each other?" Hannah seemed inordinately excited by this turn of events. "This is good — perhaps we can focus on you for the article?" Hannah pointed her pen at Meg.

Meg's eyes widened. "Me?"

Adele nodded. "We were just talking about interviewing a couple of members, chatting about our experiences of the group. I was going to suggest you and me anyhow, but seeing as you know Kate already, it's perfect." Adele paused. "How do you know each other by the way, or shouldn't I ask?" An amused smirk played on her lips.

Meg's cheeks reddened.

Kate looked down at the ground.

Adele's mouth dropped open. "Oh, God," she began, jigging about on the balls of her feet. "Me and my big mouth. Pretend I never said anything."

"No, it's fine," Meg said. "Nothing like *that*. We just met recently — Kate ordered some flowers from me for a funeral she was organising."

Kate nodded. "And Meg was more than helpful. I mean, really. She went out of her way."

Meg could see Kate was blushing too, and that she was doing all she could to avoid her gaze.

Hannah's eyes widened. "You're the famous florist?"

The look Kate flashed Hannah told Meg this was something they'd revisit later.

"Famous?" Meg shot Kate a quizzical look. "I wasn't aware I was famous."

Kate's cheeks turned the colour of beetroot.

Adele looked over to the rest of the women, then back to Meg. "I'll just go and tell them to warm up. Back in a minute."

They watched Adele go, then a noise startled the three of them. It was Hannah's phone. She plucked it from her pocket, grinned at the screen, then looked shyly over at Kate.

"I gotta take this. It's Sophie — from the other night." She let out a little shriek, then scuttled off, phone pressed to her cheek.

Which left Meg and Kate, side by side.

"So, hello again," Kate began. She smiled broadly at Meg. "Hi."

"It really is good to see you."

"You too," Meg said. "How's your hand?"

Kate held it up. "Sore, but still there, thanks to your efforts." She smiled. "I might have lost it otherwise, it was touch and go."

"I can imagine."

"But meeting you here," Kate said. "It's also illuminating."

Meg stuck her tongue into the side of her cheek. "Really?"

Kate nodded. "Yup. I mean, you're... *Here*. At a lesbian running club. You do know it's a lesbian running club, right?"

"Lesbians?" Meg paused. "You know, I thought it was weird there were no men here." Then she raised an eyebrow at Kate.

Kate laughed nervously. "But in your shop on Friday... I mean, I thought I wasn't misreading the signals, I thought there was *something*. But then your mum told you to bring Jamie to lunch and it confused me. Who's Jamie? I'm guessing he's not your boyfriend?"

Meg shook her head, laughter lighting up her face. "No, Jamie is not my boyfriend — Jamie is my brother. Which is why my mum was suggesting bringing him." Meg smiled and shook her head at Kate. "You have worse gaydar than me — and why didn't you just ask me who Jamie was?" She paused. "I knew you were a lesbian right away."

Kate raised an eyebrow. "Really?"

"Yup."

"Am I that obvious?" Kate said.

"Kinda," Meg laughed, before quickly adding. "I'm joking! You're not. You've just... Got a lesbian air about you."

"A lesbian air?" Kate was laughing now. "And what exactly is a lesbian air?" she asked, putting the last two words in air quotes with her fingers.

Meg shrugged. "You know — a certain swagger, cool hair, hands in pockets." She paused, putting her mouth close to Kate's ear. "And also, when you nearly kissed me on Friday, that was a bit of a giveaway, too."

Kate closed her eyes and blushed.

Meg straightened up and took a step backwards, sizing Kate up. "Why did you run away after the customer came in? I thought you might have stuck around."

Kate took a moment to answer. "Because I thought there was a Jamie."

Meg gave her a slow smile. "Jamie will love this when I tell him."

"Don't make me sound like a loser before I've even met him."

Meg's mouth dropped open. "You're planning to meet him?"

Kate blushed fire engine red this time, before regaining some of her composure. "So to save any further misunderstandings, let's get this straight—"

"—So to speak."

Kate grinned. "So to speak. Jamie is your brother and not your boyfriend, correct?"

"Correct."

"And you're gay and single? I really hope that last part is true by the way."

Meg reflected Kate's grin and stepped towards her. When she answered, she was close enough that Kate could feel Meg's breath on her face. "Yes to all three. Not an only child, 100 per cent gay and no girlfriend."

"So if I went to kiss you now, as on Friday, you wouldn't back away?" Kate dropped her gaze to Meg's lips.

They were now inches apart, the gap aching to be closed. Meg could smell Kate's citrus-like perfume, and the gentle breeze tickled her skin.

"No backing away. I'd stay right here." Meg tilted her head. "Is this a hypothetical question?"

Kate opened her mouth to reply, but was cut off by Adele yelling over to Meg.

"You want to do the warm-up run, Meg? Just to get the blood flowing?"

Meg looked from Adele to Kate and back, then nodded. She took Kate's hand in hers as she breezed past her, kissing her on the cheek.

"Don't go anywhere. I'll be back and we'll continue this conversation where we left it. Okay?"

Kate smiled. "I'm staying right here. Now go get all sweaty."

* * *

Kate watched Meg run towards the group, then as one, they all jogged off together, Adele shouting instructions as they went. She was entertaining thoughts of all the various shots they could do when she made Meg her cover star next to Princess Emily, when Hannah nudged her.

When Kate turned, Hannah raised both eyebrows. "What are the chances?"

"Hmmm?"

"The famous florist, running into your life. It's like a film, isn't it?"

Kate crinkled her forehead. "If you say so. But less of the famous florist, thank you. I nearly killed you when you said that earlier."

Hannah smirked. "Oh shuddup. I saw the way she looked at you. I could have called her anything and you two wouldn't have noticed. Talk about *swoon*."

Kate ran her hand through her hair. "Yeah, yeah," she replied. "Let's get everyone's details when they get back, then get some group shots when Paul gets here before they get too sweaty." Kate jogged from foot to foot. "I don't really fancy hanging around too long."

Even in the half hour they'd been at the park, the air had grown damp and heavy. Kate shivered.

Hannah gave her a look. "Not even for your famous florist?"

Kate wagged an index finger at Hannah. "If that name sticks and becomes an office fixture, I know who to blame, don't I?"

Ten minutes later, the group returned, all ruddy of cheek and out of breath. In the time it had taken them to get in some running time, the photographer Paul had turned up with his kit and the group were now ready to shoot. Luckily, the rain was still holding off, so the realism was there for all to see. Of course, they had to wait for 15 minutes while the runners gathered round somebody's compact to check their hair and make-up, but within a relatively short time they were ready to roll.

Paul spoke to them about poses, group shots, and singles, and Kate got to work helping to set them up and getting the backgrounds right. But all the while, as shots were snapped and the other members posed and looked as athletic as they possibly could, Kate only saw one member smiling back at her. Meg. Gorgeous Meg. Gorgeous, single, gay Meg.

If the gods hadn't been smiling on her previously, it looked like her fortunes were about to take an upward turn.

* * *

Despite her protestations and the cold, Kate did stick around longer than she'd intended. Something meant she found it hard to leave. Or rather, *someone*.

By 9pm the group had disbanded, but Adele and Meg had hung back chatting to Hannah, and the photographer had just packed up and left. Eventually, Hannah shook hands with the running duo and announced she was leaving.

"You coming?" she asked Kate, even though she knew the answer.

"You go ahead, I'll see you in the morning," Kate replied.

Hannah bid them farewell with a cheeky grin. Within minutes, Adele had gone too and it was just Kate and Meg.

They walked through the park side by side in the Monday night twilight.

"So that was a nice surprise tonight." Kate's feet were crunching over twigs and gravel, while the air around them creaked and coughed.

"It was," Meg agreed, shivering.

"You cold?" Kate asked. "You want my jacket?"

Meg shook her head. "It's fine."

They walked on for a while longer in heated silence.

"But you're definitely still single? Just to confirm?" Kate turned her head to Meg as she asked.

Meg smiled. "Last time I checked."

Kate cleared her throat. "How's that even possible? Not that I'm complaining... But I mean, you're beautiful, you've got your own business and have all your own teeth, too."

Kate waited for Meg to respond, but she just smiled.

"They are your own teeth, right?"

Meg gave Kate a toothy grin. "Own teeth, all present and correct."

"So why then? It doesn't make sense to me."

Meg stopped walking, then started again. "You ask a lot of questions."

"Sorry — just curious."

"It's okay." Meg kicked a stone and it bounced along the path in front of them. "It's just how it is sometimes, isn't it? I was with someone for a long time — longer than I ever should have been. And I suppose, since then, I've been a bit wary. Wary of going out and dating. Wary of opening my heart up again to something that might not work out — you know how it is." She gave Kate a rueful smile.

"I know what you mean with the dating scene," Kate said. "Like that woman I told you I was set up with. I mean, good-looking, great job, but social skills of a gnat. She was just a bit too full-on." Kate made a face like she'd just eaten something unpleasant — remembering Tanya and *that* evening was not a pleasant task. However, Meg was as far away from that as could possibly be.

"I hate women like that," Meg said. "Pushy. Sounds a bit like my ex — she knew what she wanted and she wasn't going to let anything get in her way. She wasn't like that in the beginning, but by the end, she'd turned into someone I didn't recognise. So we split up and here I am, over a year later." Meg smiled shyly at Kate. "Putting myself back out there, maybe."

"Maybe?" Kate took Meg's hand and stroked her thumb up and down her smooth skin. They'd stopped walking now and were facing each other, subtly sizing each other up. "Can I change that to a definitely maybe?"

"Maybe," Meg said.

They stared at each other for a beat and Kate's breath hitched in her throat. Meg was putting herself back out there, just like she was. Meg was right in front of her and open to offers. Kate slid her gaze down Meg's face, from her eyes to her mouth. Time wound down as Kate made her decisive move.

The kiss, when it arrived two seconds later, was soft, gentle and electric. Neither Meg or Kate had time to assess its impact fully as they both sunk into it as one, bodies moving forward, lips locked, eyes closed. The world around Kate became more vibrant, brighter as she melted into the scene, every fibre of her being standing to attention, all the blood racing down her body until she assumed she was lit up for all to see, with the epicentre somewhere between her belt and her thighs. Kate's body was humming Meg's tune, and she knew just where she wanted this to go.

Kate could vaguely hear the traffic noise from outside the park, was minimally aware of a cyclist whizzing by. But mainly, she was aware of her body, of being anchored in this moment, her feet firmly on the ground even though her heart was soaring.

Moments later, when Meg's tongue pushed against Kate's parted lips, Kate's pulse threatened to expire. What if she fainted with desire? Seriously uncool, and Meg would really think she had a fainting issue. Instead, she went with the kiss, opening herself up, exploring with her tongue too, thrilling to the rush of excitement coursing through her veins. *She was so easy.*

When Kate slowly pulled back a few minutes later, everything else was a blur — her only focus was Meg.

Meg looked drunk with emotion, her pupils swollen, her eyes watching Kate's lips. Then she flicked her gaze back and let a slow, seductive smile creep onto her face. Meg leaned forward and pressed an open-mouthed, inviting kiss onto Kate's lips, slipping her tongue slowly in and out for added impact.

It worked its magic as Kate gasped and felt the after-effects all over her body.

Meg turned up one corner of her mouth in triumph. "Well," she began. "I think that was worth the wait." Meg then licked her lips, which did nothing to calm down Kate's libido, which was already hanging off the bannisters and singing Calypso songs; now it wanted to know if they were going to drop down on the ground and go at it right here, right now.

"We should have stopped talking and started doing that the moment I came into your shop," Kate said. "All this wasted time." She kissed Meg's lips once more.

"It wasn't wasted," Meg said, rubbing a hand up and down Kate's back. "It's called build-up. Foreplay." She kissed her again, before taking a small step back. "But I'm afraid that's where it stays today as I've got an early start tomorrow, so I have to get home."

Kate pouted in response. "Tease."

Meg grinned. "That's me." She pressed a final, definite kiss on Kate's lips, then stepped back and pulled on Kate's hand, dragging her back along the path and towards the gate. Kate stumbled after her, still bewitched.

When they arrived there, the hum of traffic noise got louder, and a blue Audi passed by with its stereo blaring at full volume. Both Meg and Kate flinched.

Meg cleared her throat. "Well, I guess this is where I get off. But maybe we can meet again soon?"

"I'd like that a lot," Kate replied.

Meg's smile lit up her face. "Great. I'll call you." She paused. "And it was really great bumping into you today. Made my night, in fact."

"Mine, too."

Meg kissed Kate lightly on the lips, stole a second kiss, and then pulled away abruptly. "If I don't stop now, it could get dangerous," she said. "I'll call you." Then she kissed Kate's hand and was gone.

Kate watched her go, feeling along her lips with the tips of her fingers. They were still burning.

18

"What's got into you today?" Olivia was staring at Meg as she fiddled unsuccessfully with her latest bouquet of flowers, trying to fulfil the morning orders before their new delivery driver Stan came back for the next batch. "Yesterday you were Mrs Morose, today you're Mrs Crackpot." Olivia put her hand to her chin. "You're not pregnant, are you?"

Meg gave her a look. "Yes Mum, I'm pregnant. That's the obvious conclusion to jump to for your lesbian daughter. I just slipped up, had sex with a magic lesbian and now I'm pregnant with twins. Hence the mood swings."

Olivia laughed and nudged her daughter with her hip. "Got you smiling at least." She paired some dahlia and astrantia with some hypericum berries — a classic seasonal birthday bouquet. "Is it Tanya?"

Meg said nothing, which just invited more questioning.

"It's Tanya, isn't it? With her size two brain and her size ten mouth? I wish you'd let me come round and sort it out. Have you put the house on the market yet?"

Olivia licked her finger, selected two sheets of wrapping paper from the pile and put the finishing touches to the bouquet, slicing some Sellotape from the roller on the counter to fix the wrapping securely. Then she consulted the order book again, and walked across the shop to begin the next bunch. She stopped at a bucket of freesias and looked over at Meg, who was deep in thought.

"Meg?"

Meg looked up startled. "Sorry, miles away." She smiled apologetically.

"I can tell. There I was going on about Tanya, and you said nothing. It's a first for you, not defending the situation. I almost think that might be progress. So has there been progress?" Olivia raised an eyebrow.

Meg chewed the end of a biro and shrugged, but Olivia saw the grin that had crept onto her face.

"You've put the house on the market *finally*?"

Meg shook her head. "No, but I will. Soon. You're right — it's time." Meg raised her eyes and looked her mum square in the eye.

Olivia's cheeks flushed. "It certainly is."

"Especially now," Meg whispered.

Olivia walked back to the counter and arranged some lilies on the cellophane sheet. *"Especially* now?"

This time when she looked at her daughter, Meg was grinning in a way that Olivia hadn't seen in quite some time. Not that she wasn't thrilled to see her daughter crack a genuine, honest-to-goodness smile that lit up her whole face. It was just she hadn't seen it for ages, so it took her by surprise.

"What's going on?"

Meg was still smiling. "Do you remember that woman who was in here a couple of weeks ago? I did the flowers for her uncle's funeral?"

Olivia squinted. "Maybe."

"Well, I liked her. And then last night, she came to our running club to do a feature on us. She works for a fitness magazine." Meg paused. "So now she knows I'm a lesbian."

"Platinum hair, the one that fell over?"

Meg nodded.

Olivia smiled. "Yes, I remember her." She wagged a finger

at Meg. "I also remember the look you were giving her. So are you going on a date?"

Meg glanced at her. "We haven't got that far yet. We only just established we were both gay and single last night. I was thinking coffee. I don't want to scare her off. What do you think?"

Olivia rubbed her daughter's back in slow, thoughtful strokes. "Coffee sounds perfect. It's casual, and then if you get on you can invite her for something more. Candlelit dinner. Wine. Romance." She shook her head. "Oh, you're making an old woman pine for what she hasn't had in quite a long time."

Meg nudged her mum with her elbow. "*Stop it*. You've been out on more dates than me in the past few years. So even a coffee is a step in the right direction."

"She might even buy it for you. And a cake."

Meg grinned. "She already did that the other day."

Olivia raised her eyebrows. "Then it's only a short step to romance and wine for you." She put her arm around her daughter and squeezed her tight. "I'm so pleased sweetheart. You've had a tough year. Let's hope — what's her name?"

"Kate."

"Let's hope Kate can bring a smile back to your sad face."

"Mum…"

Olivia laughed, and went to get more flowers to flesh out the bouquet she was making. "Some eucalyptus and palm with the lilies?" She held up the flowers to Meg.

Meg looked at the semi-done bouquet on the counter and nodded her head. "Should work well."

* * *

Later that day, when her mum had gone on an errand, Meg took her courage in her hands and sat on it before it could escape. It wasn't like her to make the first move, to go after what she wanted. However, although she loved her mum dearly, Meg didn't want to end up like her — alone.

She took Kate's business card from her counter draw and spun it between her thumb and index fingers. Art Editor — it sounded official, grand. Meg grabbed her phone before she could change her mind and plugged in the number.

"Hello?"

"Hi Kate — it's Meg."

There was a slight pause, then Kate cleared her throat. "Oh, hi." She sounded nervous. "How are you?"

"Good. You?"

"Very good. Particularly now you've called."

Meg laughed — she couldn't help it. "Smooth."

Meg heard movement, rustling down the phone. "Is this a bad time?"

"Nope, not at all. Just taking you into a meeting room for a bit of privacy."

Meg heard a door slam, then Kate's breathing evened out. "Okay?"

"Yep." Kate paused. "It was great to see you last night."

"You too." Meg had a flashback to the kiss, which caused a flush down her whole body. She cleared her throat. "And I was wondering if you wanted to do it again? But maybe this time without me in Lycra."

Kate chuckled. "I quite liked you in Lycra."

Meg laughed too. "We can talk about your fetishes another time," she said. "But for now, I was thinking a coffee after work. Either round here, or I could meet you halfway?"

"A coffee," Kate said. "Sure, I could do a coffee, and happy to come to you."

"Great." Meg smiled down the phone. "Tomorrow night — about sixish?"

"I can make it for 6.15."

Meg nodded and then realised she was on the phone. "Perfect. Pick me up at the shop?"

"It's a date," Kate said.

"This one certainly is," Meg replied. "See you tomorrow."

"I'll look forward to it."

Meg pressed the red button and stood smiling at her phone. This week was certainly looking up compared to the last one, the one before that and the one before that. In fact, her last date had been with someone she met online and she'd done coffee with her too. Only then, she'd pressed the eject button after ten minutes — right about the part where the woman told her she had six dogs. One dog, Meg could cope with. But six? No, thanks.

19

Wednesday night was a fine one when Kate left her work, a tall glass cruise ship of a building situated near the Thames, affording her views across the city direct from her desk. She was lucky — many of her friends in the media worked in basements and didn't see daylight for hours on end.

Kate's offices, on the other hand, had been built within the last five years and were still so new, they gleamed. Security staff patrolled the building making sure none of the staff scuffed the floor or dropped litter. Every glass door sparkled, the desks remained unscratched, carpets were still buoyant and chairs bouncy. Kate mounted her bike and rode out of the backstreet that the cycling bay backed onto, careful not to get oil on her freshly washed skinny jeans.

The London traffic was its usual busy self as she swung out onto the main road and raced along beside the cars, senses hyper-aware as she weaved around pedestrians, parked cars and the odd delivery van. Historic buildings rose up on either side of her and she breathed in the familiar scent of sunshine and exhaust fumes. She was glad she had her shades on, because the sun still held a fierce glare and she'd seen plenty of near-misses with cyclists and drivers.

Kate had been a proper London cyclist for a fair few years now. It was after being stranded on the top deck of a stationary bus one day that she had impulsively jumped off and gone into a bike shop. Before she knew what she was doing, she was having an in-depth chat with the woman behind the counter, and within half an hour she'd left with a serious-looking racer. Within two months it'd been stolen, but she'd caught the bug and bought another.

Kate's mum was not a fan of her bike-riding, considering it another risk her daughter simply didn't need to take. However, Kate loved the independence, speed and agility bike-riding afforded her in London traffic, and over the years she'd seen the ranks of fellow cyclists swell as people looked for other ways of commuting. She could get to most places quicker than by public transport and she could take her bike out to wider spaces at the weekends and really stretch her legs. Kate had never been a fan of running, but cycling suited her perfectly.

She negotiated the roundabout at the bottom of Waterloo Bridge, swung around the queue of cars and stood up in her pedals as the slight incline kicked in. She wiggled her shoulder to adjust the strap on her rucksack, then rode onto the bridge, up and over the Thames.

Waterloo Bridge was her favourite in London and now she was working nearby, she had the perfect excuse to cross it daily. She loved it in misty mornings and chilly winter evenings, but most of all, she loved it on days like today, with the sun sinking low in a clear sky and the river high, flowing to both sides.

On her left, the London Eye rotated slowly, and the South Bank heaved with tourists and artwork; while on the opposite bank stood Big Ben and the Houses Of Parliament, London's shimmering golden palaces. A glance right and she saw the top of the Oxo Tower, the rounded dome of St Paul's Cathedral and the city skyline piercing the evening sky. It was a view she never tired of. The vibrant scent of the river coated her nostrils as she passed over it — a mix of diluted ocean, oil and heat.

Half an hour later and Kate was nearing her destination. Jess had tried to stop her from cycling today, telling her she didn't really want to arrive for her coffee date sweaty. But Kate had overruled her, saying she'd rather arrive a bit hot and bothered from a bike ride than hot, bothered and irritated from public transport. Anyway, she wasn't daft; she was going to stop off at her mum's house first so she could dump her bike and freshen up.

Kate was executing her plan to the letter as she turned up at her family home around 5.45pm. She knew her mum wouldn't be home from work yet, so she let herself in with her key, lifted her bike through the hallway and kitchen, then into the utility room out the back. In the kitchen, she was surprised to see mugs on the side, the bread out of its bin and the butter standing on the counter, a knife balanced against it as if someone was about to whip up some toast at any second. Her mum must have been in a hurry to get to work this morning. Out of habit, Kate put the knife in the dishwasher and the butter back in the fridge. She checked her watch — she needed to get going.

She grabbed her bag, ducked into the downstairs bathroom and set about sorting her helmet hair and touching up her make-up. She was glad she'd managed a cool nine hours sleep the night before — her skin looked taut and fresh. However, when she emerged from the bathroom, she walked straight into her mum, clad only in her pink dressing gown.

Kate's heart nearly burst from her chest, while a small scream escaped her mouth.

Her mum took her by the shoulders, bundled her into the kitchen and shut the door.

Maureen looked flushed and a tiny bit cross. "What are you doing here?" Yep, definitely cross.

Kate, however, was still recovering. "What am I doing here? What are you doing here?"

"It's my house."

Her mum had a point. "But you're normally still at

work." Kate put both hands on her thighs as she bent over, her breathing heavy.

Maureen's face flushed.

"And why are you in your dressing gown?" Kate paused. "Are you sick? You should have called if you were sick, I could have brought some stuff round."

Her mum shook her head. "No, I'm not sick." She ran a hand through her hair. "Lawrence is here." She said it in a stage whisper.

Kate's eyes widened and her mouth fell open.

Her mum continued, avoiding meeting her gaze. "We went out for dinner last night and he came back." Maureen trailed off. "And you know, he's still here." She looked down at the floor, then at Kate, the hint of a triumphant grin playing at the corners of her mouth.

Kate began to laugh, shaking her head the whole time. "I think this might be the definition of awkward if you look it up in the dictionary." She grinned and nudged her mum with her elbow. *What was the etiquette in these situations?* It was all new to her.

Maureen smiled at her, but then tensed up. "But whatever you do, can you not tell Vicky just yet?" Maureen winced to back up her point. "You know what she's like. She's having a hard enough time with this already, I don't want to send her into a full-blown tizz by telling her we're sleeping together. I mean, we weren't sleeping together, but now it looks like we kind of are." And despite herself, Maureen smiled again.

"And while I'd love to stand around and chat about you and Lawrence sleeping together, I have to leave to get to a date of my own. A far more innocent coffee date this time." Kate squeezed her mum's forearm. "But don't worry, your secret's safe with me." Kate paused. "But you know she's going to find out."

Maureen pulled her dressing gown tighter around her. "I

know that, but I'd like to keep this private for at least a little while. You wouldn't know if you weren't here, so just keep it that way. Let Vicky get more used to the idea of us first."

Kate nodded. "Okay." She opened the door to the hallway and walked down it, her mum following close behind. "By the way, I'll be coming back to get my bike later, that alright?" Kate turned as she spoke.

Her mum nodded. "Fine." She pursed her lips. "He has to go home later anyway, so we'll probably just have some dinner and he'll head off."

Kate smiled, then leaned in to peck her mum on the cheek, taking her hand as she did. "You know, I'm really happy for you. And Vicky will come round — just give her time."

Maureen pulled her in for a hug. "I hope you're right."

As Kate stepped back from her mum's embrace, her mum's eyes had welled up. Kate checked her watch — 6.05pm — she really had to run. She squeezed her mum's hand and gave her a peck on the cheek. "Love you," she told her, before disappearing out of the front door and into the calm world outside.

Kate laughed as she walked up the drive, shaking her head at the recent turn of events. If she wanted something to take her mind off being too nervous about her date, then here it was. Her mum was sleeping with Lawrence.

* * *

Kate knocked on Fabulous Flowers' glass front door at 6.20pm. Meg was sitting at the counter, peering at her phone. She looked up and Kate's stomach did a flip. She was stunning.

"Sorry I'm late." Kate flexed her shoulders as Meg opened the door.

Meg gave a shrug. "S'fine. I was just catching up with the world of Facebook, so you saved me another five minutes of looking at other people's apparently fabulous lives." Meg treated Kate to a full-on grin. "Just let me grab my bag and we can go." Meg ran back into the florist, hit all the lights, grabbed her black tote bag and locked the door behind her. Then she turned to Kate. "And now, I'm all yours."

That sounded just about perfect.

They walked for five minutes down the High Street, sharing stories of their day, Kate leaving out the details of her most recent family transaction — that could wait, she reasoned. She'd asked Meg where they were headed and she'd been told it was one of Meg's favourite places, a little café down a side street. And when they walked in the door, Kate could see why Meg loved it — mismatched furniture, industrial lighting and low-slung couches mingled with delicious-looking cakes and bakes. Immediately, Kate felt at home.

"You see what I mean?" Meg asked as she sat on a cracked leather sofa pushed against the back wall. "I love it because it feels so unlike a chain. And the coffee is to die for." She wriggled around till she got comfortable, then smiled at Kate. "But they do beer or wine too if you'd prefer. It's my market day tomorrow, so I have to be up at 4am — hence the early coffee date rather than the normal food-and-wine date."

Kate narrowed her eyes. "Like in My Fair Lady? You're going down the flower market?"

Meg nodded. "My skirts are a little less flared, though. And I don't wear a bonnet anymore — too tight under the chin."

"So where is this flower market at 3.30am?" Kate sat forward, interest piqued. She couldn't imagine having to get up that early for a job — hitting her 9.30am start was hard enough.

"Covent Garden." Meg rubbed her cheek. "We try to only do it about once a week now, for all the key produce, sometimes twice. You might think it sounds glamorous, but try getting up tomorrow that early and tell me the same thing."

"But you love it?"

Meg beamed. "I do — I've never done anything else. I started working with Mum straight from school — she didn't want me to, but I wouldn't take no for an answer. School and me didn't really mix." Meg shrugged. "So I learned on the job — best way. Then she sent me to evening classes to learn about floristry — but that was okay, that was the kind of school I could handle."

Kate smiled. "So you get all your flowers from the market?"

Meg shook her head. "Just the run of the mill stuff. We have a specialist supplier who gets us all the particular things we need for weddings — that stuff has to be exact. If you go to the market, you can only have what's there at the time."

Kate nodded. "It's impressive, running your own business. I guess I've never really thought about where flowers come from — they just appear in the shops and then magically in my vase at home."

"And I bet you buy them from the supermarket, too." Meg sounded peeved, her brow furrowed.

Guilt coated Kate's features. "No, never! I always buy them from my cute local florist."

"Liar," Meg replied. "But our margins are way tighter these days, what with everyone now selling flowers. When I started, people came to us to buy their weekly flowers. Now, we survive far more on occasions — weddings, funerals, anniversaries and birthdays."

Kate held up one hand, palm out, and twisted to face Meg. "I promise, on my life, I will never buy flowers from a supermarket ever again."

Meg laughed, flashing Kate her glorious smile once again. "Don't make promises you can't keep. Don't worry, even my brother does it sometimes. It's inevitable." Meg paused, looking Kate directly in the eye. "But you used us for your funeral, and I'm more pleased you walked through the door than any other customer this year."

And just as quickly as Meg laid down a killer line, she put her hand on Kate's thigh and pushed herself upwards, wallet in hand. "Enough shop talk. What can I get you?"

Kate looked up at Meg and the first answer that arrived in her brain wasn't appropriate — so she went with answer number two. "Whatever you're having."

"Coffee — but you have yours white, correct?"

Kate nodded.

"Two secs," Meg said, before scooting to the counter.

Kate watched her go and couldn't stop a smile forming on her lips. Smart, sexy and accomplished in business — plus, she dressed well too. Today, Meg was wearing skinny denim jeans with a light blue top and navy jacket. She had a yellow scarf around her neck, but it was still small enough for Kate to see the gentle ebb of her collar bone and the smooth, tanned skin above.

Looking at it now, Kate wanted to get up, put her hands on Meg's slim hips and place gentle kisses all the way up her neck. But she thought that might be considered inappropriate, especially as this was a coffee date and Meg had to get up tomorrow. Maybe next time.

After a few minutes, Meg returned with two coffees. She placed them on the low wooden table in front of the sofa, then returned to the counter and came back with two chocolate tiffins.

"These are delicious." Meg took a bite and licked her lips.

Kate was transfixed.

"Honestly — Daisy who makes them should really branch out — she'd make a fortune. Whenever I work with Mum, she insists on buying two of these every time to see us through the afternoon coffee break."

"Sounds like the best kind of work environment."

"Until you realise it's with your mum." Meg rolled her eyes and sat forward to drink her coffee. She turned to say something to Kate, stopped, then sipped her drink again.

Kate took the lead. "So tell me a bit about your family."

Meg stuck her lip out before proceeding. "Not much to tell. You've met my mum — who approves by the way."

"Really?" Kate grinned.

"Really. And there's my brother Jamie who is, wait for it, also gay."

"The famous Jamie is gay too? Your mum must have the gayest genes ever."

"She does," Meg said, laughing. "I think for a while she was a bit perplexed by that, but now she's fine with it." Meg shrugged. "Just wants us to be happy, like all mums."

Kate smiled. "What about your dad?"

Sadness fell briefly on Meg's face, before she replaced it with a sigh. "My dad is a moot point. He left when we were little because he didn't like family life." Meg put the last bit of her sentence in air quotes. "Bit late to figure that out after having two kids, but hey. We were an army family till then, but then Mum came back to the UK and set up the florist with the money Dad gave her. I see him very occasionally; he's back here now too." She took a sip of her coffee. "I'm trying to forgive him and be Zen about it, and he seems to want a relationship with us now. But it's hard."

"I never understand how people can do that — up and leave their families. I look at my nephews now who are three and four and I'd hate to miss out on their lives — and I'm only their aunty, not their parent."

Meg nodded. "Plenty of people do, but I agree with you. I have friends with kids and it baffles me. Not the kids bit, but the leaving them bit."

"But you get on well with your mum?"

"As well as we can, working together. So actually, by that barometer, we get on amazingly." Meg laughed and flopped back on the sofa. "She's great — she had a lot to do, left on her own with me and Jamie, but she just got on with it — own business, bringing up two kids. Until she had a heart attack this year."

"A heart attack?"

Meg nodded. "Yup — out of the blue. I mean, she didn't drop down or anything, but she just felt really short of breath and she got pains in her jaw and her right arm. It was at the shop. We called an ambulance and they diagnosed a mild heart defect and gave her pills. But it was a shock to everyone."

"I bet — she doesn't look like a heart attack victim."

"That's what everyone says. But she's fine now, touch wood." Meg leaned forward and tapped the table. "Back to normal — well, as normal as she can be."

Kate shifted in her seat. "A relief for you." She paused. "And your mum never met anyone else after your dad left?"

Meg shook her head. "No, never. I think she was wary when we were kids and now, she's just used to being on her own. It'd be nice if she did, though."

"Be careful what you wish for."

There was a pause.

"So I was just thinking." Meg tucked a stray hair behind her ear. "About when we could go out on a proper date. With drinks, food, waiters, that sort of thing." She paused. "Actually, one of my best friends is having a party on Friday night if you're free and fancy that? It's his thirty-three-and-a-third birthday — don't ask." She sipped her coffee again and raised her eyes to Kate.

"Thirty three and a third?" Kate grinned. "That sounds like something to celebrate."

"I know it's not very romantic, but my friends are all lovely and I know you'll get on with them." Meg paused, chewing the inside of her cheek. "That is, if you're free."

Was Kate free? She was now. Even though she actually wasn't. But she only had work drinks lined up and frankly, none of her workmates had the same effect on her as Meg — so Meg won, hands down.

"I'm free," she smiled, her gaze dropping to Meg's lips,

imagining putting her own on them. "And I'd love to come." Kate held up her index finger. "But with one condition."

Meg was now also staring at Kate's lips and subtly moving towards them, but Kate's sentence brought her up short.

"Name it." Meg's eyes were back on the prize, waiting and watching for the words to fall from Kate's mouth.

"That the following week — whatever day suits you — we go out on a proper date, just the two of us, with dinner and drinks included. Deal?"

Kate held out her hand for Meg to shake, never taking her eyes from Meg's delicate features.

But instead of shaking her hand, Meg moved closer to Kate, stopping when she knew Kate could feel her breath on her face. "Deal." And with that said, Meg closed the final distance between them and kissed Kate lightly.

An electric charge shot through Kate and she closed her eyes to quell the dizziness.

Kate knew Meg felt it too as she jolted too.

When Kate opened her eyes again, Meg placed her lips against Kate's, locking them together.

Kate's whole body throbbed as sensation flowed through her veins — she had wondered if she'd just imagined how good their last kiss had been, but no, this one was just as good. If not better, because she was experiencing it right now.

What's more, Meg was taking charge, pressing her body into Kate on the sofa, winding an arm around her waist and pulling her closer. Kate had nowhere to hide, which suited her just fine.

She wilted as Meg slipped her tongue between her lips and all her remaining blood supply plummeted south. If Meg wanted to mount her right this moment, Kate wouldn't have many objections. Meg's hand drifted up to Kate's neck, caressing it as she kissed her, pulling Kate close.

After some time, Meg pulled back and held Kate's gaze.

Kate's mouth wasn't gaping, but it felt like it was. "I could get used to this," she said, her breathing still ragged.

Meg gave her another peck on the lips. "That makes two of us."

They held each other's gaze for a few beats, before turning their attention back to their coffee, still both grinning like idiots. All around them, nobody was batting an eyelid — clearly, kissing in this café was the done thing.

Then, half an hour later, they were on the move.

"So Friday night around 8ish? I'll text you the details tomorrow," Meg said.

"Sounds perfect." Kate followed Meg out the café door.

"You know your way back to the tube?"

Kate nodded. "I know this area like the back of my hand."

They both took a deep breath and exhaled at the same time. Then they both laughed.

"I'll see you Friday." Meg kissed Kate on the lips once more, squeezed her hand and walked off, turning to wave not once, but twice.

"Have fun with the flowers tomorrow," Kate shouted, before skipping to the tube like a giddy kipper.

20

The next day Kate woke flushed with positivity. After more than a year in the dating wilderness, life was finally looking up. If all went well with Meg this Friday, she wouldn't have to look at another dating app any time soon. She'd had a lifetime's worth of GSOH and supposedly fantastic careers, only to find that the woman in question had never actually moved out of her parents' house and still believed in Santa Claus. Even worse was the born-again Christian who didn't believe in sex before marriage — Kate had definitely preferred the woman who believed in Santa Claus.

But this morning, life was abuzz with possibility. She'd met a woman who made her swoon and whose kisses might halt a war, and she had her Uncle Mike to thank for it. Funny how in life he'd been less than useless, but his death had proved beneficial in more ways than one for both her and her mum.

She jumped out of bed, aware she had things to do today — cleaning, dental check-up and then the doctor for her dreaded smear test. Oh, the glamour. She'd taken the day off work as a personal day, and had promised to call in to see Jess for a late lunch at her work. If she was going to make that deadline, she'd have to get a move on.

* * *

Five hours later Kate walked into Porter's, the light and airy café Jess worked in. Jess had started working here when she moved back from Australia and everyone had raised their eyebrows. However, Jess had ignored them all — she loved the café, the owner Matt and everything about it. And even though Kate was firmly entrenched in publishing, she could see the appeal. Porter's was one of the best cafés around, serving great food at reasonable prices. What's more, it was a total suntrap, lit up by massive windows everywhere you looked and stylish Swedish-style furniture. The place was modern, sleek and inviting.

It was Matt who greeted Kate first today, with Jess nowhere to be seen. He gave Kate a wave from behind the counter where he was serving a customer, alongside his cousin Beth who also gave Kate a wide smile. Beth was the kind of woman you'd want on your side in a tug of war.

"She left you?" Kate asked, leaning against the counter.

"Making a phone call down the alley." Mark heated some milk before he finished the end of his sentence, his sandy hair falling into his eyes. "Should be back soon. The usual?"

"Yes, please." Kate indicated with her head. "I'll be over there." She perched on a stool by the window, leaning her elbows on the shallow ledge that stuck out, deep enough to fit your food and coffee. Sure enough, within a minute Jess appeared on the other side of the massive windows, giving Kate a wave and sticking her tongue out as she strolled past. Kate responded by sticking her tongue out too. Somehow, even though they weren't blood siblings, Kate and Jess often behaved like them.

Jess walked straight up to Kate, gave her a kiss on the cheek and plonked herself down on the stool beside her. She had her phone in her hand and was wearing a sticky grin.

"From the look on your face, I'm guessing that was Lucy." Kate smiled at her flatmate.

Jess gave her a full-beam smile in return. "You are correct, that was the gorgeous Lucy." Jess paused, waving her phone in the air. "And she's still in love with me!"

"No accounting for taste."

Jess ignored the comment and jumped up, her red Converse hitting the floor. "Shall I get us something to eat?"

Kate nodded. "Yes, please — I'll have whatever you're having."

Ten minutes later they were both chewing over an Asian salmon salad, coffees perched, days being discussed.

"How was your lovely smear test?" An amused grin played on Jess's face as she rolled her shoulders.

"It was a stellar experience, as usual." Kate pursed her lips. "I mean, just put on file I'm a lesbian. I don't care, and I've told them often enough. But no, every three years I go in there and they ask me if I'm having sex and what type of birth control I'm using. It's *so* annoying." Kate rolled her eyes to emphasise the point.

"So what kind of birth control did you say? Coil? Condoms?" Jess raised an eyebrow.

"I told the nurse my birth control was sleeping with women."

Jess choked on a bit of sliced carrot. "And what did she say?"

Kate began to laugh. "She looked me up and down, nodded her head and said 'Thought so'."

Jess let out a spiralling laugh that was soon out of her control. When she'd wiped away the tears rolling down her cheeks, she spoke again. "Rumbled by the nurse." She wiped away another tear, a wide grin still splitting her features. "And did you tell them you *were* having sex?"

"Well, kinda…" Kate paused. "I mean, if everything goes well this week, I *could well* be having sex."

"Tempting fate a bit, aren't you?"

Kate gave Jess a look. "No such thing. I'm an optimist and I have control of my own destiny. And my destiny is calling."

"Thank you, Mystic Meg."

"You're welcome."

The pair grinned at each other.

Jess let out another belated howl, leaned forward and took a lungful of air.

"Let me know whenever you're finished laughing at my misfortune," Kate said, but she was still smiling.

"It might be a minute." Jess coughed, ate some salmon, regained her composure and began again. "So you think you might be in? How did it go last night?" She took a sip of her coffee.

Kate jiggled her knee up and down on her stool. "It went well. And where were you last night when I came home to discuss it?"

"Having sex with my girlfriend," Jess said.

"Too much information."

"You asked."

"You're right, I did." Kate paused. "So, last night. We had coffee. We snogged in the café where we had coffee. And then she left because she had to get up at crazy o'clock this morning to buy flowers."

Jess cocked her head. "How romantic."

Kate smiled. "That's what I said. But she didn't agree — she reckons getting up at 4am is anything but. But I still stand by my original prognosis."

"So you snogged?"

Kate nodded.

"With tongues?"

Kate gave Jess a stern look. "Can we stop being 12-year-olds, please?"

Jess pouted. "And did you tell her the real story about you falling at her feet in front of her shop the other day?" Jess began to laugh again.

Kate pursed her lips. "That is to go no further," she whispered, shaking a finger at Jess. "I told you that in *confidence*."

"Oh come on, you'd laugh if it happened to me," Jess said. She put a hand on Kate's shoulder to emphasise her point. "It's hysterical. You have to tell her — she'd *love* it. I know I would. It's cute. Kind of."

Kate couldn't help but grin. "If she ever finds out, I know where it's come from."

"My lips are sealed," Jess replied, miming zipping up her lips. "Unless we go out and you feed me too much tequila." She paused and wriggled on her stool. "Anyway, back to you two kissing last night."

Kate refocused. "She's invited me to a party tomorrow night at her friend's house." She paused. "But is it weird that she's invited me for coffee, then to a house party, but not out on a proper one-on-one date? Or am I reading too much into it?"

"You're reading too much into it."

"I knew you'd say that." Now it was Kate's turn to pout. "So I'm going to a house party tomorrow. In Stoke Newington. I am going to have to dress uber-gay."

Jess snorted. "Er, hello — I think you might have that covered." Jess waved her hand up and down Kate's body. "You don't exactly scream 'I'm straight, find me a man!'." Jess paused. "And anyway, let's rewind. You're going out in Stoke Newington."

Kate nodded.

"Which isn't that far from us. So if things go well, we could have a florist back in our flat tomorrow night."

Kate smiled and held up her fingers — they were crossed. "You have to say special hopeful chants for the rest of the day, okay?"

"Why? I thought your destiny was in your own hands?" Jess smirked at her flatmate.

Kate shook her head. "I've no idea why I come in here for reassurance."

"Because you love me?"

Kate rolled her eyes.

Matt chose that moment to wander over and take their plates, giving Kate a kiss on the cheek now he was out from behind the counter. He had long been one of Kate's favourite men, being that he was always clearing up and was an excellent cook. If she was straight, she would have married Matt on the spot.

"Everything okay, ladies?" Matt stacked the plates expertly on his strong, hairy arm.

"Delicious as always," Kate replied.

"Can I interest you in some cake for dessert? We've got coffee & walnut or salted caramel."

Kate's ears pricked up. "Salted caramel? Did you make it?"

Matt nodded.

"In that case, I'll have an extra-large slice."

Matt bowed as he turned. "Coming right up," he said over his shoulder.

"I wish I had your boss, mine just offers me Kit Kats," Kate told Jess as they watched him go. Then her mouth fell open and she covered it with her hand.

"OMG — I forgot to tell you what else happened yesterday."

Alarm spread across Jess's features. "What?"

Kate went to say it, then started to laugh, convulsing till she was red in the face and doubled over on her stool.

"What? What is it?"

"So before I went to meet Meg, I dropped my bike off at Mum's." Kate was still trying to regain her poise. "I thought she'd still be at work, but she wasn't. She was there. Having sex with Lawrence." Kate began to hiccup as she said the final part.

"You're kidding." Jess's eyes were wide with surprise.

Kate shook her head, then hiccupped again.

"Well I never."

More hiccupping. "I know." Kate paused. "I was actually kinda proud, once I'd got over the embarrassment."

Jess smiled. "And how has Vicky taken the news?"

Kate shook her head. "She doesn't know yet, and Mum doesn't want her to. Vicky still thinks Lawrence is about to run off with Mum's money and leave us all destitute. If she knew this had happened, she'd think it was all part of his cunning plan."

"Has your mum got that much money to run off with?" Jess said.

"Exactly." Kate hiccupped.

Right at that moment, Matt appeared beside them, bearing two slices of cake and a glass of water for Kate.

She hiccupped, before gulping down the offered water in one. She then took a bite of Matt's cake, chewed and her eyes fluttered shut. When she reopened them, the world had changed, but only for the better.

"Have I told you lately that I love you?" she asked Matt.

He winked at her. "Join the queue. If I'd known the effect of salted caramel cake on women, I'd have started making it years ago."

21

Friday afternoon, and Meg was in her kitchen eating a banana and having a coffee. The sun was streaming in the large window which had made her and Tanya fall in love with this house in the first place. Meg still recalled the first time they'd sat at the kitchen table planning their future together — kids, cats, the lot. Much time and incident had passed since then, but the one thing that had remained constant was the window and the light it cast on their lives, filling the kitchen with hope, daily.

Sometimes, on afternoons like this in a quiet house with the kitchen tidy and Tanya-less, Meg could even dream that her ex wasn't here anymore, that she'd moved out and Meg had been able to afford to keep the house herself. In her dreams, Meg had the house and a cat. Tonight, she hoped she'd get the girl.

When she and Tanya did eventually go their separate ways, Meg was going to get a cat, for sure. They'd had one briefly, but then it had disappeared and Meg hadn't been able to bear the thought of getting another. Today though, there was an unfamiliar cautious optimism flooding her mood. Maybe she would eventually have someone to share the cat with.

She got up to put her banana skin in the tall, metallic bin when she heard the front door slam. Her body immediately tensed up. Whether she would get happy Tanya or sneering Tanya was something she was about to find out. Meg took a sip of her coffee and turned to face the door.

However, it wasn't Tanya whose face appeared at the kitchen doorway, but rather an attractive brunette with a strong, jutting chin and rolled-up jeans. If this was a burglar, Meg was fairly sure she was one of the most attractive she'd ever seen. Meg had watched enough Crimewatch in her time and the photos never once fitted this description — but then, perhaps hipster lesbian burglars were the new thing.

"Hi!" said the woman. Friendly. Almost flirty. She trailed her eyes up and down Meg's frame and, clearly pleased with what she saw, smiled more broadly and then winked at Meg. In Meg's kitchen, in Meg's house.

"Hi." Meg put down her coffee and placed a hand on her hip. Despite herself, the wink had impressed Meg. She reminded herself this could be a burglar and stood up straighter. "I'm Meg, I live here." She paused, sucking on her bottom lip. "You are?"

The woman clapped her hands and let out a peal of laughter. "Right — you don't know me! I forgot." She smiled at Meg, who still had an eyebrow raised. Then the woman stepped forward and held out a hand. "Chris — friend of Tanya. She's told me all about you."

Meg regarded Chris's hand, hovering in front of her.

"All good, of course," Chris continued.

Meg took Chris's hand and shook it warily. "So you're still going to have to fill in some blanks for me here." Meg paused. "Why do you have a key to my house when I have no idea who you are? I've met most of Tanya's friends over the years, but you are new to me."

"Right." Chris was nodding emphatically. "Yes, I'm a recent acquisition." Chris hesitated, went to say something, then seemed to change her mind at the last minute. "We met last weekend at a club. We're going out again tonight and I work not too far away, so Tanya gave me her key to save me going home." Chris swung around to show Meg the backpack on her shoulder. "Got my stuff for later."

Meg narrowed her eyes. *Great.* Tanya was giving out keys to their house to random strangers she'd just met. More things to add to the ever-growing list of Tanya issues.

Meg sighed. "Well, nice to meet you Chris." Meg walked towards the doorway and brushed her house guest. She caught a waft of cigarettes. "I'm going to get ready for my evening out." Meg hoped her clipped tone demonstrated to Chris that her intrusion on her evening was not wholly welcome.

"Going anywhere nice?"

Chris clearly wasn't very good at picking up signals.

"A friend's birthday." Meg was already wording the fight she was going to have with Tanya as soon as she got in. "Now, if you'll excuse me." Meg gave Chris a weak smile before wearily climbing the stairs and slamming her door. She wanted to scream, but she knew that wouldn't be a satisfactory course of action for anybody, and would only give the cheery Chris something to tell Tanya later.

Why hadn't she sorted this out earlier? Taken everyone's advice? Why was she such a coward when it came to this sort of thing? And to top it all, she'd left her coffee in the kitchen.

"For fuck's sake," Meg muttered, before flinging herself face first on the bed like a toddler having a tantrum. Her good mood of earlier had evaporated into thin air, replaced by familiar self-loathing.

* * *

However, ten minutes later, the self-loathing had turned into anger as Meg heard the front door slam again. Was this Tanya coming home? Or had she had a few keys cut, and their kitchen was now teeming with fresh lesbians?

Meg stood up and eyed herself in the mirror: bloodshot eyes, toothpaste on her T-shirt, dry skin. She needed a shower, fresh clothes, new make-up and a new attitude before she stepped out of the door to meet Kate. However, she was also aware that would only come if she dealt with the problem at hand. She absolutely did not need this headache today. However, she'd put it off far too long already. Meg rubbed her palms up and down her face, saw her mouth twitch in her reflection, then yanked open her door.

Taking the stairs two at a time, she heard voices in the kitchen. Meg strode in, to be met with the sight of Tanya and Chris in a clinch.

Meg was not to be put off. "Tanya, I need to speak to you."

At Meg's stern tone, Tanya dropped her hands from their current target and twisted around. She looked at Meg with surprise.

"Now. On our own." She looked directly at Chris. "If you don't mind." It was an order and Chris knew it.

"Not at all," Chris said, walking past Tanya and then Meg. "I'll be in the lounge."

Meg waited until Chris's footsteps had retreated, shut the kitchen door and scowled at Tanya.

"Is it your time of the month?" Tanya folded her arms across her chest.

"Don't be smart, I don't have time for it today."

Tanya backed into the kitchen table. Surprise registered on her face.

"There's a lot we need to sort out. *A lot.*" Meg's mouth twitched. "But first things first — when did you start giving out keys to strangers you've just met?"

Tanya's mouth fell open slightly. "Sorry?"

"Chris? She just walked into the house today when I was having my coffee. A complete stranger who you met this week. I mean, come on Tanya, even you must read the papers. London is full of nutters. You do not give them keys to your house a few days after meeting them."

In response, Tanya put her index finger to her lips. "She's only next door," she said in a heightened stage whisper.

"I don't care where she is, the point is, she came into our house without you! And I had no idea who she was. She could steal all our stuff, she could kill me…"

"She doesn't really look like a killer, now does she?"

"How the fuck should I know? And you don't either. You've shagged her what, once, twice, three times?"

"I don't like to brag." Tanya smirked. Actually smirked. "And anyway, she's not a stranger, she's my girlfriend."

Meg wanted to punch her. "For today at least." Meg exhaled. "I'll cut straight to the point, Romeo. Do not — I repeat, *do not* — give out keys to our house. It's bad enough you're traipsing half of lesbian London through here every other day. Do you understand me?" Meg's face had turned purple as she spoke, her eyes fixed on Tanya.

Tanya held up a hand in defence and nodded. "I hear you, I hear you," she repeated. "But it just made sense today. She works around here, we're going out tonight, so I gave her my key. And she's not a serial killer. Or a thief. I guarantee it."

Meg closed both her eyes. When she opened them again, Tanya was staring at her, trying to assess her. This outburst was unusual, as Meg normally opted out of conflict. Today, necessity had made her choose her nemesis.

"This situation," Meg continued, circling the kitchen with her hand, "is going to change. I'm putting the house on the market and we are going to move on with both of our lives." She gulped in air, her breathing now staggered as she ploughed on. "And in the meantime, you are not going to give out keys to any more strangers. Am I making myself clear?"

Tanya went to say something, stopped, then reassessed. "You have my word — no more giving out keys. Promise."

Meg let her shoulders drop and relaxed somewhat.

"But as for the other thing — now's not the right time to sell. Everyone's saying it. So we should just sit tight and wait for the market to pick up. It's the sensible thing to do in the long run."

Meg sat down at the dining table and slumped forward, putting her head in her hands. The voice that came out of her mouth this time wasn't as strong as it had been. The wind had been knocked out of her, but she was still going. "Sometimes, Tanya, economical sense isn't the key criteria involved. I'm miserable living here with you, I want to move on with my life. You've met someone new and so have I. It's time. Time to make the move." She looked Tanya direct in the eye as she spoke.

This time, her ex pulled the chair out opposite and sat down facing her, her lip jutting out slightly. "You've met someone?"

Meg nodded slowly. "Early days, but it's made me see this situation isn't healthy." Meg paused, searching Tanya's eyes for a flicker of understanding. "Surely you'd prefer to be in your own place, too?"

Now it was Tanya's turn to slump. "Course. But it's not the right time."

"It *is* the right time. It is *totally* the right time." Meg's gaze never wavered.

Tanya shook her head gently. "Selling now would be idiotic — we'll hardly make any money. The market's moving — this time next year we could be sitting on a goldmine."

"Or we could be in exactly the same situation!" Meg shook her head. "I'm not waiting anymore, T. I'm calling the estate agent first thing tomorrow, and then we're listing it. And then I'm getting a cat."

"A cat?" Tanya looked confused.

Meg nodded. "Yes, a cat. My own place and a cat. Should have done it months ago." She got up, scraping back her chair. "Now if you'll excuse me, I have a date to get ready for."

Meg enjoyed saying those words to her ex and noting the effect they had on her. Squirming would be the correct term. It seemed that Tanya could give it out, but she wasn't all that good at being on the receiving end.

She'd better get used to it, though, because Meg was ready to shake things up and get behind the controls of her life — whether Tanya liked it or not.

22

Kate couldn't spot Meg on a first glance around the room. Bad news. She'd been let in by a girl in a baseball jacket who'd been on her way out, so Kate had no clue who Meg's friend Nathan was or what he looked like. Considering it was his party, that put her at a slight disadvantage. Whoever he was, though, he was clearly paid well as this flat looked massive by London standards: Kate had already passed a roomy bathroom with a jacuzzi bath, double shower and bidet. Honestly, who had room for a bidet in London?

The lounge was low-lit and held six people. Two large couches stood against the walls, one leather, one fabric, and a coffee table had been pushed to one side to allow for dancing later. There was a bubble machine working overtime, and brightly coloured lights danced on one wall. The music was classic disco.

Kate stood clutching a blue carrier bag filled with bottles of beer, struck by a bout of shyness. To her right, two men with crew cuts were rolling cigarettes; in front of her, a Muscle Mary and a baby dyke were in avid conversation, not noticing her at all.

Kate was just deciding on her next course of action when a lanky man with a lazy swagger approached her from across the room. He was wearing thick-rimmed glasses that were far too big for his face and when he got closer, Kate saw they were just for show — there were no actual lenses in them. His floppy hair was thick, the colour of treacle.

"Hi." He held out his hand. "I'm Nathan, I live here." He paused. "If you're a gatecrasher, you look like a nice one."

"Kate," she said, shaking his hand. "Friend of Meg — she invited me. I'm just glad I'm at the right place as I couldn't see her."

Nathan's eyebrows shot up. "Aha. The famous Kate!" He bowed and swept an arm through the air. "Welcome." He stood upright. "And it's hair, by the way."

"Sorry?"

Nathan twiddled a finger above his head. "Meg. She's having a hair malfunction." He put an arm on Kate's elbow and guided her through the centre of the room, ending their short journey at the kitchen. "Help yourself to a drink and I'll go see if I can grab her."

Nathan disappeared out of the lounge and Kate walked into the heaving kitchen. Music throbbed in her ears, glasses clinked and the counter-top in front of her was covered in a mysterious sticky liquid. So far, so house party.

Kate squeezed a couple of bottles of her beer into the fridge and located an opener. Then, beer in hand, she ventured back out into the main room where Kylie was now being pumped out at top volume, and a throng of gay men were bumping, grinding and dancing as one.

"Kylie fan?"

Kate turned to be greeted by a wonky smile attached to a stunningly attractive man, all twinkly blue eyes and a light sheen of sweat coating his brow.

"Who isn't?" she replied.

It seemed to be the right answer as the man lifted his beer bottle and clinked it against hers. "Dean," he smiled. "You're a friend of Nathan's, I presume?"

"Not really," Kate replied. "Friend of Meg. Although I only met her recently, so not even sure friend is an appropriate term. Hopeful contender, maybe?"

Dean gave Kate a knowing grin. "I think you might stand a chance, delightful Kate. You've got my blessing, at least."

Just at that moment, Dean grinned over Kate's shoulder which made her turn — and there was Meg walking into the lounge, her face full of promise, her hair like polished sunshine. She was just as good as Kate recalled, if not better.

"You came." Meg kissed Kate's cheek — it glowed hot straight away. "It's good to see you."

"Of course I came." Kate blushed as she said it and was glad of the low-lighting. "I wouldn't have missed it for the world."

"Lucky me." Meg looked down. "You got a drink?"

Kate nodded. "And a new friend in Dean."

Dean stepped between them and gave Meg a hug.

"Now don't move, and don't believe a word he says while I get a drink, okay?" Meg fixed Kate with her piercing gaze.

Kate swallowed hard. "Staying right here," she said.

Meg squeezed Kate's hand as she brushed past her and Kate's nostrils filled with her musky perfume. *Just when had Meg turned into a femme fatale?* Out of her running gear and out of the florist, she could well have been mistaken for a film star — and tonight she was Kate's date. This was going *very* well.

* * *

Two hours later, they'd had cake and sung happy birthday to the non-birthday boy. Kate had been by Meg's side for most of it, her proximity making every one of Meg's nerve endings stand to attention. She watched Kate now, approaching her from across the room, a secret smile playing on her lips. She was carrying a bottle of beer for herself and a white wine for Meg.

"Thanks." Meg leaned in so her breath tickled Kate's ear. "I was thinking, maybe we could stay a little longer, but then perhaps go somewhere a little less busy. Just you and me?"

Kate gulped. "I would love that."

Meg clinked her glass to Kate's bottle. "Good." Meg's gaze

didn't falter from Kate's, her eyes drinking her in. She put her wine down as her heart clattered in her chest and their eyes locked. Meg readied herself for the impact of Kate's lips, her warm kiss.

Only it never came. Instead, there was a shriek from nearby and before she knew it, Nathan was in between them, his arms around Meg, using her as a human shield.

"Make him stop, Meg!" he screamed.

Kate looked up and saw Kylie fan Dean dashing towards them with a can of squirty cream, quite a bit of it already adorning his head and shoulders.

"Get out here, Davis, you pussy!" Dean rounded Meg, who was staggering backwards and turning, as Nathan pulled and twisted her body to where he wanted it to be.

Kate stepped to the side, not a fan of squirty cream.

"Get off me, Nathan!" Meg was trying to break free, but Nathan wasn't easy to shake.

Seeing an in, Dean dodged into the space that Kate had vacated, shook and squirted. It hit Meg on her side.

"Hey!" Meg tried to move out of the way but Nathan had her held firm.

"You little shit, Davis," Dean shouted. He jigged some more and took aim.

Seeing what was coming, Meg's eyes widened. "Don't you dare…"

But Dean had already begun to squirt again, aiming at Nathan who had just stood up beside Meg. Nathan let go and made a dash for it, Meg unfortunately moved slightly to her left into the space Nathan had just vacated, and the cream hit Meg square in the face, also ending up in her open mouth.

Seeing Nathan escape, Dean gave chase, pausing briefly to shout, "Sorry Meg!"

Meg didn't believe it for a second. She stood, tongue licking the cream from her face and scooping it off her shirt.

Clare Lydon

"Can you believe this? I'm going to kill them both when I get my hands on them." She looked around the room, touching her face and looking at her hand, now covered in cream too.

Kate checked the lounge doorway. "They've run out the front door — trying to cream each other." She stepped forward, taking Meg's hand and tugging her across the room. "Come on, let's get you cleaned up." Kate led Meg down the hall and into the plush bathroom. She closed the door and handed Meg a spare toilet roll from the stack by the toilet.

Meg took them gratefully and began wiping the cream from her face, eyeing herself in the over-the-sink mirror as she did.

Kate stood behind her, grinning every time Meg caught her eye.

"You can stop laughing so much anytime you want," Meg said, even though she was laughing too. "Honestly, do men ever grow up?" Meg shook her head. "I suppose I should be glad it's squirty cream and not actual cream or anything worse. At least this kinda disintegrates." She wiped the last evidence from her face and licked her lips again. "And it leaves me tasting sweet."

Kate stepped forward so she was at Meg's side and pointed at her cheek. "You missed a bit."

"Did I?" Meg looked back in the mirror, frowned, then turned back to Kate. "I didn't."

Kate nodded. "You did." And then she leaned forward and gave Meg a light peck on the cheek. "And you missed a bit here too." Kate brushed Meg's lips lightly with her own, then leaned back, assessing. "Nope, still some there."

This time, her kiss lasted a couple of seconds, before Kate stood up straight, smiling.

"I don't think you're telling the whole truth." Meg smiled and put a finger to Kate's lips. "I think you used the cream as a trick to kiss me. Am I right?"

Kate took Meg's finger gently into her mouth and circled it gently with her tongue. "You'll never make it stick in court."

Meg's body vibrated, right down to the soles of her feet. Eventually, she withdrew her finger and pressed her lips lightly to Kate's, before running her tongue along Kate's bottom lip. She stood back to admire her work, as Kate opened her eyes slowly.

Neither of them drew a breath for a moment.

"Now unless you fancy getting down in the jacuzzi bath, I suggest we finish our drinks and make a run for it. I've done my duty for Nathan's party — and it's not even his bloody birthday. Now I think it's time for us to get to know each other better, don't you?"

Kate let a slow smile wend across her face. "A drink at a pub then?" She was talking to Meg's back as she followed her into the bedroom to get her jacket.

"I was hoping not — yours is closer, isn't it?"

Kate nodded, surprised. "Yep — we can have a drink there instead."

Meg took Kate's hand in response and gave it a squeeze. "Sounds perfect."

And it was. For the first time in a very long time, Meg was telling the truth when she said she wanted to go back to a woman's house — and that was something that, in her darkest hours, she had often questioned would ever happen again. Yet here she was.

Meg gathered her wits as they got in the lift to take them down to street level. Her last great love affair had dismantled her, stripped her bare and left her in pieces. She was still trying to piece herself back together fully and she knew it would never happen until she and Tanya sold the house and moved on.

Kate squeezed her hand. "You okay?"

Meg turned her head and nodded. "Yeah, I'm great."

They were out of Nathan's building now and had come to a main road where the traffic was hurtling by at speed.

Meg zipped up her jacket and smiled at Kate as they walked towards the bus stop. She wasn't about to tell her what she'd been thinking about — Tanya was not high on her list of priorities right now. Meg forced herself back into the present.

"Because if this isn't what you want... You seem a bit preoccupied." Kate frowned as she spoke.

Meg saw the doubt in her expression and squeezed her hand again. "I promise you, the only thing I'm preoccupied with is getting to yours and kissing you into oblivion."

A slow grin appeared on Kate's face. "Oblivion, you say?" Meg nodded.

"In that case, let's get a cab, it's quicker."

Before Meg could argue, Kate's hand was up in the air and the yellow light on top of the cab coming towards them was extinguished. The driver lowered his window and looked at the pair expectantly.

Kate opened the back door, shouting "Old Street, quick as you can please!"

They slammed into the back seat at the same time, hands entwined, gazes fixed.

It was going to be a long journey, however he took it.

23

"When you said you lived central, you weren't joking." Meg sounded impressed as she climbed out of the cab and onto the cobbled street. The cab's engine was still running, so a claggy diesel noise cluttered the night air. "You actually live a *stone's throw* from the tube." Meg frowned. "It makes me feel like I really do live in the burbs."

Kate climbed out of the back of the cab and paid the driver.

"Which one do you live at?" Meg looked up and down the street as the cab drove off.

"This one right here." Kate indicated the door right in front of them with the number 73 emblazoned on it in chrome fixtures.

Meg looked sideways at Kate, who was digging in her pocket for her key. "Are you really rich and you haven't told me yet? I didn't think publishing paid well enough to afford a flat here."

Kate laughed nervously — she hated this conversation. "Nah — I had some inheritance and also a chunk of savings. Right place, right time." Kate shrugged as she opened the door and walked around her bike, before stepping aside to let Meg up in front of her. "After you."

Kate was pleased that Meg seemed satisfied with her answer and wasn't pushing for more information. Sometimes in the past, she'd pretended she rented her flat just because it seemed easier and put her on a par with all the other 30-somethings in the city: struggling to get by, paying money to greedy landlords.

But the fact was, Kate had always been a good worker and an even better saver, and she'd already had the deposit for her first flat saved up when her dad died unexpectedly, and then that deposit got a bit larger. Kate had seen the flat and thought, why not? It needed a crazy amount of work doing to it when she'd bought it, but Kate knew her way around a toolbox and was happy to take it on.

With the help of family and friends, she'd ended up with a lovely, central London home which didn't bankrupt her and was now worth a packet. However, it still pained Kate to tell the truth for numerous reasons. She didn't want to appear to be a spoilt rich kid, even though she knew she'd worked damn hard.

Kate showed Meg through to the lounge. Meg sat down on the sofa, then instantly got up, biting her top lip. She put a hand on her hip and went to say something, then checked herself.

"You okay?" Kate asked.

Meg nodded. "Fine. It's just — I'm still fairly sticky." She patted her not-quite-so-shiny hair, before holding out her shirt. "Can I be cheeky and have a quick shower?"

Kate was leaning on the doorframe of the lounge. "Sure — be my guest," she said. "This way." Kate walked down the hallway, with Meg following behind. "Towels are on the shelf." Kate indicated the metal shelf on the wall stacked with towels. "And do you want another top to wear afterwards?"

Meg thought for a moment. "That would be brilliant."

Kate disappeared into her room, then made it back to the bathroom to give Meg a T-shirt.

"Thanks — I won't be long." She paused. "And I don't normally get naked within five minutes of walking into someone's flat," Meg said. "Just so you know."

"No complaints here." Kate kissed Meg on the lips. "You want to give me your top and I'll rinse it for you?"

Meg did a double-take, before grinning at Kate. "That would be lovely."

Kate was still smiling as she walked down the hall and knocked on Jess's door. No answer. She poked her head around the door — her flatmate was nowhere to be seen. Kate crossed her fingers that Jess would be out late or, even better, staying at Lucy's. She strolled back to the kitchen, just as the boiler chugged to life, which told Kate the shower was on.

Meg was naked, just the other side of this wall — the thought brought an epic smile to Kate's face. She was still holding Meg's top in her hands, so Kate got out the handwash and cleaned it as best she could, before wringing it out and hanging it over the hallway radiator. If that didn't score her brownie points, she had no idea what would.

She was in the lounge with a bottle of Heineken, reading foodie magazine Scrumptious, when Meg reappeared some ten minutes later. Her jeans clung to her shapely legs, while the T-shirt Kate had given her had a low-cut V-neck. Meg had combed her wet hair, which was now slicked back and side-parted. She looked like a Calvin Klein model. Kate blinked rapidly.

"Hi." Meg was clutching the doorframe uncertainly.

"Hello again," Kate replied. She cleared her throat. "Can I get you a drink. White wine?"

Meg nodded. "That would be great."

Kate got up and slunk past Meg, almost too scared to touch her for fear it might all turn out to be a dream. In the kitchen, she levelled her breathing and tried to calm her mind. But before she knew it, there was Meg, leaning against her fridge, looking delicious.

"Everything okay?" Kate's stomach flip-flopped again as she surveyed Meg again — intense, turquoise eyes, honeyed skin, soft lips. *Those lips.* Yes, she remembered kissing those earlier. In fact, every part of her body remembered kissing them earlier.

"Everything's just fine." Meg stepped into Kate's personal space and snaked an arm around her waist. "Only I remember at the party promising to kiss you into oblivion and I just thought, we may as well start sooner rather than later. Shall we bypass the wine and go straight to the bedroom?"

Honestly, Kate had been dreaming about a woman saying something like that to her for about 34 years. Yep, since around the time she was born.

Kate was about to respond, but Meg had already made the decision for them.

Her question was rhetorical.

Kate was a fast learner.

Meg pressed her lips onto Kate's.

Kate's body shook. *Literally*. Meg's kiss created a mini-earthquake on Planet Kate and she was helpless to stop it. Was she coming across as too much of a juddering mess to her potential new lover? Kate hoped not. She'd forgotten to check the list of possible don't-dos on a first date, but she was pretty sure 'constant vibrating' would come pretty close to the top.

Still, Kate managed to shove these thoughts to the back of her brain and concentrate on the here and now. Meg was kissing her into oblivion, so it was only polite she should be present and engaged.

Kate increased the pressure of her lips on Meg's, then slipped her tongue slowly in and out of Meg's inviting mouth.

And that was when Kate felt Meg shake and she knew the playing field was level.

And then their kissing escalated. Kate's hands were under Meg's top, tracing the outline of her nipple through the lace, the other grasping her bum through her jeans. And all the while, their lips were joined, their bodies aching with want.

Then Meg's hand was pressing into Kate's crotch, her

thigh behind it increasing the pressure. Meg sank even deeper into their kiss which made Kate's head spin, then with her right hand she stealthily popped open Kate's jeans. Before Kate knew it, Meg's hand was in her pants.

Kate had no time to think about it, no time to process — she simply gasped at the turn of events. Kate had no idea whether to applaud such bravado or be appalled at her speed. But her body was certainly not appalled as Meg's hand moved and Kate's eyes widened — she gasped again.

Meg was inside her.

Kate's reaction was to press down. And then groan into Meg's mouth.

Meg's reaction was to go deeper.

Kate let out another a groan of desire, but then pulled back and looked into Meg's eyes, her pupils wide and dilated. She could barely stand, let alone get some words out — but she was going to give it a shot. She cleared her throat, aware her face was probably flushed pink by now, as well as her brain scrambled.

"Didn't you say we should go to the bedroom?" Kate's voice had a rugged cadence.

"I suppose we should." Meg's tone matched Kate's right back.

Kate let her gaze wander downwards, then up again to Meg. Then she raised both eyebrows.

Meg took the hint, before whispering: "I don't normally do this so quick, either — it just happened." Her expression spelt 'bashful' as she extracted her right hand from Kate. "You make me behave abnormally."

Kate sucked in breath. "Don't worry, I'm not complaining." Kate took Meg's hand in hers and pulled her into the hallway.

And it was then they heard the front door slam. Kate turned and saw Lucy coming up the stairs, followed by Jess.

Neither Kate nor Meg moved — they were like two deer caught in the headlights, not knowing which way to turn.

"Hi guys! Didn't expect you home so early." Jess stood at the top of the stairs and assessed the new addition to the flat. She smiled at the pair, as did Lucy.

Neither Kate nor Meg said a word.

"I'm Kate's flatmate Jess, by the way, seeing as she seems to have been struck dumb." Jess held out her hand to Meg.

Meg raised her right hand to offer to Jess, but then froze. She stared at her right hand, quickly retracted it and held out her left instead.

Kate stifled a laugh.

Meg, however, simply blinked, then slipped back into social mode. "Meg — lovely to meet you, I've heard a lot about you. And you must be Lucy." Meg turned her dazzling smile on Lucy, who projected one straight back.

"Great to meet you, too." Lucy shook Meg's hand warmly.

"Right, well, lovely to see you, but now we've got to carry on down the hall and have mind-blowing sex. In fact, you just interrupted us on the way there. So if you don't mind, can you not take your jackets off, turn around, go back down the stairs and head over to Lucy's house for the night."

That, of course, was what Kate *wanted* to say, but she didn't.

"How was the party?" Lucy hung her coat up on the rack and wandered into the kitchen. Not waiting for an answer, she opened the fridge door and looked up at the threesome who were watching her from the hallway. "Shall I grab two beers or four?"

However, Jess stepped forward and grabbed Lucy's hand, shutting the fridge door before her girlfriend could pluck anything from its shelves.

"Babe, we don't really have time. We're meeting Anna and Max at that bar, remember?" Jess was drilling her eyes into Lucy, but her girlfriend just looked confused.

"We are?"

"Yes — at the new cocktail bar." Jess dragged a perplexed Lucy from the kitchen, giving her back the coat she'd just hung up. "Fabulous margaritas, apparently, and who doesn't love a tequila?"

The whole group muttered their approval.

Jess winked at Kate, then started down the stairs, taking Lucy with her. "So you guys just get back to doing whatever it was you were doing, and we'll see you later," Jess shouted. Five seconds later, the front door banged shut.

Kate and Meg were left looking downwards, then they burst out laughing, doubling over and literally holding their sides.

"I can't breathe!" Kate wheezed. "When you held out your hand…"

"Don't," Meg said.

Kate placed a soft kiss on Meg's lips. "You looked adorable," she said, before clearing her throat. "Now then, where were we?" Kate took hold of Meg's hand and led her down the corridor and into her bedroom.

"Just about to get caught having sex in the kitchen," Meg said. "I can't believe I did that." A pause. "Are they coming back?"

Kate shut her bedroom door behind them and drew Meg closer to her. "I don't know and I don't care." Kate pressed her lips to Meg's and her body lit up with joy. "But I'm hoping she got the message from my eyebrow movement and penetrating stares that they should stay at Lucy's tonight. After all, I'm the landlord, surely I get some perks."

"I'm sure we can sort some perks out for you." With that said, Meg pushed Kate down onto her king-sized bed and surveyed the room. "Nice décor, by the way — very minimal, New York loft."

Kate sat up and stared at Meg. "Are we really doing design critique now?"

Meg smiled down at Kate, then kissed her full on the lips. "You're right — I'll save it till after we've had sex. But I like to make sure you have some taste first."

Kate pulled Meg down on top of her.

Meg squealed.

"I have a whole bunch of taste — I chose you for starters." Kate let her hands land on Meg's naked back as she slid them under her top. Then her hands were roaming over Meg's butt, before coming back up and cupping her face, looking into her eyes.

"I want to get naked with you — I have since the moment I laid eyes on you. So can we make that happen now?"

A slow smile spread across Meg's features as she nodded her head. "We can definitely make that happen."

With that, Meg stood up and slowly, deliberately peeled off her T-shirt, revealing a perfectly toned stomach with jeans that clung deliciously to her thighs.

Kate hiked herself up onto her elbows to ensure her view was solidly clear and that she was paying the utmost attention.

Meg's gaze was intense as she reached around to tug open her bra with ease. The white lace dropped silently to the floor, leaving Meg's deliciously rounded, pert breasts exposed, both nipples erect.

Kate drew in a breath — she was spellbound. Every part of her body wanted to reach out and touch Meg, especially her breasts, but she also wanted this particular show to get to its climax. Because Kate knew that after that, there were more climaxes to follow.

With that thought roaming her mind, Kate forgot to balance properly, her left elbow gave way and she collapsed on the bed. When she opened her eyes, Meg was leaning over her, her breasts inches from Kate's face.

Kate reached out a hand.

Meg slapped it away. "Uh-uh. You wanted to see me naked, but there's no touching allowed yet." Meg stood up, pulling a dazed Kate with her. "And if that was a trick to get me on top of you, I wasn't born yesterday."

Kate simply licked her lips and stared.

Meg leaned forward and kissed Kate's lips lightly. "Now, where were we?" She paused. "Why don't you sit on the end of the bed?"

Kate did as she was told.

Meg walked closer to Kate, until she was just inches from her, Kate's eyes level with Meg's belt. Meg put her fingers to her belt buckle and tugged the loose end, freeing the buckle with a lazy clunk. It hung loose as she then popped open the button on her jeans, before slowly, ever so slowly, guiding her zip downwards and open.

Kate's eyes were now so wide she thought they might start spinning or pop out at any minute. To say this was erotic would be an understatement.

Then Meg slowly stripped off her jeans.

Whoa. Kate stared anew at Meg's lacy knickers, so unlike anything she would ever wear. She glimpsed the skin below and gulped in some air.

"You want me to leave them on?"

Kate stared and vaguely nodded her head.

"Just let me know — I want to get to know you." Meg's tone was suddenly two octaves lower.

No more words were said — they didn't need to be. Kate stared straight ahead, focused on white lace. She put her hands out to cup Meg's buttocks, drawing Meg to her. She ran her fingers across Meg's stomach and kissed her way up Meg's body, getting to her feet to finally hold Meg's breasts, feel their weight, their warmth, their beauty. Kate held it together long enough to allow Meg to remove her shirt, discard her jeans and throw her pants to one side.

And then it was Meg's turn to gasp at Kate's body, acquaint herself, feel her back, her breasts, her soft thatch of hair. Of course, Kate already knew what it felt like to have Meg inside her. But just to have her standing next to her, her hand cupping Kate — it was all-consuming.

And then, unlike earlier, Kate took control. She eased Meg onto the bed and prowled over her, this time kissing *her* into oblivion. Meg's lips were soft, her body smooth and warm as Kate settled on top of her, the sheer bliss of their naked bodies connecting making her brain explode into tiny pieces.

Kate moved her weight slightly off Meg and slid her right hand down her body, down to where she felt lace. She ran a light finger inside the top of Meg's pants, before gently travelling downwards, moving the material aside and trailing her finger through Meg's hot core.

Meg broke the kiss and slammed her head into the pillow, moving her hips to meet Kate's touch. She groaned and wriggled out of her pants.

Kate gave Meg a sultry smile as she threw the final item of Meg's clothing onto her bedroom floor.

* * *

As Kate slipped her fingers inside Meg, Meg let her eyelids flutter downwards, pushing her body upwards to take Kate in as far as she possibly could. The rush that shot through her body shattered every nerve ending she had.

Honest-to-god fireworks.

Meg sunk into the moment, feeling the warmth envelop her as Kate moved inside her. Then Kate's body was on top of her again, their lips entwined, and Kate was thrusting and moving in a sensuous, seamless motion. Meg was powerless as wave after wave of desire crashed over her body and her mind stopped being able to process exactly what was going on, such was its power, its presence. Was Kate who she'd been waiting for?

That thought made Meg open her eyes in surprise.

Kate was still on top of her, still inside her.

Kate simply stared down at Meg, the moment glowing between them. Then she kissed Meg softly, gently.

And then Kate took Meg's hand, kissed it and pushed it gently to herself, lifting herself up on top of Meg, on her knees, almost begging. She didn't need to — Meg was happy to comply.

Kate gasped as Meg slid her fingers inside her, Meg turning her wrist to gain the best access, her mind a mess as Kate began to move inside her again. Now they matched each other move for move, their actions becoming ever more frantic and urgent as the feeling built, the heat increased. Then they were tumbling, changing positions, resuming their beat, filling each other deliciously.

Meg groaned, then crashed her head into the pillow as Kate used her thumb to swipe across her clit. All bets were off. Meg's blood thundered down her body.

Kate circled and then pressed into Meg, letting her know there was no escape — she was hers. Kate increased her speed, and within a few seconds Meg's chest flushed, something popped in her brain and a climax ripped through her body. With it, she let out a strangled cry. It came from deep within her and was laced with emotion Meg hadn't even known she possessed until tonight.

This was all new for both of them, but fresh in such a rich, deep way for Meg, she wanted to weep. But she knew better than that — crying at first-time sex was not the done thing. However, when Meg opened her eyes, refocused and felt Kate's gaze drilling into her, she was pretty sure Kate felt it too. This shift, this other realm they'd opened up, one that Meg knew would be very hard to contain now it was out of the box. Their first time, and it was like they'd known each other their whole lives.

Hot damn.

* * *

But there was no time to dwell on matters — Meg was still

in the zone and Kate knew it. She went to give her more, but was stopped when Meg brushed her hand away.

"We've got all night." Meg's voice was low, bass-like. "And I want to see if you taste as sweet as you look."

Kate's stomach lurched. Could this night get any better? She had a feeling it could.

Meg reversed their positions and watched as Kate stretched and squirmed beneath her. Meg sucked each nipple gently, kissed her way down her stomach before settling between Kate's legs, breathing heavily to indicate her intentions.

Kate cast her eyes downwards — her stomach was rising and falling rapidly, her breathing heavy.

"You're going to kill me, you know." Kate's voice was a gentle whisper.

Meg licked the inside of Kate's left thigh, then her right. "Well, just think of the story I get to tell the ambulance crew." The whole time she spoke, Meg's mouth was placed directly in front of Kate's clit, so Kate felt the heat of every word. "I'm the ultimate stud and you get to die in the ultimate fashion. I think we all come out covered in glory, don't you? Or covered in something."

Before Kate had a chance to respond, Meg flicked her tongue and delved into Kate, licking around and around, in and out, up and down. Kate put her hands out grasping for something, but there was nothing there — she was in freefall. Somehow, though, she knew Meg was her parachute.

Kate was on the edge, as Meg ramped up her particular brand of charm offensive, sucking Kate into her mouth gently, then applying pressure where she knew it was needed. Meg's tongue was a weapon of mass destruction.

In a matter of minutes, Kate came with a shuddering rush as her body shattered into hundreds of glittering fragments, before magically fusing itself back together again. She spun and spun for what seemed like forever, the stars circling above her, before she sailed down to Earth on a cloud of emotion, sailing up and down as Meg continued her masterpiece. Eventually, everything stopped, the only sound being Kate's chest wheezing up and down.

And then there was Meg, head on Kate's thigh, chin glistening, grin firmly in place.

After a few seconds she crawled up Kate's hot body, kissing Kate's soft skin as she went, then fell onto the bed beside her. Neither of them spoke for a few minutes, just kissing hair, hands, arms, cheeks, not wanting to acknowledge the feeling pulsing between them. However, even if they weren't ready just yet, the emotion was wholly present, spinning above them, categorising this moment in their lives as a date to remember. Flick to this date in the future and it might say: found Narnia, hit up Nirvana. This was the day bliss came calling and left a card at both their doors.

Kate's shattered body was a testament to that.

* * *

Three hours later and Kate was on her feet, walking down the hallway in a daze. She was half-dressed and half-drunk on sex, so she hoped Jess or Lucy weren't home. If they appeared now, they wouldn't get much sense out of her.

She took a glass from the cupboard and filled it with water, then drank it down in one. Sex was thirsty work — particularly this kind. She was still woozy from it, still reeling from their compatibility, not quite believing tonight had finally happened. But it had, and she was living, breathing proof you could walk into a florist one day and find the woman of your dreams. She kicked herself for not being more of a flower-buying girl sooner.

But Kate was a big believer that everything happened for a reason, and Meg had come along just when Kate's faith in love was wavering. In just a few weeks, Meg had reaffirmed

Kate's belief there was someone out there just for her. Kate hoped Meg felt the same way, because right now, Kate didn't want to be anywhere else.

She filled her glass again, then got another and filled that, before heading back to the bedroom with water for her and Meg.

Her Meg, she hoped.

24

Meg's phone alarm blared at 6am.

Kate untangled herself from Meg and rolled over, slamming her alarm clock. The noise continued. Then suddenly stopped.

"What day is it?" Kate rolled onto her back, before turning her head slowly towards Meg, peering out from bloodshot eyes. "Sorry — I'm not a morning person." She scooped Meg back up into her arms and kissed her still-warm neck.

"Neither am I this morning, believe me. I need more sleep, you need more sleep…"

Meg was silenced by Kate's lips covering hers, Kate's hands roaming over her naked butt, up her naked back. She groaned as Kate slipped her tongue into her mouth and then just as swiftly back out again. Meg was ready to be had all over again at a single touch from this new lover. *Again and again.*

After a few minutes, Kate pulled back and stared at Meg. "Wait, did you set the alarm so we could have early morning sex? I'm confused. Couldn't it have waited until at least 8am when normal people are awake?"

Meg's body shook as she laughed. "Sorry — this is the life of dating a florist. We have a big day today and I have to get up and help Mum. Saturdays are not days we can take off."

Kate's face dropped. "What if I tie you to the bed and hold you hostage?"

"You'd have to face the wrath of my mother and I don't think you'd come out a winner." Meg had a rueful smile on her face. "It's been tried before and nobody ever comes out of it well." Meg kissed Kate lightly on the mouth before hopping out of the bed with a groan. "Can I have a quick shower to wake myself up?"

Kate rolled backwards and nodded. "You're the cleanest person in this house right now." A pause. "My dressing gown is on the back of my door." Kate pointed towards her grey towelling robe that was hanging next to a baseball jacket. "I like your tattoo by the way."

Meg shrugged on the dressing gown, then came back and stood beside the bed. "You mentioned that last night when we were drifting off."

"I did?"

"Uh-huh. Said sunflowers were your favourite."

"Well, now you know I wasn't lying." Kate snuck a hand out and grazed Meg's thigh.

In return, Meg kissed her. "Just so you know, you're hard to leave. Especially because I know what we could be getting up to today." Meg grinned widely, last night's scenarios playing through her head. Every inch of her body wanted to stay and play, but she knew she had to get going. Work called.

Kate groaned and her eyelids fluttered shut, then back open again.

Meg placed a passionate kiss on her lips, before straightening up. "At least you'll have sweet dreams when I'm gone."

"That much I can guarantee."

* * *

True to her reliable self, Meg was at the shop by 7.30am — but her mind was still replaying last night. Her body was humming in a way it hadn't in over a year and she was more than a little proud of herself. Sparks of desire cascaded through her as she recalled Kate's lips on her body, Kate inside her, Kate on top of her, Kate all around her. Meg wore the resulting smile as she unlocked the front door and switched on the shop lights, before dumping her bag behind the counter and sitting down.

She was still in that very same position when Olivia walked in two minutes later. Meg raised her eyes and quickly tried to erase all the images currently parading through her head, lest her mum somehow see a digital readout on a magical screen above her head. Olivia sometimes seemed to possess such psychic powers, so Meg was taking no chances.

"Morning, daughter!" Olivia put her bag underneath the counter next to Meg's and fiddled with her golden hair. "Bit blowy out there this morning — you'd never guess I just spent ten minutes styling my hair before I left the house, would you?"

"You look gorgeous as ever, mother," Meg said. And then she winked. At her own mum. WTF? Meg needed to reset her brain from sexy mode to normal mode. Plus, she was determined not to wink at her mum again.

"You okay this morning?" Olivia scratched her chin and regarded Meg with caution.

Meg nodded and jumped up off her chair — movement should shake her out of her loved-up reverie, surely? "All good, but in need of coffee. Shall I do the honours?" Meg didn't wait for an answer, she was already off and into the back of the shop to fill the coffee machine.

"Did you make a start on the Dylan order?" her mum shouted.

Meg flicked the switch on the machine so it glowed orange, then walked back to the shop. "Not yet," she mumbled.

Olivia gave her a look. "Okay, but you're acting very strange this morning. Anything I should know?" As she said it, Olivia consulted the order book, then walked around to start gathering the relevant foliage for the wedding. The star flowers were set to be delivered by their supplier in half an hour, so their job now was to get the supporting cast perfect.

Meg shook her head. "Nope," she said, disappearing into the back again. Of course, she wanted to share her triumph with her mum, but it was a bit soon. She needed to give what had happened a chance to breathe, a chance to live on its own before she shared it with anybody else. At least another ten minutes before she blurted it all out. Perhaps 15 if she was lucky.

The trouble was, it was all a bit too soon since she'd tumbled out of Kate's flat and taken the tube to work. She could still touch and taste Kate, still feel how fantastic it'd been to wake up in someone's arms again. In Kate's arms, to be precise.

Out the window of the kitchen, Dave from the next door estate agents' walked by — he waved at Meg, mouthing "Morning!"

Meg waved — had Dave been able to read her thoughts? No, of course he hadn't, she was being stupid. She grabbed two white china mugs from the cupboard over the sink. A few minutes later, she filled them with hot, black coffee, adding a splash of milk for her mum and a lump of sugar. She hesitated, then added a lump of sugar into her own too. She figured she could do with the energy.

She walked into the shop, where her mum had put on the radio in the background and was cracking through the first wedding order at some speed.

"Blimey — you're on fire this morning." Meg put the coffee down beside her mum and resumed her position on the chair.

Her mum glanced back at her. "Someone has to be, seeing as you're on a go-slow. I take it last night was a heavy one? Wasn't it Nathan's party?"

Meg nodded, taking a sip of her coffee. "It was. And yes, it was a late one."

Olivia sighed. "What have I told you about Friday nights? Leave the drinking till Saturday — we need you alert today." But then she smiled. "But I'll let you off this once, seeing as you're normally the model daughter."

"I am?"

Olivia turned and smiled at Meg. "You are." She paused. "Anything else I should know?" She swept her eyes up and down her daughter's frame.

Meg adopted her best innocent face. "No, why?"

Olivia raised an eyebrow. "Because, darling sleepy daughter, those are the clothes you were wearing when you nipped round to mine en route to the party last night. So either you were feeling very lazy when you woke up this morning and just stepped into whatever was on the floor — which is very unlike you — or you never made it home last night. Am I warm?"

Meg looked down at the floor, drummed her fingers on her mug, then looked back up at her mum. "Never work with your family. I should know this, shouldn't I? I should go around schools warning of the dangers of going into the family business." She hugged her mug with both hands.

"And?"

Meg smiled. "Yes, you are correct. I went to Nathan's party last night, and Kate came too, and then I went back to Kate's flat."

Olivia put down the scissors she was using to curl some peach ribbon, walked over to Meg and hugged her. Full-on, take-your-breath-away hug. Then she held her at arm's length and smiled a smile that only a mother can.

"I'm proud of you — well done."

Meg looked alarmed. "For having sex?"

Olivia laughed. "For getting out there and giving it a go again. I know it hasn't been easy for you this past year, but meeting someone else is exactly what you need to put a bit of sparkle back in your life — and when I walked in here this morning and saw that goofy grin on your face, I knew what had happened. If Kate was here right now, I'd kiss her myself."

"That would be awkward."

Olivia let go of Meg and returned to her ribbon curling. "Nonsense — the woman who's put the smile back on my baby's face deserves nothing less." She paused and her face tensed. Olivia drew in a deep breath and rubbed her chest.

Meg crinkled her forehead. "You okay? Are you having pains?"

Olivia closed her eyes, exhaled and rubbed some more, shaking her head. "Just indigestion I'm sure, almost nothing. Honestly, every time I get heartburn is not a heart attack." But Olivia still wasn't smiling.

"Well excuse me for looking out for my mother," Meg said. "Sit down when you've done that, have a break, I can do the rest." Meg got up and put an arm around Olivia, who shook it off just as quickly.

"Even with heartburn I can do this better than you because I haven't been up half the night, have I?" Olivia smiled gently, but Meg could see she was still in pain.

Olivia changed the subject swiftly. "And what about the other one — does she know about this? Might knock the smile off her cocky features too."

Meg shrugged. "Well, I guess she might have an idea if she's home when I rock up later in the same clothes. Plus, I did tell her I had a date before I went out, and also that we needed to get the house on the market and start moving on with our lives."

This time, Olivia dropped the scissors. They fell with a clatter onto the polished wooden floor. "You told her that?"

Meg nodded, before hugging her mum to her. "And please don't drop the scissors like that when you've just said you're having twinges — you nearly gave me a heart attack. I expected you to sink to the floor at any second."

Olivia laughed in her ear. "The younger generation are so dramatic! You and your brother both." Olivia rubbed Meg's back. "But back to Tanya — let's hope she gets the message into that thick skull of hers once and for all. But it might take a couple of goes, because it is pretty thick."

Olivia shook her head, then grinned. "Anyway, let's not worry about her today — you've got far happier things to be thinking about." She turned back to the job in hand, then back to Meg. "But now, we need to get going with these orders — so do you feel like giving me a hand like you said you would when you thought I was dying a minute ago?"

Meg grabbed the order book. "I'm on it."

25

Monday evening, and autumn had crept up on Meg like a tap on the shoulder. All around, the leaves were turning red and brown and attaching themselves to the pavement, making running treacherous. But Meg wasn't put off — the evening sun was just going down when she stepped out of the shop and set off running to the park.

Meg loved the feeling of her body clicking into gear when she ran. It was one of those moments she so rarely had in life where she felt suddenly free, her mind clear, and she concentrated on just what was happening to her at that specific moment — the mechanics of running. Her feet pounding the pavement, her legs somehow attached, her upper body processing the airflow. At moments like this, her body felt like a miracle of modern science.

This week, her body had already been put through a workout — Kate had made sure of that. After leaving on Saturday morning, Kate had texted Meg throughout the day, making her smile and blush in happy union. After work, Meg had gone back to Kate's with the intention of going out for dinner, but they'd never made it out the front door. A rush rumbled from Meg's head to her toes as she recalled their evening and night spent together.

On Sunday, they'd ventured out to one of Kate's favourite places for brunch. London had seemed brighter, warmer, fitter and fresher than it had for the past year, and Meg was well aware why. She loved walking down the road holding hands with Kate, breathing her in, feeling part of a couple.

Sure, this was how you were supposed to feel in the first throes of romance, but honestly, Kate threw up other feelings altogether for Meg. More rounded feelings. A flicker that Meg had never truly felt before.

It was something she was well aware of, but also petrified of.

* * *

After running with her club for over an hour, Meg made her way home through the dusky night air. It was nearly 8pm. *What was Kate doing now?* Having spent Friday and Saturday in her bed, last night had felt quite bereft without her.

As she rounded the corner of her road, Meg's buttocks tweaked and she cast her mind forward to dinner and a hot bath — her body deserved it. She slowed to a walk to let her heart rate recover as she made her way up her road.

The smell of roast chicken hit her nose as she stepped into the house. Then there was laughter from the kitchen which meant Tanya was entertaining. *Again.* Meg had arranged for the estate agent to come round and value the house today and Tanya had agreed to cover it. She might as well get the conversation over with.

She found Tanya at the stove, fussing over asparagus and green beans, with Chris seated at the dining table.

"Hey! You've been running — you always make me feel bad when you go running." Tanya smiled a wide greeting at Meg, which threw her off her game slightly. She'd come in prepared for a fight.

"Lovely night for it." Meg walked over and grabbed a glass from the cupboard, before filling it and gulping down the water in one. She needed that. "Anyhow, how did today go?" She refilled the glass and waited for an answer.

Tanya turned her head. "Today?"

Meg nodded slowly and took another sip of water. "The estate agent."

Tanya's eyes widened.

Meg's eyes narrowed. "Don't tell me you forgot."

Tanya screwed up her face. "I knew there was something. Shit, I'm sorry."

Meg exhaled and tried not to throw her glass of water all over Tanya. It took supreme effort. "I told you last night and I texted you — what happened in the interim?"

"Sorry — I really am. I did mean to be here, but there was a last-minute schedule change…"

Meg banged her glass on the counter-top with more vigour than she intended, which made Chris jump.

"It's funny how there always seems to be a schedule change whenever something important needs to be done, isn't it?" Meg turned to Chris, who at least had the good grace to be looking away.

"And you." Meg was pointing. "I hope you know what you're letting yourself in for. Because this is it. Work comes first, and life always has to revolve around what Tanya wants."

Meg turned back to her ex. "I'll reschedule and make sure I'm here next time. This is going to happen, T, whether you like it or not."

She left the kitchen and clattered up the stairs, a headache limbering up, every muscle clenched. So much for her relaxing run and leisurely dinner. She'd have to do that when the kitchen was clear and she'd calmed down somewhat. For now, a hot bath and much exhalation was needed.

26

The current issue of Female Health & Fitness was in its final stages of production, with most pages laid out and the cover nearly done. Kate was attempting to line up the picture of Princess Emily in sports gear beside their '30 Ways To Lose Those Pounds' feature, but getting the princess's head to work around the '30' was proving tricky. She'd have to consult Dawn.

Kate swivelled in her chair but couldn't spot her editor — she must have slipped out for lunch. Kate had tried to get a picture of Meg on the cover, but it hadn't really worked, so she'd settled for Meg's dazzling bone structure inside instead.

Meg had done a sequence of early starts this week, all of which meant they hadn't seen each other since Sunday — and today was Thursday. Which must mean Kate was getting more mature, not spending every second of every day with the person you'd just slept with. She'd been there, bought the T-shirt. Now, she was ready to take things slowly. Well, slowish.

Today was a good day, though, because Meg was coming in to meet her from work and also to finalise some quotes with Hannah — that was the last feature to lay out tomorrow and Kate was going to take extra-special care with it.

A noise from behind startled her — she turned and there was Dawn, just plucking a Kit Kat from her drawer to have with her cup of tea.

"There you are." Kate spun round in her chair, rolling her shoulders after all that hunching over her screen. She let a momentary dizzy spell pass before she spoke again. "I wanted to chat about the cover lines — the '30' keeps hitting the princess in the nose."

Dawn peered at Kate's screen. "Can't you make her nose smaller?"

"Not without making her look demented."

"Can Harry not help?"

Harry was the company's go-to wonder boy when it came to massaging images. If you needed to cover up a spot, add some make-up, lift someone's bust or add some highlights, Harry was your guy.

"I don't think so," Kate said. "I don't want to stray too far from the truth, seeing as it's royalty. Plus, I think her PR might reject it at approval stage. Can't we just change the words?" Kate turned back to her screen to assess the image.

Behind her, she heard Dawn sigh dramatically. "Okay. Let me just finish my lunch, then we'll get right on it. Honestly, you're an award-winner, you think you'd be able to fix this..."

Kate spun back to her, sticking her tongue out at Dawn.

Dawn smirked in reply.

"And that's your lunch?" Kate wagged a finger at Dawn's Kit Kat.

In return, Dawn lifted her middle finger. "Bite me," she said. "As far as everyone else is concerned, I follow all our magazine's advice to the letter. And if there ever comes a day where it shows otherwise, there's always Harry to make me look gorgeous." Dawn winked at Kate as she prodded her in the back. "Anyway, isn't the famous florist due in today? I can't wait to meet her!"

Kate sighed. "Due later, so the wait is nearly over. And please don't call her the famous florist."

* * *

Meg breezed through the doors of the magazine company just after 5pm, black handbag hitched over her right shoulder, a frisson of excitement flashing through her veins. She'd spent all day looking forward to seeing Kate again, but now it was here, she had to admit to feeling some anxiety. The idea of being in a national magazine was a bit daunting after all, but she tried to allay her fears.

The building was everything she'd anticipated: cool, white and modern, with floors so shiny it was almost a shame to walk on them. She informed the receptionist who she was here to see, and he instructed her to wait in an uncomfortable-looking armchair. Meg perched delicately, taking in the constant comings and goings of this vast company. It made a busy day at her shop look anything but.

A few minutes later, one of four shiny lifts spat out Kate, and she walked towards Meg, beckoning her over to the barriers. Kate used her security pass to tag Meg in, getting a withering look from the security guard in the process. She gave him a wink, then turned her attention to Meg.

"You look lovely," she said, kissing Meg on the cheek.

Meg looked down at herself: ripped black jeans, black boots, white top and a tuxedo jacket. She should look lovely, she'd spent a good hour putting this outfit and its accessories together.

"So do you." Butterflies rose in Meg's stomach as she smiled at Kate.

They might have stood like that for some time too, had there not been a queue developing at the barriers behind them. Kate tugged on Meg's hand and led her towards the lift, which Meg was disappointed to see they had to share with four other people. No sly snogging in here, then.

They got out at floor nine and Meg followed Kate along the carpeted corridors, taking in the glass doors and walls, the chrome chairs, the sleek furnishings.

"It's all very shiny, isn't it?"

Kate turned to her, taking her hand. "It is now. You should have seen our old office — it was a nightmare. Now we're working in this, it's a complete turnaround." The collar of Kate's green shirt was stuck up at an awkward angle, but Meg stopped herself from reaching out and fixing it.

They arrived at the magazine and Kate introduced Meg around, Hannah shaking her hand warmly and Dawn arriving just in time to press some flesh.

"Heard so much about you, it's a real treat to finally meet you." Dawn stood in front of Meg, her eyes not-so-subtly assessing her as if she were about to slap on a price tag.

"You too — it's a real thrill to be featured in the magazine. My mum's very excited."

"You'll have to give us her address and we'll send her a special copy," Dawn said, all smiles.

* * *

While Hannah dragged Meg off to a meeting room to finish up the article, Dawn grabbed Kate's arm and steered her into one of their side offices, making big eyes at her as she did. Dawn closed the door and sat on the small table, letting out a low whistle as she did before punching Kate lightly on the upper arm.

"What?"

"*What?*" Dawn replied. "You didn't tell me the bit about the famous florist also being a hot florist! I mean, I've seen her in running gear, but that is nothing compared to her in the flesh. Where did you pick her up, the florist runway? That girl is drop-dead, hold-onto-your-hat gorgeous." Dawn stood up and walked over to Kate, poking her in the chest. "You have been holding back. I want to dump my husband and run off with her. Forget about the baby-making. We can adopt some from Vietnam just like Angelina and be perfectly happy. That okay with you?"

Laughter creased Kate's face. "Sorry, did you need input from me? You seemed to be doing fine on your own." Kate tapped Dawn on the arm. "Now let's go back out there so you can fantasise about my new..." Kate paused. "Well, it's early days."

Dawn grabbed Kate's arm again and hung onto it. "Girlfriend! She's your girlfriend! Go on, say it."

Kate raised an eyebrow. "You can be so childish sometimes, you know that?"

"And that's why you love me," Dawn replied. "But seriously, girl — she is smokin'!"

Kate froze. "If you say she's hot like a George Foreman grill, I'll deck you."

Dawn was understandably confused. "What?" she asked.

Kate shook her head. "Nothing — just forget it."

* * *

"So did you like the photos?" Kate fell into an easy stride alongside Meg as they headed out of Kate's office and down towards the Thames. Sunset was yet to happen so they'd agreed on dinner and a ride on the London Eye, which, despite living in London, neither of them had ever done.

"I did — they were really flattering. Did you touch them up when nobody was looking?" Meg smiled at Kate as she said it.

Kate glanced sideways. "No need — you're gorgeous just the way you are."

"You're making me blush."

They walked along for a few more seconds dodging other pedestrians on the busy pavement, before hitting the river itself and turning left, heading towards the South Bank. Beside them, the river Thames was flat and glassy, the sun shimmering off its surface as it made its way south. Joggers padded by them, office workers hurried towards buses and tubes, and thick chunks of teenagers laughed as they passed by.

"It's great to see you, by the way." Meg paused as she considered the next words. She took Kate's hand as she spoke them. "I've been thinking about you — us — all week. My mind's been a whir of flowers and sex. I love flowers, don't get me wrong, but sex trumps them every time."

Kate smiled and squeezed Meg's hand. "What about sex on top of flowers? A bed full of red rose petals to get jiggy on, that sort of thing."

"How very American Beauty." Meg stopped in her tracks. "But promise me, if you ever feel the need to do that, you'll get white rose petals?"

Kate laughed. "Not red?"

"Never red." Meg shook her head, grinning. "Looks great on film, a nightmare to get the red stains out of your bedding. Plus, red's a bit corny, don't you think?"

Kate raised an eyebrow and smiled. "Should I be looking for aged red stains when I stay over at yours then?"

Meg's face fell. *When she stays over at mine.*

"It was a joke — you okay?" Kate asked.

Meg swallowed and rallied. "Fine. And you won't find any red stains — I promise." She picked up her pace, changing the subject without any words.

"So, you'll be surprised to hear that I've been thinking about us, too." Kate looked at Meg. "My mind hasn't been many other places apart from in my bedroom with us in it."

Meg kissed Kate's hand as they walked. "What happens when you actually go into your bedroom?"

"My mind explodes and I have to lie down for at least ten seconds every time."

* * *

Fifteen minutes later, they were in a surprisingly short queue to take a ride on the London Eye, the giant white metal wheel that casts its shadow over the river Thames. Their pod, one of 32 on the wheel, was egg-shaped like all the rest, with an oval-shaped wooden bench in the centre, the shell made of reinforced glass.

It might have been romantic had the pair been on their own, with a glass of Champagne and poetic sonnets at the ready. Instead, they were locked in a pod with ten over-excited Italian teenagers, all chattering at such a high pitch that Kate and Meg pressed themselves against the glass at the far end, as if that would somehow lower the volume. It didn't.

The London Eye moved at glacial speed. As the pod made its way upwards, Kate eyed London sprawling out on every side of her, the Houses Of Parliament that had seemed so large on the ground now a speck in her eyeline. From here, they could see landmarks like St Paul's Cathedral, Buckingham Palace and the Gherkin, and witness the wiggle of the river as it meandered across the city.

"Shame we're not here on our own, isn't it?" Kate said.

Meg turned her head and raised an eyebrow.

Kate laughed. "Not like that." She nudged Meg with her hip. "I was more thinking perhaps a spot of dancing on the bench like in the Sound Of Music bandstand scene, then a glass of bubbles to round things off as we hold hands and watch the sun set."

Meg smiled and placed her hand on the small of Kate's back. "You old romantic." She paused. "But that does sound great. I love The Sound Of Music and I'm all for a glass of fizz. Champagne always makes things feel special, don't you think?"

Kate took Meg's hand. "I agree. But as it is, we're here with a load of teenagers. So no dancing and no Champagne, but we can do the hand-holding bit." She squeezed Meg's hand.

Meg squeezed hers right back.

They twisted and turned as the pod made its way round, pointing out landmarks they'd once worked at or passed on the bus.

"If you look really closely — I mean squint — you can probably see my old school from here." Meg pointed northwards.

"Really?" Kate squinted obediently.

"No."

Kate laughed. "What school did you go to? You never told me the other night."

"It wasn't really top of my list of topics." Meg smiled.

"You had a list of topics?"

Meg nodded. "Course — just in case things went badly. You know, favourite films, favourite bands, favourite sexual position. What school we went to barely grazed the top 30."

Kate put a hand on Meg's waist and held her gaze. "So what are your answers?"

Meg licked her lips and thought for a moment. "Let's see," she said, counting on her fingers. "One, The Sound Of Music. Two, toss up between The Backstreet Boys and Fleetwood Mac. Three — I'll let you know later." Meg kissed Kate on the lips and lingered, before pulling back slightly. "As for schools, I went to Westbourne and then Borough." Meg smiled. "You went to the grammar school, didn't you?"

Kate nodded.

"Full of geeks. We were by far the cooler school."

"Oh really?" Kate said. "Cooler than this lot you think?" She indicated the Italian teenagers all around them.

"Definitely. This lot have far too many colours. We were muted, sophisticated. At least, we thought so at the time." Meg paused. "And what about your favourite things?"

"I'll tell you over dinner," Kate replied.

As their pod reached the highest point at the top of the wheel, the teenagers all began squealing in high-pitched excitement, pressing their faces against the glass and hugging each other.

Meg had to laugh. "It's pretty magical, though, isn't it?"

Kate kissed her hand. "I wouldn't want to be here with

anyone else." She paused. "Including all of this lot. Shall we invite them to dinner with us?" Her eyes sparkled as she beamed at Meg.

Meg let out a bark of laughter. "Perhaps a step too far."

Soon, the ride was over and the pair were disembarking, being thanked by a man dressed in an ill-fitting royal blue jacket and with far too much gel in his hair.

"Worth the wait?" Kate asked as they fell into step on solid ground, this time hand in hand.

Meg slung a glance her way, before giving a firm nod of the head. "Definitely."

* * *

Two hours later and they had just finished a surprisingly good pizza, washed down with a bottle of Sauvignon Blanc from the Marlborough region. Spanish red was more Kate's style, but she was a versatile wine drinker. Out the restaurant window, the view across the river in the twilight saw a London skyline smeared with lights, illuminating the city for the night ahead.

"That was delicious."

"It was," Kate agreed.

"And I was thinking — I told you all about my family the other night, but you didn't tell me about yours."

Kate smiled warmly. "What do you want to know? We're small but perfectly formed. There's my sister Vicky who married Jess's brother Jack, and they've got two sons — Luke and Freddie. They're all great. And there's my mum, who's a trooper." Kate smiled sadly. "My dad was amazing, but he died in a car crash five years ago. Only 56. I still miss him every day."

Meg reached over the table and took Kate's hand. "I'm so sorry." She paused. "Out of the blue like that must have been awful."

"It was." Kate's mind floated back to that time. It was now

in soft focus, consigned to the part marked 'Revisit Sparingly'. Those first few months had been the worst, but it had taken her a few years to deal with the grief and manage it. Nobody warns you the impact of the death of a loved one, especially sudden death.

Kate shuddered as she remembered fully. "But life goes on, and we're all good now." She paused. "In fact, my mum has just started seeing someone. Met him at my uncle's funeral, would you believe."

"Really? Now that is a scandal."

"It certainly is — especially where my sister Vicky is concerned. She's convinced he's out to steal Mum's house and money, whereas I think he seems like a genuine bloke. We agree to differ."

Meg nodded. "Must be hard to accept someone after your dad has been taken so abruptly."

Kate shook her head. "It would have been if it happened a few months after. But it's been five years now. I'm happy for my mum and Vicky should be, too. She's not in my good books right now."

Meg smiled. "Everyone accepts things at different speeds. I'm sure she'll come round."

"I hope so," Kate replied. "Because Mum really likes him. And I've had dinner with him and he seems like a normal guy — and you can't hope for more than that. Plus, he's got grown-up kids too, so he gets family." She sucked her top lip for a moment. "I'm more dreading meeting them — what if it turns out to be the kid who bullied me at school?"

Meg's face fell. "You were bullied at school?" Concern shone in her eyes.

"No — it just sounded like a good line."

Meg smacked Kate on the back of her hand. "You bugger." Meg sat back. "I envy you, though."

"For being such a good liar?"

"For having a dad — one you can think of fondly. And even though he's gone, you still had loads of years with him, which you should treasure. Me and Jamie never had that. My dad was never there."

"Is it too late to try to get to know him now?" Kate put her elbow on the table as she spoke.

Meg shrugged. "He's tried to get in contact. But with Mum so fragile, I don't want to do anything to upset her. Not now."

Kate nodded. "I get that. But I'm sure she'd understand too. He is your dad, after all."

Meg pursed her lips. "That's the thing though, I'm not sure that means much to me. He was never there, so my 'dad' feelings are fairly non-existent. I don't *feel* any connection to him."

Kate watched Meg's features droop with sadness. She wanted to lean over and kiss it better. So she did.

Meg raised the side of her mouth in a half-smile. "What was that for?"

"You just looked so sad, I wanted to cheer you up. Did it work?"

"You certainly derailed my morbid train of thought." Meg shook her head and blinked twice.

Kate leaned over the table again and repeated her trick. A hot flush swelled in her body. Her mind had gone a bit blank now, too.

"Shall we get the bill and get out of here?" Kate said.

Meg nodded in response.

"Shall we go to your place for a change?" Kate asked.

The grin fell off Meg's face. "Nah," she said, hoping it sounded casual. "Your place is closer." Now it was her turn to kiss Kate. "Plus, it's been pretty successful so far."

And Kate had to agree, it had been.

She put up her hand to get the waiter's attention.

27

The following week and the weather gods had decreed rain, by the bucketload. Outside, the wet stuff was sheeting down, the surface of the Thames churning like a hot wash on extra spin. Inside, however, the mood was upbeat as the first copies of the new magazine were back from the printers. Kate and Dawn were sat at their desks admiring it.

Dawn held the cover at arm's length and tilted her head. "It looks fantastic Kate, really good. I'd say this could be another award-winner — although I don't want to put a jinx on it."

Kate put her head next to Dawn's. "You could be right. Would have looked better with Meg's face peering out of it, but what can you do?"

"I agree — that girl is a cover star. Maybe we can put her on the next one?"

"I did suggest it to her, but she said no." Kate shrugged and smiled.

Dawn put the magazine on her desk and turned to Kate. "So it's all going swimmingly? What is it now — two weeks?"

Kate shook her head. "Three — and everything is still fine. I keep waiting for it all to fall apart, but I can't see it happening. I just can't see a fault in this girl and I'm the expert in finding them."

Dawn crinkled her forehead. "So it could be serious then?"

Kate cleared her throat. "A bit like the cover, I don't want to jinx it. But who knows? If everything keeps cracking along as it has been, you might need to dust off your hat before too long."

Dawn grabbed Kate's arm and stood up. "Oh my — you're talking marriage after only three weeks! You are smitten, girl." She paused. "But then, I suppose that's the good thing about lesbian relationships, isn't it? In straight relationships, it's usually the girl who thinks of marriage before the man and freaks him out. Does that happen with lesbians?"

Kate chuckled. "Oh, you'd be surprised. I'm only sharing the wedding thing with you, not Meg — I'm not a total nutter. Mention the M word and that's a sure way to see her running for the hills." Kate paused. "I don't even know whether she likes ketchup or brown sauce on her bacon sandwich yet. Could be a deal-breaker if she prefers brown."

"True, very true. These are far more important issues. So when are you seeing her again?" Dawn picked up her trusty diary and notepad, before turning back to Kate for an answer. "Meeting with ads," she said, pointing over her shoulder.

Kate looked at her watch — nearly 4pm. "Well, I wasn't meant to be seeing her till Saturday, but I might stop by her shop later and drop in a magazine on the off-chance. I know she really wanted to see it."

Dawn looked amused. "All casual like, just passing etc."

"Exactly." Kate paused, then looked at Dawn. "Not too obvious, is it?"

"Not at all." Dawn patted Kate's shoulder, smirking as she strolled off.

* * *

And so it was just over an hour later, Kate clocked off work early and got on the tube, magazine in bag. Meg was going to love her — she'd been going on about little else ever since the shoot and the interview, which endeared her all the more to Kate. After so many years in magazines, Kate was sometimes blasé about it, forgetting how exciting her job was to strangers. When they'd been out the previous week and Kate had told Meg that Hannah had arranged to interview a recent gold medal winner, Meg had been beyond excited. Kate couldn't wait to see Meg's gorgeous face when she saw herself in print.

The tube was packed so Kate had to stand. It was now October, so scarves were being let out of their hibernation and coats dusted off as the autumn evenings kicked the sun into touch and the air cooled. However, on the tube, it was the opposite — still stuffy, with everyone sweating in their cold weather gear.

Kate was no different, shedding her grey scarf as the first beads of sweat dripped down her back. She hated getting the tube and not biking, but turning up looking like a drowned rat was not a good look in anyone's book. Kate ticked off the stops as the train juddered on its journey, the crowd thinning out as they passed through major interchanges. When she got off at Finchley, she was glad to breathe in the wet, tarmac-scented air.

Kate put up her brolly and strolled down the main road, her eyes taking in the brightly lit signs for fried chicken, a cool new café and more estate agents than were strictly necessary. Cars swooshed by kicking up wet spray, while people huddled in shop doorways to avoid getting too wet. The nights were closing in — it would soon be time for the clocks to go back.

Within five minutes Kate was at Fabulous Flowers and this time there was no dithering. She pushed open the door, pausing to shake her umbrella onto the pavement. The bell rang as Kate knew it would, and then a woman emerged from the back of the shop — but it was neither Meg nor Olivia. Rather, she was Asian with shiny, liquorice hair and a pink shirt that looked fresh out of the packet, judging by its starched collar.

"Hi there — can I help?"

"Hi," Kate said. "I'm after Meg — is she around?"

The woman turned up the corners of her mouth and shook her head. "Nope — she had some stuff to do today so it's just me. Can I pass on a message?" The woman rummaged on the counter and picked up a pad and pen, before looking back at Kate.

Kate had a brief flashback of nearly kissing Meg right up against that counter, but put it to the back of her mind. Instead, she held up the bag containing the magazine. "I just wanted to drop something off to her. Is she due back today?"

The woman shook her head again. "She was going straight home — said she had stuff to do, what with putting her house on the market and everything."

Kate blinked. Meg was putting her house on the market? This was news to her — but then, so were many things in Meg's world. Kate had opened up to Meg with surprising ease, whereas Meg had been far more guarded. Now Kate came to think about it, she didn't even know where she lived apart from somewhere around here.

"Perhaps I'll just drop this off to her at home." Kate smiled her A-list smile. "I'm Kate by the way, Meg's girlfriend." It was the first time Kate had said those words out loud, but she styled it out with aplomb. Kate held out her hand and the woman shook it warmly.

"Anya — part-time help here." Anya seemed to have no qualms at all that Kate might indeed be Meg's girlfriend. Perhaps Meg had been standing in this very spot earlier, waxing lyrical about how fantastic Kate was. It was a warming thought.

"Nice to meet you." Kate turned to leave, but then twisted back, her foot squeaking on the slate-tiled floor. "By the way, I always get it wrong — what number is Meg's house again?"

Anya frowned, then consulted a large book on the counter. "133." She smiled again at Kate.

Kate clicked her fingers. "133. Must write it in my phone."

She rolled her eyes at Anya. "And the road again? Only been there twice — went to the wrong street the first time."

Anya chuckled. "It's easily done — they all look the same around here." She consulted the book again. "Blair Avenue. It's the one with the pub on the corner."

"Great — you've saved me getting lost again," Kate said. She was a worryingly convincing liar when she wanted to be.

"Catch the 245 if you want to stay dry," Anya advised as Kate walked out the door.

Kate plugged the address into her phone and Google showed her Meg lived about a five minute walk from her mum, five minutes from the house she'd grown up in. Who would have thought? There was Kate, always thinking she had to move to central London to meet the exciting woman of her dreams, when all along, she was almost the girl next door.

* * *

Meg was really pleased with how the valuation of the house had gone. Despite Tanya's misgivings, if they sold and took an equal split, they'd make a tidy sum to help them both start again. That was all she really wanted, and she hoped Tanya would see it that way, too. Yes, there were a few issues the agent had asked her to sort, but with those done, the woman had told her it should be plain sailing — an ideal family home. Meg hoped whoever bought it had more luck than them.

She flicked on the kettle and glanced at the clock — nearly 6pm. Outside, the sky was the colour of lead and the rain was sheeting down as well as drumming on the overhead skylight. Viewed through the skylight, the weather was always dramatic — either blistering sunshine or thundering rain.

Meg crossed her fingers that Tanya would be out tonight, as she fancied doing a spot of cooking, perhaps even baking some biscuits. She hadn't baked any since life got complicated and Tanya had taken over the kitchen. However, now she was taking steps to get her life back on track, Meg was remembering who she was and what she liked. Running, baking, reading. And even going out for a meal with a hot woman on her arm. Yes, she certainly enjoyed doing that.

A smile slipped onto her face as she grabbed a mug and made her tea. But then her dreams of a Tanya-free evening were shattered as she heard the door slam. Just at that moment, her ex poked her head around the door.

"Hi." Tanya's cheeks were glowing red. An umbrella dripped silently onto the carpet by her side, but her hair was bone dry.

"Hey." The word curdled on Meg's lips.

"So it went well today?"

Meg walked over and took the umbrella from Tanya's hand, dumping it in the sink. "You remembered."

"I told you I was sorry about last time."

Meg bit back a response, trying to keep the exchange civil. "Yeah, it was good. You got my text about the price?"

Tanya nodded.

"If we sell at what they valued it at, we'll both make enough to start again." Meg didn't take her eyes off Tanya as she spoke.

Tanya slumped against the doorframe and chewed the inside of her cheek. After a few seconds, she nodded. "Sounds ideal." She sighed. "You know, this isn't really what I ever wanted, us splitting up and selling the house, but maybe you're right. Maybe it's time to move on. So I'm not going to put up any more barriers. If this is what you want, I'm happy to go along with it."

Meg steadied herself on the counter-top as her mouth fell open. "Just like that? You've seen the light?" She tilted her head. "What's the catch?"

Tanya shook her head and smiled. "No catch. You can

actually thank Chris — she was on your side." She shrugged. "You're right, we should move on with our lives. When does it go on the market?"

"From tomorrow." Meg pushed her hair off her forehead.

"Great. You can fill me in on the details in a bit — just let me get out of my wet clothes."

The doorbell interrupted their conversation and Tanya turned. "I'll go."

Meg stood in the kitchen, not quite believing what she'd just heard. Perhaps she could invite Kate over sooner than she thought. Make her a lovely dinner, then have her for dessert. She smiled and sat down at the table, waiting for Tanya to deal with whoever was at the door.

It would be the first time they'd sat down civilly in nearly a year.

* * *

Kate stood on the doorstep of number 133, an excited smile on her face. But that was quickly wiped off when her failed blind date of some weeks earlier opened the door. Tina? Or was it Tanya? Even though she couldn't recall her name, Kate recalled her demeanour very well. What she was doing at Meg's house, Kate had no idea. Her stomach plummeted and some rain tracked down the back of her neck. Kate had a bad feeling about this.

"Well, hello," Tina/Tanya said, licking her lips. "Has it taken you this whole time to track me down and see the error of your ways? And in the driving rain, too." She raised an eyebrow. "It's almost romantic."

Kate shifted her weight onto her other foot and pursed her lips. "Very funny. I was looking for Meg. Is she in?" Kate peered over Tanya's shoulder.

An amused look passed over Tanya's face. "She is." She

stepped back to allow Kate into the house. "How do you two know each other?"

Kate shook out her umbrella for the second time in half an hour and stepped into the hallway. "We're kinda seeing each other."

Tanya's face registered surprise. "Really?" She stretched the word out like an elastic band.

Kate nodded.

"You and Meg?"

"That's right."

At that moment, Meg appeared in the doorway.

Kate looked up and smiled — she couldn't help it.

In contrast, the colour drained from Meg's face like it had a crack in it.

"Hey." Kate couldn't quite pick up on the vibe circling the hallway, but she was pretty sure she didn't like it.

"What are you doing here?" Meg was frozen to the spot, her eyes darting between Tanya and Kate.

"That's just what I asked her," Tanya said. "I tried to pick her up a few weeks ago, now I find she's your new date." She smiled at Meg. "We were lovers, and now we're attracted to the same woman. Perhaps we should have a threesome at some point to square the circle, so to speak." Tanya shut the front door, looking very pleased with herself. She leaned against the wall, her arms folded across her chest.

"You two *were together*?" Kate stared at Meg, beseeching her to say no. Only, she knew she wouldn't.

Meg nodded slowly, her brow furrowed. "And you two know each other?" She pointed at Tanya, then at Kate.

Tanya nodded. "We met a few weeks ago, had a drink together."

"I wouldn't say we had a drink together — I'd say you were overbearing. Good to see you're consistent." Kate paused. "And this was before anything happened with us," she told Meg, holding up a palm. Then Kate shook her head. "Although why I'm explaining this to *you* when you *slept* with her is anyone's guess."

Meg shook her head at Tanya. "I can't believe you tried to hit on the first woman I've liked in *ages*."

Tanya shrugged. "My charms didn't work though, so you won."

Nobody said a word for a few seconds and the silence was deafening.

Kate was still frowning. "But you still haven't filled me in totally — how long were you together?"

Tanya was happy to fill in the blanks. "Years — we bought this house together. Funny how these things work out, isn't it? I must say though, most of the décor is Meg's doing — she's the one with the design eye. When we first moved in, it was a right state, wasn't it, honey?"

Kate's face was frozen in frown mode. This wasn't making sense to her and she hoped she could iron out the wrinkles in this story without ruining her evening. In her hand, the umbrella dripped steadily onto the beige carpet. She glanced at Meg, who was still lacking in colour, still saying nothing.

Kate was clutching the magazine in her hand, which somehow didn't seem so important now. She could taste fear on her tongue.

"And you're — just visiting tonight?" Kate asked Tanya. "Stopping by on the way home from work?" She winced as she said it.

But Tanya shook her head. "We both still live here. Still here after — what is it now, Meg? Nearly six years?" Tanya threw a hand in the air to emphasise her point. "Time flies when you're having fun."

"Yes, okay, Tanya, you've made your point." Meg's voice cut in with stony authority. But then she turned to Kate, and her tone softened considerably. "Look, we went out, we bought this house and we both still live in it." Meg cast her eyes down to the floor briefly, then she took a deep breath and refocused. "But we haven't *been* together for a year and we both live *very* separate lives."

"Nine months, a year, give or take." Tanya moved her hands as if juggling time.

"What were we just saying in the kitchen before Kate arrived?" Meg's tone had gone a notch higher as she addressed her ex.

"Do tell me, because I'm all ears." Kate was loosening her shoulders like a boxer in her corner. "Was it a mutual pact to make me look like an idiot? Because it's working *really well* if that was your intention."

"No! That's not what we were saying," Meg said. "I really *like* you, and I was telling Tanya that — and that we need to sell this house and move on. You've got it all wrong." Her voice was brittle, cracking as it hit the air.

"We're moving on — we are," Tanya said. "But there's an *awful* lot of history to sieve through first."

Kate let out a bark of indignation. "You're telling me." She shook her head in disbelief before turning a granite gaze on Meg. "I can't quite wrap my head around the fact you both still live here *and* bought this house together. It never occurred to you once to tell me this in all the time we've been seeing each other?" Kate's vision blurred, her cheeks flushed scarlet. "Not once?"

"I was going to tell you this weekend — it just never came up before." Meg's eyes were wide.

Her words scratched Kate's skin like they were an irritant. Kate laughed. "It *never came up*? I should put this on my checklist now, should I? Do you have a girlfriend and are you still living with her?" She almost choked on her own words. "Can you hear what you're saying?"

"You haven't *told her*?" Tanya let out a low whistle.

"You're not still holding a torch for me, are you? Because really, we should have chatted about this before we put the house on the market and everything."

Meg clapped both hands over her ears as she shouted. "Shut up! Just shut up, Tanya — I've had just about enough of you."

"Me too," Kate said. "And I only met you a few weeks ago."

Tanya opened her mouth to say something, but Meg's stare was still drilling into her, so she closed it and said nothing.

Kate shifted from one foot to the other, took a deep breath and addressed Meg. "I thought it'd be a nice surprise for you to bring this round tonight." She held out the magazine, still in her work carrier bag. "But honestly? I wish I hadn't bothered."

"What is it?" Meg grasped the carrier bag like it held a bomb.

"The magazine."

"It's already out?" Meg flicked her gaze to Kate.

"Early copy." Kate shook her head. "But it turns out I've walked into a domestic that my own — girlfriend, can I call you that? — is having with her ex. In the house they bought, that they still live in. That she never told me about." Kate bit her lip, before glancing at Tanya, then Meg.

"You never thought this might be something you should mention? That you were living with your ex? What else are you not telling me? Is there an ex-husband or any children waiting in the wings?" Kate sighed loudly and held up her hand as if stopping traffic. "Never mind, don't even answer that. I think I'd better go. Leave you two... to... Whatever." Kate moved the bottom half of her jaw one way, the top part the other way and then back again. "I need some air."

Kate turned and put her hand on the front door latch. However, before she had a chance to open it, Meg was beside her, a hand on Kate's arm.

"Don't go." Her voice was almost a whisper. "*Please*. I'd like to explain."

Kate looked down and shook her head. "You had plenty of chances to explain. And now I understand why you never wanted to bring me back, and why you were always herding us back to mine — because you already had a girlfriend here."

"Ex — she's my ex!" Meg turned to Tanya. "Aren't you?"

Kate followed Meg's gaze.

Tanya nodded.

Meg exhaled. "It was just... Never the right time. And I thought maybe we might sell the house before you came round, and then it wouldn't be so awkward."

Kate faced Meg, their mouths just inches apart. Kate allowed her gaze to drop, before she picked it back up and shook her head with a sad laugh.

"And it's not awkward at all now, is it?" Kate swallowed down a lump in her throat. "I thought you were different, I thought I could trust you. Turns out, you're just like all the others."

Meg recoiled as Kate's words hit home.

As she opened the door, Kate could still feel Meg's hand around her arm. She shook her off, before turning and shaking out her umbrella. The mechanism jammed. There was an excruciating few seconds while Kate wrestled with it.

"Do you want me to help?" Meg stepped forward.

Kate's whole body stiffened at Meg's proximity. She turned and looked her in the eye. "I think you've done enough for one day."

She finally got the umbrella up. "You're on page 49. You look stunning. As always." Kate dropped her head. "See you around," she said, before turning away, rain — and tears — misting her vision as she walked up the path.

Kate didn't look back.

* * *

Meg watched the door slam shut and closed her eyes. Was she still breathing? She checked and she was. Was Tanya still breathing? Yes, unfortunately. Had the world's roof caved in? For her, perhaps. Poor Kate, getting drenched in the rain.

Meg opened her eyes and twisted to face Tanya. "You happy? Was that what you wanted?"

Tanya was having none of it. She turned up a corner of her mouth before answering. "Before you blame me, I think you need to look in the mirror. Why didn't you just tell her you were still living with me? It's hardly the crime of the century. We haven't sold the house, we *have* to live here." Tanya stroked her chin and paused. "So really, why? I mean, you've made it pretty clear we're over. I'm not standing in your way. But *you are*. It's high time you stopped blaming me and started looking at yourself. You made this mess, and it's yours to clean up."

Tanya pushed herself off the hallway wall and looked at Meg. "She's worth trying to keep hold of — so you might want to start thinking of a way to salvage this. Putting the house on the market was step one. Sorting your own life out is step two." Tanya shook her head. "Anyway, I'm going to get changed. Let me know if you want to talk about the valuation later."

"Yeah, I'm sure to want to talk about *that* tonight," Meg spat.

"It's all part of sorting things out. It's all connected."

Meg watched Tanya disappear upstairs to her room, forming a ton of comebacks and cutting comments in her head. But somehow, they never came out of her mouth. Because logically, she knew Tanya was right. Yes, her ex hadn't wanted to sell originally, but if Meg had pushed, she would have. She wasn't a terrible person.

Meg just hoped she could sort it out with Kate before it was too late.

28

"So why am I coming with you again?"

"Because you love me, and because I offered to buy you coffee and cake. And because I'm having a crisis."

Jess kicked the pavement and smiled as the pair wheeled Kate's bike down the road to Bikes & Bakes. In this day and age, bike shops couldn't simply be bike shops — they had to diversify.

"What's up with Beryl?"

"Dodgy brakes," Kate replied. "Which wasn't so good when I was cruising down Hampstead Heath recently."

Jess laughed. "Cruising on the heath? What did I tell you about that?"

"Ha ha," Kate replied.

Once inside, Jess nabbed the last available table, while all around her, conversation was being traded at full pelt. Kate handed over her bike and within five minutes, she was back with coffee and cake.

Kate sat down opposite Jess, the late evening sun streaming in through the window and making her squint. The weather had bucked up today, the city now painted in autumnal sunshine.

Jess took a sip of her cappuccino. "So come on, then — the suspense is killing me. Your crisis. Is it a world-dooming crisis, or something that's eminently sort-outable?" Jess took a bite of her carrot cake as she waited for Kate to answer.

"Any good?" Kate asked, avoiding the question.

Jess nodded, rescuing a stray crumb from her lip. "Nearly as good as mine." She paused. "Now spill."

Kate took a deep breath. "You won't believe it when I tell you."

Jess raised her eyebrows in response.

"So last night, I went to Meg's place for the first time. She's been quite evasive about me going round there, but I didn't really think anything of it. I mean, I had *no reason* to. She wasn't exhibiting the signs of someone who was hiding anything or having an affair — and I *know* those signs, I've seen them before."

Jess grimaced and paused mid-chew. "But she is?"

Kate shook her head slowly. "Not exactly." She exhaled. "But she is still living with her ex-girlfriend, which she'd conveniently failed to mention."

"Ah," Jess replied, through a mouthful of cake.

"Yes, ah." Kate sipped her coffee. "But the best is yet to come. Guess who said ex-girlfriend is?"

Jess sucked on her bottom lip before answering. "That woman from Orange Is The New Black?"

Kate gave her a withering look.

Jess thought for a moment, before her features filled with alarm. "Not Caroline?" she whispered.

Kate choked on her coffee. "God, no! But perhaps worse." Kate sat back to deliver the news with maximum impact. "Remember Lucy's mate who you tried to set me up with and she cracked on to me at dizzying speed?"

Jess sat upright and tapped the table. "In that bar?"

Kate nodded. "Tanya."

"Tanya is Meg's ex?"

Kate nodded again.

"*Oh. My. God.*" Jess covered her mouth with her right hand. "And she's still living with her?"

More nodding.

"But I'm assuming not in the biblical sense?"

Kate exhaled before replying. "I don't think so. I mean, I believe her when she tells me that. *I think*. But the thing is, they went out for a few years, and they split up over a year ago. So just when exactly are they thinking of going their separate ways?"

Jess looked thoughtful. "I can see what you mean about crisis. I mean, you *like* this girl."

Kate nodded sadly. "I do. I *really* do. But now I'm thinking, is she really available? Does she still have feelings for Tanya and she can't make up her mind?" Kate shuddered. "And, more importantly, can I really be going out with someone who went out with someone like that in the first place?"

Jess patted Kate's arm. "Don't think like that. Everyone's allowed to fall for the wrong person at least once in their life. Whether they then stay living with them forever — well, that's another story. But maybe they just had trouble selling — it happens."

"I know all that, but it still puts a spanner in the works." Kate sighed. "I'm just not all that comfortable going out with someone who's going home to their ex every night. I know they're not *together* anymore, but it still feels weird. Why didn't she just tell me?"

Jess shrugged. "I don't know, that's something you should ask her. And if she thinks this is going somewhere, she'll try to make the change."

"I know." Kate sighed again. "But it feels wrong. And I think I'd feel this way if it were anyone, but the fact it's Tanya makes it doubly worse. I'm just glad I didn't drink way too much tequila and sleep with her that night." Kate shook her head just thinking about it.

"Never a truer word spoken," Jess smiled. "But if you want my professional opinion—"

"—You're a professional now?" Kate had her elbow on the table and was leaning her cheek on her balled fist.

"Certainly am — I listen to people's problems all day long in the café, don't I? And in my professional opinion, this crisis is very sort-outable." Jess paused, wagging a finger at Kate. "If you'd slept with Tanya, it might not be, but you didn't, so pat yourself on the back for not being a slut."

"Well done me. But that's easy for you to say."

"Is it?"

"Yeah," Kate said. "Because even if I can get over the fact she went out with Tanya and is still living with her, why didn't she just tell me? We had conversations about our lives — family, what we do, where we live. Just drop it in, then it's not a big deal. But the fact she didn't *makes* it a big deal. So now I think, can I really trust her? Look at my last relationship — Caroline cheated on me." Kate pushed her plate to one side and slumped forward, head in hands.

In response, Jess tapped her on the head and pointed at Kate's slice of carrot cake. "Are you going to eat that, by the way?"

Kate sat up. "I'm having a crisis and you're trying to take the food off my plate?"

"I just thought you might not feel like it in your heartbroken state."

Kate pushed the plate towards Jess.

"I stand by what I said, though." Jess took a bite of the cake. "This is sort-outable. *Really*. Meg is not Caroline — Caroline was just not in the same place as you. Caroline cheating on you was not your fault." Jess leaned over and took Kate's hand in hers. "Meg is not cheating on you." Jess paused for added emphasis. "She's not. She just has a housing situation, that's all."

Kate's eyes clouded over with sadness. "Then why does it feel like she is?"

There was a beat as neither of them spoke. Beside them at the end of their long table, two men in chequered shirts and big hair sat down with an iPad and started discussing gigabytes and RAM. Jess and Kate gave them the once over, then tuned them out.

"Anyway, you will sort this out, I know you will." Jess paused, chewing at her fingernails. "And I know this might not be the *exact* right time to tell you this, but I have some news."

"Oh?" Kate sat up straight.

"Yeah," Jess said. "Thing is, Lucy and I have been talking and... Well, there's no easy way to say this, but I'm moving in with her. And so moving out from you." Jess bit her lip as she waited for Kate's reaction.

Kate smiled ruefully. "Wow. I'm breaking up and you're moving in. Congratulations."

Jess winced. "I know it's not brilliant timing, but I thought I should let you know." She scratched the top of her head. "Even though I'm sad. I've loved living with you — I'm really gonna miss you."

"Sounds like we're never going to see each other again."

"Ha!" Jess said. "You don't get rid of me that easily."

"Good." Kate fiddled with her teaspoon, eyes down. At the counter, someone smashed some crockery and the café cheered as one, like they were all back in school.

"But drinks soon to celebrate the end of a beautiful living arrangement?" Jess asked, turning her head from the commotion.

Kate nodded. "Absolutely. And I am really pleased for you. Despite everything going on with me. It's a big step."

"It is. I'll miss my zone one postcode, though."

Kate held up her now empty coffee cup. "Here's to you, then — new beginnings."

Jess tapped Kate's cup with her own. "New beginnings. And to you sorting this mess out."

Kate raised both eyebrows up, and then down again. "We'll see."

29

The following Monday and Meg was in the shop, chin resting on her palm, staring into space. Her mum had called to say she wasn't feeling very well this morning, so Meg had dispatched Jamie round to check up on her. If everything else in her life seemed to be stalling, at least Meg could rely on her family. Jamie had just texted to say Mum seemed fine, and he'd left her with some lunch and fresh magazines.

She'd relayed the bad news about Kate to Jamie over the weekend, but he'd been stoic about it. Jamie's view was she'd come round, and if she didn't, it was never meant to be. As far as Jamie was concerned, if Kate couldn't get over this small bump in the road, how was she ever going to navigate anything else?

Meg hoped it was that easy, but it'd been five days now and no contact — the text messages had dried up, the impromptu calls into the shop were no more. And now, Meg was staring at the door, willing Kate to walk through it — or at the very least collapse in front of it.

Instead, the bell rang and in walked Mr Davis.

"Hello," Meg said. "Everything okay? It's not Saturday already, is it?"

He shook his head, but the spring was gone from his step. "It's not. Just want some flowers for Sheila. My wife."

No wise cracks. No jokes. Meg walked around the desk and stood next to him, both staring at a bucket full of yellow roses.

"For any particular occasion?" Meg asked.

Mr Davis shook his head and smoothed down the lapel on his suit jacket. "She's not feeling great, so just to tell her I love her. That's all." He turned to face Meg. "Women need to be shown, don't they? I tell her all the time, but sometimes I feel she doesn't take it in. So I thought, flowers midweek would do the trick. Flowers always make her smile. She loves flowers."

Meg smiled. "Flowers normally make *most* people's days — something that says love." Meg rested a hand on her hip. "I know you always get a seasonal bouquet every week, but is there something your wife likes?"

Mr Davis turned and walked to the other side of the shop. "Irises." He stood in front of a bucket. "She loves irises. Always has."

Meg nodded and walked over to collect a bunch of irises: purple, pink and pale yellow. She tied them with paper and a bow and gave Mr Davis a card to write to accompany them.

"Are you okay today?"

Meg was at the till about to register his purchase.

She looked up and blinked. "I'm fine," she lied.

Mr Davis pursed his lips. "You don't seem it. Perhaps you need some flowers. Has anyone sent you any recently?" He put a hand on the counter and studied Meg.

Meg stopped, finger poised over the till, then she shook her head. "People are scared to send flowers to florists — they think it's a waste of time." She took Mr Davis's offered cash and rang up the sale.

"And what do you think?"

Meg eyed him, before handing over his change and giving him his flowers.

"I think that flowers are never a waste of time."

"That's what I thought." He beamed at her. "See you Saturday — I'll have a new film star for you by then."

Meg watched Mr Davis leave and looked around her shop. Flowers. It was true nobody ever sent Meg flowers, but she was used to that. But it was also true that all women liked flowers — she'd never met one yet who didn't melt a little on receipt.

It had to be worth a try in her own life, didn't it?

30

Vicky was sat on Kate's leather sofa, moving one way, then the other. She frowned. "I think you might need a new one."

"Life? Relationship? Or sofa?"

Vicky shot her a look. "God, you can be dramatic. I hardly think a woman chasing you and sending you flowers seven days in a row is something to be downhearted about. It's not even like she cheated on you. She was just economical with the truth. Give her a break." Vicky paused. "And I meant your sofa — bit saggy now, isn't it?"

"That's why I've got all the cushions." Kate picked up one from her armchair opposite and chucked it as her sister's head.

"Hey! Don't throw missiles at the messenger." Vicky studied her fingernails, then looked back up at Kate. "So have you decided to forgive Meg?"

Kate rolled her neck. "Some days yes, other days no."

"One bunch of flowers would do me."

"Yes, but you're not dating a florist."

"True." Vicky shifted again. "But it wasn't the crime of the century and you do like her — surely that's worth considering. Are you miserable without her?"

Kate nodded slowly.

"Do you miss her?"

Another nod.

Vicky sighed. "Then stop being such a wombat and go round there."

"That's what Jess said."

"And it's not often I say to take Jess's advice, but in this case, I'll agree with her."

That made Kate chuckle. "Maybe tomorrow when I cycle over to see Mum."

Vicky cleared her throat and sat forward. "And in the spirit of forgiveness and moving forward, I'm having a birthday party next week and you're invited — with Meg of course, I have faith in love even if you don't." Vicky paused and lowered her voice like she was telling Kate some MI6-style secrets. "And I've also invited Mum and Lawrence."

Kate's eyes widened and she clicked her tongue twice. "Mum and Lawrence too? Why are you whispering?"

"I'm not whispering." Vicky crossed her arms over her chest and frowned.

"Not now. Now you're sulking," Kate said. "So he's not the pariah you first thought?"

Vicky exhaled. "Laugh all you like, but I was just looking out for Mum's safety. But yes, maybe I was a bit harsh on him. This is me holding out an olive branch to Mum, so they better be able to make it."

"I'm sure Lawrence could think of nowhere else he'd rather be."

31

Friday night and Meg was so over this week. Her mum hadn't been feeling well again, so Meg had been stretched to her limit, although Jamie and Anya had been brilliant. On top of that, she'd had no word from Kate even though she'd now sent her a bunch of flowers for seven days straight. If the shoe was on the other foot, seven bunches of flowers would make Meg react. But clearly, Kate took a different shoe size.

Still, at least Meg had a Friday night dinner planned with Jamie and Greg — she could be waited on hand and foot, with gay men at her beck and call. Jamie lived in Crouch End, which was now a well-heeled area of north London. It had also undergone a significant amount of gentrification, judging by the cool bars and restaurants Meg spotted on every corner. And inside every single one, Meg looked for Kate. Kate sitting in the window, Kate standing at a bar, Kate browsing in a boutique. She just needed to see her and explain. Perhaps she should go round to her house — she knew where she lived after all.

But then again, Kate had ignored the flowers, so perhaps that was a sign. *A sign to stay away.*

Meg walked on up the main road towards her brother's flat, passing two craft beer pubs and an artisan bakery. A few minutes later, Meg pressed Jamie's bell. She was greeted by his boyfriend, Greg.

"You've shaved your beard off." Meg stepped through the door and reached up to Greg's chin. Greg had a thick head of wiry, tightly sprung hair and his physique was so buff, it would instantly pass an army inspection. His skin was fake-tanned to the colour of mahogany and he looked at least five years younger without his beard.

"I always said you were observant." Greg gave her a hug and ushered her into their immaculate pad — clean lines and muted shades of blue, green and grey, with just the right amount of harsh corners and soft furnishings.

"Jamie in the kitchen?" Meg followed Greg down the hallway of their converted Victorian flat and into the kitchen at the back, which overlooked the garden. Their cat Jupiter sat on the work surface beside Jamie, supervising his chopping and slicing. Jupiter was jet black, save for a white ear and chin. His long whiskers were very still as he watched Jamie, purring by his side.

"Hey sis," Jamie said, turning his head to Meg.

She kissed her brother's cheek, shrugged off her coat and sat down at their kitchen table. That was one thing she could match Jamie on — she had space for a kitchen table too. Well, she did at the moment. But he beat her in everything else — love, ambition, sanity. Okay, maybe she wasn't quite mad yet, but her current situation was starting to edge her there.

"Wine?" Greg was already opening the fridge and reaching for a bottle.

"Please," Meg said. "Have you heard from Mum today?"

Jamie nodded, without turning his head. He was chopping onions, garlic and bacon. "Yeah — I called at lunchtime and she sounded really good. I think her mate Janet was coming over tonight for dinner."

Meg's shoulders slumped. "Good — at least that's one less thing to worry about." Meg smiled as Greg placed a large glass of white on the table in front of her. "You're an angel sent from Planet Gay," she told him. "So what's happened to the beard?"

Greg stroked his chin. "Just fancied a change. Plus, I read in The Guardian that beards were going out of fashion, so I thought I should do the decent thing and get rid."

Meg made an O with her mouth. "Have you told him?" she mock-whispered, inclining her head towards her brother.

"He's ignoring it," Greg whispered back. "He's an individual who has his own style. At least, that's what he told me."

Jamie didn't even bother turning around. "I don't have a beard, I have sleekly designed stubble. There's a *world* of difference."

* * *

"So she hasn't responded at all to the flowers?" Jamie sipped his white wine and sat back. They'd just finished his spaghetti carbonara — "the lighter version with a lot less fat" — and were now digesting before dessert.

Meg shook her head.

Jamie's phone was plugged into his speakers which were currently pushing out a chilled playlist, which complemented the ambience perfectly. This evening had calmed Meg down — either that, or she'd drunk more wine than she should have.

"And how many have you sent?"

"Seven bouquets."

Greg whistled loudly. "Seven. That's damning. That's damning in the extreme. She must *really* hate you."

Meg shot Greg a look. "Not really helping."

Jamie kicked him under the table and took over. "Maybe she just needs time. Or maybe she's not for you, like I said. Some things work out, some things don't." He paused. "Maybe it's time for you to stop sending flowers and find someone else."

Meg sighed. "But I don't want anybody else. She's what I've been waiting for. Kate could have been the *one*."

Jamie raised his eyebrows and chuckled. "The *one*? Have you been reading fairytales again?"

Meg reached over and slapped him. "Stop being so cynical," she laughed. "I've seen the way you glaze over when you talk about Greg."

"You sure that's not Jupiter?" Greg intervened.

"I think it might be," Jamie concurred, before leaning over and planting a kiss on his boyfriend's lips.

"Whatever. I don't want to give this up — I want her back. We had *amazing* sex. I can't believe she's just going to walk away from that."

Now it was Jamie's turn to lean over to Meg — he stroked her arm. "Well the sad fact is, beautiful, you just might have to. Seven bouquets of flowers and no contact says something. I hope they weren't all the expensive stuff."

The music stopped as Jamie's mobile went off. He jumped up to answer it, seeing the number flash up on the screen.

"Hi, Mum." Pause. "Oh hi." Frown. "What?" Pause.

More pausing and frowning.

The hairs on Meg's neck and arms stood up. She rested her eyes on Jamie, who'd gone stiff.

"And where is she now?" Pause. "Okay, great. Yeah, let me know for sure, but probably there. Thanks for letting me know."

Jamie pressed the red button and placed his phone on the sideboard, turning the speakers off.

"Fuck." He wiped his palms up and down his thighs. "Okay, so Janet said there's no need to panic, but Mum's had another episode — they're not sure whether it's a heart attack or what. But Janet's called an ambulance — it'd just arrived and now they're going to hospital."

Meg's stomach dropped and a ball of carbonara worked its way up her windpipe. "But she's okay?"

"Well, she might have had a heart attack..."

Meg pushed her chair out abruptly. "You know what I mean."

Jamie looked around for his keys, wiping his mouth. "Yes, I know what you mean." He paused. "Fuck, we can't even drive now — we'll have to get a cab to the hospital."

"I'll call." Greg already had his phone in his hand.

32

Saturday dawned and Kate was on her bike, cycling through the October drizzle. First stop, Fabulous Flowers. Second stop, her mum's house. By the time she arrived, the sweat was trickling down her back and her hair was sticky as she took her helmet off. No matter. Today wasn't about looking gorgeous. Today was about seeing if there was a way forward with Meg.

Kate's heart was pounding as she approached the florist — she was still nervous. She hit the brakes and stopped outside, putting the ball of her right foot on the pavement, but frowned when she saw the shutters were still down. She glanced at her watch — 10.15am. Meg should be here, it was a Saturday. Kate's heart jumped into her throat. Surely Meg would get staff in to cover unless something awful had happened? Kate's stomach lurched as her mind ran through the possible scenarios. She should have replied to the flowers and not played so hard to get. What an idiot.

Five minutes later, her knock on Meg's front door was answered by a pyjama-clad Tanya.

"It's you." Tanya yawned, curling up her bare toes.

Kate was in a hurry. "Is Meg in? I just went to the shop and it's closed."

"Want me to check my bed?" Tanya asked.

Kate glowered.

Tanya smiled sleepily. "Just a little joke to lighten the mood," she said. "She's at the hospital — her mum was rushed in last night with another suspected heart attack. She left early to see her this morning."

The blood drained from Kate's face. "Shit." She paused. "But she's okay?"

Tanya nodded. "I think so — she's at the Memorial. You know the way?"

Images of Kate's dash to the exact same hospital to be greeted by her dead father flashed through her brain. She knew the way.

"You should go — she'd love to see you." Tanya pursed her lips. "She's been a mess all week."

"That makes two of us."

* * *

Kate jammed her bike lock into place and walked into the hospital, breathing in the heady mix of germs, grime and bleach skating on the scuffed floors. She'd texted Meg and they'd agreed to meet in the café at 11am. Kate got directions from reception and went straight there, scoring a table in the corner.

When Meg walked in, Kate's well-rehearsed talk of future honesty and no more secrets flew out the window. Meg's face was drawn, her eyes were puffy and she looked broken.

Kate remembered that exact feeling.

Meg approached the table cautiously, dragging her feet.

Kate was having none of it. She got up and went to meet her, wrapping her arms around Meg.

In return, Meg collapsed into her and wept on her shoulder.

Kate held her tighter.

After a while, Meg sniffed, brushing her hand across her nose, leaving a glistening stain on her wrist.

Kate reached into her bag and offered her a tissue.

Meg smiled. "Sorry about that," she began. "It's been a long 24 hours."

"I bet," Kate said. "How is she?"

Meg blew her nose strongly, the noise making the people at the next table look over. "She's hanging in there. Not critical, but not out of the woods." Meg shook her head. "I've been letting her do too much, but from now on, none of that. She's resting in front of the TV if I have anything to do with it." Meg put her head in her hands. "It's just such a shock." She spoke through her fingers. "She was fine — she seemed fine."

Kate nodded. "I know."

Meg reached out and took Kate's hand. She stared at it, then slowly, she brought it up to her mouth and kissed it. "I'm so glad you're here. I wanted to call you, but with everything..."

Kate squeezed Meg's hand, taking in her watery eyes and red nose. "None of that matters now. It was stupid." Kate paused. "And you look ridiculously cute with a red nose, by the way."

The corners of Meg's mouth turned upwards. "Don't — I look a right mess." She smoothed her top down with her hands.

Kate shook her head. "You could never look a mess."

Meg's features crumpled, but she pulled it back together at the last minute and took a deep breath. "Stop being so nice to me or I'll cry." She blew her nose again. Her eyes settled on the coffee cup in front of her.

"Is that for me?" Meg turned to Kate, her eyes glistening.

"Black Americano for the lady. Straight up, just the way you like it."

Meg took another deep breath and burst into tears.

* * *

"The hospital food — honestly. I mean, they gave me a menu this morning and I chose from it, but I thought it was odd that I was only being allowed puréed food." Olivia tried to sit up further, but couldn't quite manage it.

"You want some help?" Meg was up and had a hold of the pillows, getting them to where Olivia wanted them before sitting back down.

"But now they're telling me that was a mistake — they gave me the wrong menu! I had puréed breakfast and lunch, so I'm pretty pleased I get to have a solid dinner tonight."

"You want us to run out and get you a McDonald's?" Kate asked.

Olivia laughed. "I've got a dicky heart, not dicky tastebuds." She had the latest edition of Female Health & Fitness on her bed and picked it up, flicking to the article with Meg's photo.

"And I hear you're responsible for making my daughter famous? She looks pretty snazzy, doesn't she? My gorgeous girl." Olivia smiled at Meg, then stroked her jaw.

"She's certainly that," Kate said, rubbing Meg's thigh. "Did you read the article?"

Olivia nodded. "It's good. I also like the fitness secrets of Princess Emily. But I have to say, I wouldn't like to live without my Custard Creams. Sounds like too much of a regimented diet to me."

Olivia was doing remarkably well and the doctors were amazed at her progress. Meg insisted it was just because they wanted the bed back, but Olivia was thrilled, whatever the reason. She raised a quizzical eyebrow at Kate and Meg now over her reading glasses, laying the magazine across her knees.

"So are you two back on? Resolved your differences? Going to live happily ever after?" There was a twinkle in her eye as she asked.

"Mum!" Meg shook her head. "Sorry — a near-death experience and she thinks she can say what she likes."

"Well. You might die tomorrow, so you may as well make today happy."

"Very true." Kate smiled hesitantly at Meg. "And yes, I think we're back on track, aren't we?"

In reply, Meg kissed her cheek and looked back at Olivia. "Very much so."

"Good," Olivia picked up the magazine again, before lowering it slightly to look at Kate. "Because I like you."

"Glad to hear it." Kate blushed.

"Are we disturbing the coven?"

All three women looked over towards the doorway, where Jamie and Greg stood with a bunch of flowers and a box of Black Magic, Olivia's favourites.

"Did you buy those at the gift shop?" Olivia pursed her lips.

"We're not open, so I had no choice." Jamie put the flowers on the end of Olivia's bed, along with the chocolates, then walked over and kissed his mum on the cheek. "And glad to see you're feeling better, you cantankerous old woman."

Olivia smiled at him. "Less of the old, thank you."

Greg stepped forward to kiss Olivia, then Meg introduced Kate to the boys.

Jamie's grin was wide. "It's a shame it took Mum being rushed into hospital to meet you, but it's lovely to finally do so."

Kate shook his hand. "You, too." Jamie didn't look at all how she'd imagined — somehow, she'd pictured tall, blonde, handsome. Not that he wasn't handsome, but Jamie was more distinctive in his looks: paper-thin skin and thick hair, the colour of loose change. Kate was drawn to him immediately.

"I can't believe it was only last night Meg was telling us all about how you hadn't responded to her flower assault…" Greg was cut off as Jamie kicked him in the shin.

Greg bent down to rub his leg, then stood up, looking sheepish. "Sorry," he told Meg.

Meg simply shook her head.

Kate smiled. "I was planning to react, I was just waiting to see how many she was going to send. I actually cycled round to the florist this morning to call off the flower war as I've run out of vases, but then it wasn't open and all roads led to here."

* * *

Meg and Kate walked out of the hospital two hours later, leaving Olivia to get some rest. Jamie and Greg were coming back for evening visiting, and Olivia had urged Meg to take a break and spend time with Kate. Meg had reluctantly agreed and now here they were, hand in hand, passing under the hospital's entrance awning.

Meg looked straight ahead as she began to talk. "So I'm not sure what to do now. This morning we weren't talking and now we're together in hospital. Bit odd, isn't it?"

Kate squeezed Meg's hand. "You could say that. But look at it this way — we've got a whole day ahead of us and we can do what we like. Together." Kate stopped walking. "I've got an idea — you happy to follow?"

Meg nodded. "I don't want to make any decisions today, so I'm all yours."

* * *

A London village on the Thames, Greenwich was the perfect backdrop for an impromptu date. Stepping off the boat was like stepping onto a giant film set, with history and glamour oozing from every building, choreographed green spaces and sunlight glinting off every surface. Yes, even the weather was better in Greenwich — when they'd boarded the water taxi in central London, the air had been lank and greasy.

"I haven't been here in ages," Meg said, as they strolled up the boat ramp. "I came for lunch with Jamie a few years back when he was doing a property down here, but not since then."

"I love it." Kate paused. "Still in central London but you really could be in a seaside town. It's a breath of fresh air and I thought we could do with that today. Wipe the slate clean. Start afresh?"

A warm surge flowed through Meg's body. "I like the sound of that."

Their feet crunched on the gravel in the university grounds as they strode across it, the strained sound of an out-of-tune trumpet floating from the window of the music building. The gloriously statuesque buildings were light grey in colour, with intricate stone work, thick wooden doors and grand arches, history compressed into their bricks.

They chose an historic riverside pub and snagged a table by the window — so close to the river they could smell its maritime glaze. Over doorstep sandwiches filled with smoked salmon and cream cheese alongside hot, salty chips, Meg noted the rise and fall of Kate's chest as she spoke, and imagined her delicate skin beneath her top. She ran her tongue across her bottom teeth as Kate chatted about work, her colleagues and her past week. Meg listened, as well as taking in the wrinkles around Kate's piercing aqua eyes, the square of her jawline, her strong neck and her calm, assured presence.

When they'd finished eating and were feeling more human — neither had eaten breakfast — Kate led Meg out of the university grounds and up into the royal park. They passed a packed kids' playground and skirted a myriad of dogs and runners, walking up the steep incline to the top of the park. From this vantage point, London was laid out before them across the river, looking larger than life.

Meg fixed her scarf tighter around her neck as she surveyed the scene. "You think there are some people squinting out from one of the pods on the London Eye right now, trying to make us out in the distance?"

Kate's body shook as she laughed. "Nah, they're probably just trying to tune out the bunch of teenagers they've got in the pod with them."

Higher up now, the wind swirled around the pair and when Meg shivered, Kate put an arm around her.

After some moments taking in the sprawling, widescreen view, Meg spoke. "I'm glad they worked, you know."

Kate turned her head. "Worked?"

"The flowers."

Kate smiled. "Me too."

"I'm sorry everything got so messed up. I'm sorry I wasn't honest with you in the first place." Meg moved her jaw one way, then the other. She kept looking straight ahead — it was easier that way.

"Me too." Kate matched her stance, looking into the distance. "Why weren't you, though? I mean, living with your ex isn't unheard of."

Meg paused, looking pensive. "I think I was embarrassed. I didn't think I'd ever meet someone again and I wasn't really pushing Tanya to sell the house. It kinda... Suited me a bit, I guess. And then when you came along, I panicked. I thought you'd think less of me for still living with her. So I figured I could hide it and get her to move out before you found out."

Kate laughed. "That's a lot of thinking."

"Not the best thought-out plan, I'll admit." Meg paused. "And that was certainly the case when you turned up on our doorstep that night. God, I wanted the ground to swallow me up."

Kate tightened her grip around Meg's shoulders, risking a glance right. "And what do you think now?"

Meg glanced left. "That I was stupid. That I should never have done it. And that I'm glad we're here together today, that my mum's on the mend and I'm not home alone feeling miserable."

Kate placed a kiss on Meg's rosy cheek. "That makes two of us."

They turned and walked along one of the many paths available, which eventually brought them out near to the park bandstand. Kate grabbed Meg's hand and ran towards it, pulling Meg with her. She kissed her knuckles and bowed, before motioning for Meg to get up on one of the benches that lined the bandstand's interior.

"What?" Meg narrowed her eyes at Kate.

"Up," was Kate's simple instruction.

"Why?"

"Why?" Kate's tone was raised. "We were only talking about The Sound Of Music recently. It's your favourite film, isn't it?"

Meg laughed, before getting up on the bench. "Don't tell me you want to re-enact the scene, line by line."

"If you could do that, I'd be forever impressed."

"Be careful what you wish for, captain." And with that, Meg began walking around the edge of the bench, leaping dramatically when she came to the end of one and had to make it to the next, even though the gap was almost non-existent. "So are you going to start, or shall I?"

Kate held out her hand and Meg took it as she continued her movement around the circle of the bandstand, atop the circular arrangement of benches.

"Start what?" Kate asked.

"The singing." Meg had a wicked grin on her face.

Kate stopped moving. "You really want to sing?" Her mouth had dropped open slightly.

Meg started walking again, which jolted Kate into action as she accompanied her around the bandstand.

"Okay, I'll start." Meg cleared her throat. "I am 32 going on 33, and I really like to pose," she sang. Meg broke out some model poses, before carrying on.

Kate began to laugh as she continued to follow Meg around.

Meg grinned at her delight. "Women in caps, and jeans and hi-tops, honey I know of those!"

Kate laughed loudly, dropping Meg's hand to clap her. "Making it your own, Ms Harding." Kate still walked beside her.

"I am 32 going on 33," Meg continued, punching the air. "But I'm hoping, I've met my match." She pointed at Kate. "She's sexy and great, makes my heart beat at rate, I think she's quite the catch."

With that, Meg jumped down from the bench, bowed to Kate and kissed her hand. "Madam," she said, bowing again.

"That was some performance," Kate said.

"No performance," Meg replied, shaking her head. Her heart truly was thumping in her chest. "I meant every single word."

They were standing in the centre of the bandstand now, facing each other. Meg was breathing heavily, getting her breath back. After a few seconds she joined her hands with Kate and they stood, staring at each other.

"It's kinda apt being here, isn't it." Meg motioned with her head at their surroundings. "A grand space, full of possibility. Just like our relationship so far, wouldn't you say?"

Kate nodded her head. "I would."

Meg stared into Kate's eyes, ensuring she felt the connection too. If the spark behind Kate's pupils was anything to go by, Meg was pretty sure she did.

"The past week has been a rainy parade of what-ifs and coming to terms with the fact that you might not want to see me again." Meg gulped in some air. "But whatever the outcome, the house is on the market and I'm ready to move on." Meg met Kate's gaze full-on and entwined their fingers even tighter. "I can do it on my own, but I'd rather not. I'd rather do it with you by my side. So what do you say, captain Carter? Shall we give it another go? Double or quits?" Meg stroked her thumb up and down Kate's hand.

Kate's features softened, and outside the bandstand, she heard some children arguing over a ball. She tuned them out. "I'm not much of a gambler, so double or quits isn't my style," she said.

Meg's face dropped. "Oh."

"However, I'm pretty confident this isn't a gamble. Not if what my heart is telling me is anything to go by."

Meg held on tight. "And what's your heart telling you?"

Kate allowed a smile to form on her lips. "It's telling me I really missed you this week. It's telling me you're pretty hot. And it's telling me we should get out of this bandstand before we're ambushed by kids."

They looked around and sure enough, five kids were running towards them. Meg tugged on Kate's arm and they ran off into the park, laughing.

* * *

They got the tube back to the hospital to see Olivia, who'd looked tired and in need of a good rest — rather like the whole family. They'd lounged lazily around her bed until she'd shooed them out, telling them to go and have a Saturday night out "like young people should".

Jamie, Greg, Kate and Meg had left the hospital and decamped to the Bull & Bush to talk over the day, eat cheeseburgers and drink large glasses of soothing Rioja. It was the topic of much hilarity that this was their first time out as a foursome, and what a picture they must have painted. But Meg was pleased that Kate was there, and the evening sailed by in a river of good humour which was just the tonic they all needed.

They kissed goodnight outside the pub and the men headed towards the tube, the women towards Meg's place. Meg was feeling somewhat apprehensive about that, even though her big secret was now out in the open.

"You know that Tanya might be there," she told Kate, as they turned into her street and strolled along the rows of terraced houses with small front lawns.

"I know, but we're big girls, we can handle her. You point out something up high and I'll rugby-tackle her. Simple." Kate glanced at Meg with a smile as she said the last bit.

"And there was me worrying you wouldn't know how to act."

They walked on side by side in silence for a few moments before eventually arriving at Meg's door. She got her keys from her bag and turned to Kate. "Ready?"

"I'm right behind you — literally and metaphorically."

However, after all Meg's fretting, Tanya wasn't in the house today — the lounge was tidy, the kitchen wiped and everything was presentable. She was audibly relieved — she desperately wanted to make a good first impression on Kate, especially after last time. Meg was also sending up a small prayer of thanks to whatever goddess it was who'd made her change her bed sheets only two days ago.

They went through to the kitchen where the clock read 10.45pm. Meg was beyond exhausted. She leaned against the kitchen counter as Kate stood beside her.

"You want a drink or something? Or shall we just go to bed?"

Kate raised an eyebrow.

"And I might even mean to sleep, more's the pity — didn't get much last night, strangely." Meg slumped into Kate, all at once overwhelmed with the day.

"I'm all for sleep." Kate placed a kiss on Meg's blonde head. "Especially if it involves sleeping with you."

"No tea? Or a beer? I don't want you accusing me of being a bad host."

Kate stroked Meg's face. "So long as it's me and you, I don't care what we do."

"Then I'm knackered — let's go to bed."

Meg was asleep within eight minutes.

* * *

The following morning, and Meg was awake before Kate — it was a florist thing. But waking up to a hot body in her own bed was a novel and most welcome situation. Meg kissed

Kate's shoulder lightly but she didn't stir. From the sounds outside, she guessed it was still fairly early — pre-9am at least. No lawn mowers were deadening the air, no children shouting, and only the odd car engine could be heard chugging by. Meg allowed herself a moment to relax, sinking into the bed.

Until she remembered her mum. In the hospital. After her heart attack. It was that few seconds in the morning where she didn't remember and then — boom! A lightning bolt in her brain.

She grabbed her phone from the bedside table and held it up — it needed a charge. She had a text. Meg drew in a deep breath and clicked on it. But then the phone fell out of her hand and landed on her nose, bouncing off it and onto the bedding.

"Fuck!" Meg was holding her face — that always hurt more than she thought.

Beside her, Kate stuck her head up and peered out of one eye at Meg. "You alright?"

"Yeah, my phone just attacked me." Meg sat up a bit more and retrieved it.

Kate closed her eyes again and moved to be nearer to Meg.

Meg clicked, read, sighed, then smiled. "She's okay."

Kate opened an eye again. "Your mum?"

"Yep."

Kate gave Meg a squeeze. "Awesome." Her hand wended its way up under the covers, and under Meg's T-shirt. Kate stroked along Meg's pelvic bone and slid over her belly button, before settling on her stomach. She raised herself up on her elbow and kissed Meg's shoulder, then with a bit more effort, her lips.

"Good morning." Meg kissed Kate right back, placing her phone back on her bedside table. Then she put an arm around Kate, who huddled into her, still half-asleep.

Sex was on the horizon this morning, Meg was certain,

but she also revelled in these times of calm that she'd forgotten existed. The sleepy morning moments. Humid skin. Quiet stillness. Hot, lazy breath. Heavy limbs. Foggy thoughts. At this moment, Meg was totally at one with the weight of Kate's body on hers — Meg could taste the contentment on her tongue, could feel her bones sighing as they squeezed it tight.

Kate scooched closer and opened one eye. "You okay? You're very quiet."

Meg nodded. "I'm more than okay. I was just thinking how lovely this was. You, me, the stillness."

"And no Tanya," Kate said.

Meg laughed. "You had to ruin our tranquil morning by mentioning her?"

Kate stroked Meg's stomach again and smiled. "Sorry."

They were silent for a few minutes, just enjoying each other's presence and warmth. Until the baby next door started screaming.

"Well that's spoilt the peace and quiet. But I can think of a way to block the noise out." Meg slid down the bed so her head was level with Kate, then proceeded to kiss her on the lips, on the neck, on the cheek, then back to the lips again. After a few seconds she slid her tongue into Kate's warm mouth. Meg's heart exploded in her chest, but she styled it out, riding the waves of want as they surfed down her body.

"I could well get used to waking up with you." Meg kissed Kate's face again.

Kate eased back and grinned at Meg. "Me, too."

Meg sat up, before gently nudging Kate onto her front. Then she threw a leg over Kate's bum and straddled her, running her hands up and down Kate's warm, naked back, grinding into her with her hips.

Kate was still rubbing her eyes against the pillow.

Meg leaned down, her breasts touching Kate's back, her breath hot in Kate's ear. "I know I'm more the morning person, and that's fine. You just enjoy the ride," she said. "All that sleep has left me with *bags* of energy." As she finished, Meg trailed a tongue up Kate's earlobe and around her ear.

"I love that you're a morning person." Kate's voice was rusty with sleep.

As Kate closed her eyes, Meg pressed her lips to the back of Kate's neck.

Kate shivered.

A firecracker rumbled through Meg's body, ending at her centre. She got to work, trailing her tongue up Kate's back in one long stroke. Kate's skin was hot and salty, and best of all, it covered her whole body. Meg kissed her way from Kate's shoulder blades to her butt, nibbling her cheeks, which got the desired response.

Then Meg's thigh was between Kate's legs, shifting them open. A bead of sweat trickled down Meg's back. She ground into Kate, hand stroking up and down between her legs, before eventually slipping inside her from behind.

Kate was so wet and inviting, Meg couldn't help but groan out loud. "Damn, you feel good."

Kate turned her head, struggling to speak, her body taut with anticipation. "I thought you said I could lie back and… Aaah… Enjoy the ride?"

Meg grinned and slapped her butt cheek with her free hand. "I lied."

Kate's knuckles turn white as she clenched her pillow and groaned again.

Meg increased her speed, with Kate showing she wanted more by pressing back into her. Meg thrust forward as she moved in, out, around and around, Kate moving perfectly in sync, Kate's grip tightening with every second.

The rush was building in Meg's body as she picked up her speed. She smiled down at Kate's gorgeous form, soaking up this moment of poetry. Meg pushed Kate higher and higher, until eventually her body spasmed and she flew over the edge with a strangled cry, sinking forward and then pushing back onto Meg with another cry.

But Meg didn't let up. She was still behind Kate, still going, now circling Kate's swollen clit. Very soon, Kate threw back her head and came again, riding out her orgasm to the end before collapsing under Meg.

Meg allowed Kate to lie flat before extracting herself. She then lay fully on top of her, their hot skin mingling deliciously. The sheets smelt of their warm bodies and the moment was captured in slow-motion — it was raw, intimate and blissful. Meg was folded around Kate and she wanted to stay there forever.

They lay there for a while getting their breath back, then Kate began to giggle.

"You think your neighbours heard any of that?"

Meg smiled into Kate's shoulder. "They wake me up enough, so if they did, it's about time." She kissed Kate's back and ran a hand over her bum cheek. It fitted neatly into Meg's hand, which she absolutely loved.

"That was... You are... Incredible." Kate rolled Meg off of her gently, before running a hand down the side of her face and kissing her softly.

"I know," Meg said. "You make it pretty easy, though."

"So do you," Kate replied.

They lay there, staring into each other's eyes, lost in the moment, their breathing returning to normal.

"I missed you," Kate said.

Meg kissed her lips softly. "I missed you too. More than you can possibly imagine." Kate had cinema skin, a superstar smile.

"If we ever have another disagreement, can you do me a favour?"

Meg nodded. "Whatever you like."

"Just remember this, remember us. And remember we should not be apart. Deal?"

A 100-watt smile lit up Meg's face. "That's a deal I have no problem signing up to."

Kate jumped out of bed and scrabbled in her bag.

Meg frowned. "What are you doing?"

"Getting something for us to sign." Kate scooched back onto the bed, clutching her wallet and a pen.

Meg shivered and wrapped the duvet around her again. "You're letting the cold in."

Kate produced a Sainsbury's receipt and, using her wallet as a surface, wrote on it. "I, Kate Carter," she spoke as she wrote. But the pen wasn't playing ball — Kate shook it and scribbled until the ink ran free. Then she returned to her writing space on the edge of the receipt. "I, Kate Carter, promise to remember our brilliant morning sex the next time we have a row. We should not give that up. Signed, me."

Kate offered the receipt, wallet and pen to Meg.

Meg looked at her like she'd gone mad. "You really want me to sign a Sainsbury's receipt?"

Kate nodded. "Yes. We're incredible together. We should never forget that." Kate put the pen into Meg's hand.

Meg signed her name and gave it back to Kate. "You're crazy, you know that, don't you?"

Kate smiled and put the receipt in her wallet, before grabbing Meg under the covers. "And you're a lover of crazy, if I remember correctly," she said.

Meg couldn't help but smile as she rolled her eyes.

33

One week later, and life was almost back to normality. With Olivia was out of hospital, and Kate and Meg back on, tonight was Vicky's big party.

"You think it's going to kick off tonight?" Jess was leaning in their kitchen doorway, examining her fingernails.

Kate was loading the dishwasher, filling the top tray with mugs. There was a waft of fish as she shut the door, and Kate wrinkled her nose as she straightened up.

"Vicky has talked herself off the cliff — or perhaps I should congratulate your big brother for that — and now she'll be all sweetness and light. At least in front of Mum. Plus, it's her birthday, so she's got tons of mates to distract her. It'll be fine," Kate said. "I hope. What time's your girlfriend getting here?"

Jess checked her phone. "Any minute now."

Right on cue, the doorbell rang.

Jess looked panicked. "Shit, I'm not even changed and she's bang on time. Damn her."

Kate chuckled as she heard Jess take the stairs too quick, swear as she hit Kate's bike at the bottom, then heard the sound of lips connecting.

A few seconds later Lucy appeared and gave Kate a hug. "Big night tonight!" Lucy was loosening her shoulders, as if she were about to compete in some Olympic-style javelin tournament.

"Yep — Vicky finally grows up, age 38."

"I didn't mean that — I meant you introducing Meg to the family. That's a big deal." Lucy elbowed Kate in the ribs.

Since when did she take over Jess's wind-up duties? They'd clearly been spending far too much time together.

"No biggie," Kate lied. "It might have been normally, but everyone's going to have their eyes glued to Vicky instead — there's no room for me and my new squeeze. Tonight is going to be a drama-free evening with no heart attacks or tantrums or anything else of that nature. Everybody got that?"

Jess and Lucy both nodded.

"Good," Kate said. "Anyhow, I better go and get ready. Half an hour till we leave?"

* * *

"I don't think we're in Kansas anymore, Toto." Jess swiped her Oyster card over the reader and the gate opened. Lucy and Kate followed her out.

"Finchley has its charms," Kate said.

"There are so many places on the tube that you never go to. Cockfosters. Morden. Epping. Maybe we should have a day where we go to all the places we've never been. Drink a half at the end of every tube line. What do you think?" Jess's face lit up.

"I think you'd spend half your day on the tube, and the other half in dodgy pubs. I've told you before — there's a reason we live in the inner city. It's got better stuff in it." Kate scratched her cheek as they began the walk up the High Street.

"Killjoy. What do you think?"

Lucy wrinkled her nose and took Jess's hand. "I'm with Kate on this one. Take some photos, put them on Instagram, and we'll see you back at the flat with a glass of wine." She grinned broadly at Jess.

Jess shook her head. "You can tell we're not in the honeymoon period anymore."

A couple of minutes later, Kate pointed out a couple of prime landmarks — the Pret where she'd first bought coffee for her and Meg; and then Fabulous Flowers, which they stopped in front of now, peering in the window.

"Nice display," Lucy said.

Kate smiled. "Pretty good, isn't it? Artistic." An autumnal scene played out in the window, all shades of green, mustard yellow and golden brown to the fore. "Don't ask me what they all are, but Meg's got an eye for colour."

"True," Jess said. "But while we're here, can you re-enact that day you fell over on the pavement?" Jess's shoulders shook with laughter. "Was it about here?" she asked, pointing to the pavement. She shifted marginally left. "Or about here?"

Kate pursed her lips, but couldn't stop a smile coming through. "Yes, very funny. I'm going to treat that comment with the disdain it deserves." Kate shook her head and walked away, but was still smiling.

"Spoilsport," Jess said, catching her up.

"Talking of Meg — where we meeting her?" Lucy asked.

"She's coming straight to the party, probably around nine."

"And is she bringing her housemate?" Jess backed away as she asked.

Kate gave Jess a withering look. "I hope so. Because there won't be enough tension tonight."

"I thought you said there wouldn't be any tension?" Jess said.

"It's Vicky. I lied."

They hailed a cab, stopping to pick up supplies for the party — beer, red wine, fizz. At the door, they were greeted by Jess's brother Jack, who was dressed in a vibrant floral shirt. His cheeks were flushed as he greeted the trio, taking coats and brushing cheeks with his lips.

"You're looking very Noel Edmonds tonight," Jess told him. "Are we the first here?"

"Almost — how terribly unfashionable you are," Jack said. "Where's number four?"

"She's the fashionable one, clearly." Kate gave Jack a hug.

"What you lack in timings, you more than make up for in diversity. Three lesbians to add to the party mix — we're all for equal opportunities in the suburbs."

In response, Jess whacked him on the arm.

Jack laughed in the way only brothers can, carrying the coats upstairs.

The trio walked through to the kitchen, where the table was laid with a party buffet where surprisingly, not everything was beige. As well as having two types of hummus, quiche, a whole salmon and assorted dips, there was even a cheeseboard with grapes *and* quince — terribly cosmopolitan. Vicky was busy eating cocktail sausages when they walked in — she had four empty cocktail sticks in her hand already. Cocktail sausages were Vicky's kryptonite.

"You're here!" Vicky walked around the table and hugged Kate first, before turning her attention to Jess and Lucy.

"We thought we better come." Kate brandished the present bag under her nose. "Happy 38th, older sister supreme!"

"Thanks." Vicky plucked the Champagne from the bag, then stashed it away in a cupboard. "That's not being touched — I'll save it for a special occasion." She took the bag Lucy was holding up and repeated the trick. "I've got Prosecco for tonight," Vicky confided.

"Mum here yet?" Kate asked.

Vicky nodded. "In the lounge with the boys and the other guests. And Lawrence, of course." She whispered the last bit.

"And did you play nicely?" Kate braced for the worst.

"Like a model child in a model playground," Vicky said. "No hitting, punching or kicking."

Kate gave her a hug. "Proud of you, sis."

"Early days, mind," Vicky added with a grin.

Jess opened the fridge and prised a bottle of Prosecco from the door. "Shall we get this party started, then? Got some glasses?"

Vicky rounded the table and set up four plastic flutes on the counter-top. "Saves on washing up," she said.

* * *

Half an hour later and the party was beginning to rev up, the living room stacked with starched men and bronzed women, an overspill in the hallway and kitchen. On the stereo, 70s and 80s party classics were caressing the room, Billy Joel following Kylie, Kool And The Gang cheek-to-cheek with Rick Astley.

In the kitchen, the buffet on the dining table was already half-eaten, which Kate's mum was inordinately pleased about.

"Sometimes, you put all this food out and nobody eats it. Criminal. So it's good to see it not going to waste," she'd told Kate ten minutes previous. Kate hoped she got as much pleasure from such small things when she got older — satisfaction had oozed out of her mum.

Kate checked her watch — nearly nine, so Meg should be here soon. She was looking forward to showing her off to friends and family as her girlfriend. Olivia had been released from hospital the previous day and seemed to be coping fine at home. Kate had told Meg she didn't need to come tonight if she wanted to stay with her mum, but Olivia had insisted.

"Fantastic spread, isn't it?"

A voice disturbed her thoughts as Kate's hand hovered over the home-made sausage rolls, which were delicious. She turned her head to see Lawrence smiling at her.

"Yeah, great, isn't it?" Kate's mind flashed an image of Lawrence lounging in her mum's bed, smoking a post-coital cigarette after she'd gatecrashed their slice of afternoon delight. Kate shook her head briskly, trying to dislodge the scene. Luckily, it worked.

Lawrence had a white paper plate in his left hand, already adorned with quiche, nachos, cheese and dips. "We ate before we left, but I just can't resist — I love a party buffet." He smiled broadly as he popped a cocktail sausage into his mouth. "Your young lady not here yet?"

Kate moved out of his way so he could get to the salmon. "Any minute now."

"Looking forward to meeting her."

Kate nodded and walked out into the hallway. She wasn't sure why, but that last comment grated. He wasn't her dad, so what did it matter to him about meeting Meg? Right at this moment, she had sympathy with how Vicky had been feeling. Lawrence wasn't their dad and could never replace him, but clearly he considered himself a fixture in their lives now.

Kate was still bristling when the doorbell chimed. She immediately went to open it and there stood Meg, looking tantalisingly gorgeous, giving Kate an instant smile.

"Hello beautiful," Kate said, welcoming her in.

"Back at ya," Meg replied, taking Kate into her arms and giving her a squeeze. Then she pulled back and planted her lips onto Kate's.

The usual Meg effect rippled through Kate's body, and she relaxed into it. When she opened her eyes, Meg's reed-green gaze was staring right into hers.

"Your eyes look greener today."

Meg smiled. "They do that — change colour."

Kate raised an eyebrow. "Aren't you a woman of mystery."

"I do my best," Meg said, kissing Kate on the cheek. When she pulled back, Meg held up a carrier bag that clinked when it moved. "I brought supplies — where shall I put them?"

"In the kitchen." Kate flicked her head over her right shoulder and took Meg's hand in hers. "Follow me."

As Kate entered the kitchen, Lawrence was just exiting, his plate half-full. "You still in here?" Kate's voice was light-hearted, trying to cover her earlier irritation.

But Lawrence simply looked over Kate's shoulder and said nothing. And when he dropped his plate of food, there wasn't a great clatter, with most of the contents and the plate itself being shatter-proof.

Meg dropped Kate's hand and stopped walking.

The hairs on Kate's arms stood to attention, but she had no idea why.

"Meg?" Lawrence's voice was barely audible. "What are you doing here?"

Kate turned, to find Meg's mouth hanging open, her eyes hardening.

One of Jack's friends brushed past Lawrence and Meg in the kitchen doorway with something approaching irritation, but neither Meg or Lawrence registered it.

Kate couldn't quite connect the dots. "You two know each other?"

Lawrence was still staring, as was Meg.

"We did once." And with that, Meg turned, bag of drinks in hand and coat still on. She walked towards the door.

Kate narrowed her eyes at Lawrence accusingly, then set off after Meg, who was just opening the front door to leave.

"Hey." Kate grabbed Meg's arm, but she shook her off. "What's wrong, what's going on?"

"I'm leaving." Meg shot Kate an apologetic look. "Sorry — I can't stay with him here." She yanked the door fully open just as Jess appeared in the hallway.

"You're here — finally! Super-fashionably late too." But Jess stopped talking as she approached and saw the worry etched on Kate's face. "Everything okay?"

"He's a fucker, that's what's going on," Meg told Kate, before stepping out into the October evening.

Kate held up her hand to Jess. "Give us a minute." She followed Meg out the front door and up the garden path.

Meg was already striding down the road.

"Meg! Stop!" Kate broke into a sprint to catch her up. The night air was cold on her skin and she shivered.

Meg was paying no attention to Kate's needs.

"What's he doing here? In the kitchen at your sister's party?" Meg was still walking at some pace.

Kate ran in front of her and stopped.

Meg tried to dodge round her, but Kate grabbed her arms.

"Tell me what's going on — why did you freak on when you saw Lawrence?"

"How do you know him?" Meg's eyes were wild and watery.

"He's my mum's boyfriend."

Meg let out a snort and bent over, putting down the carrier bag of beer, then her palms on her thighs. "Your mum's boyfriend. Wow. Life is certainly playing tricks on us right now." She stayed down for a few more seconds before standing up. Then she shook her head. "Go back — everyone will be wondering where you are."

Kate shook her head. "Let them wonder — I'm more concerned how you are. Will you tell me what's going on."

Meg laughed a hollow laugh. "Lawrence is my long-lost-fucking-father, that's what's going on."

The sky's blackness seemed to fall on them in that moment.

Now it was Kate's turn to be stunned. "Lawrence is your *dad*?" Even Kate couldn't quite believe it.

"Yes — and apparently he's shagging your mum. So we could become sisters. Perfect, wouldn't you say?" Meg put her fingers to her forehead and trailed them across its width, her eyes closed. When she opened them, she shook her head again.

"I can't do this — not tonight. I need to think. I don't want... Him in my life. Not now. Not with Mum so sick. It's too…" She sighed. "You take the booze back in, I'm gonna go home."

Kate put her hand to her mouth. "No — I'll come with you. I don't care about the party."

"You should," Meg said. "It's your sister's birthday."

"But she's not the one I'm in love with." Kate fixed Meg with a steely stare. Then she tried to soften it to reflect the feeling behind her words. It'd just slipped out. This wasn't the romantic moment she'd been imagining.

Meg put her hand to Kate's face and trailed her fingers down one side. She went to say something, pain written across her expression, then shook her head again.

"I can't do this." Meg's voice was metallic.

They feel into a sharp silence.

Eventually, Kate spoke in a whisper. "Do what?"

"He can't be involved — this is too messy."

"What are you saying?" Kate's voice was scrabbling to a far higher pitch than she was used to.

Meg let out a yelp of frustration. "I don't know what I'm saying, but I know it can't involve him. He walked out on us, deserted us, was never a father to us. And now he's playing happy families with you, drawing you in?" Meg licked her lips. "I have to go."

Kate grabbed Meg's arm as she went to turn.

Meg looked into Kate's eyes, then looked away.

"I don't want you to go." Kate's voice was low, almost a whisper. Her heart was hammering in her chest — the feeling was familiar where Meg was concerned.

"It's not up to you though, is it?" Meg kissed Kate's cheek, then whipped around and walked off into the night.

Kate was left looking at Meg's retreating figure.

Yep, she definitely hated Lawrence now.

34

Jamie answered the door with a tea towel in his hand. It was a slow Sunday and his sister's face was bricked with hot emotion.

Jamie paled. "Is Mum okay?" He stopped wiping his hands, leaving them suspended in the air.

Meg shook her head. "She's fine, she's fine." She stepped into the hallway and strode past Jamie with purpose.

"Come in, why don't you," he muttered as he shut the front door. He followed Meg into the lounge.

Meg circled the room, bit her finger, then looked up. "Is Greg here?"

Jamie shook his head. "At the gym."

Meg sat on the sofa and exhaled.

Jamie sat down opposite her on a green velvet armchair. "What's wrong? Why do you have a face like thunder? Are you sure Mum's okay?"

Meg nodded. "Yes, I'm sure — I spoke to her this morning and I'm going round there after this." Meg sat forward.

"Bit of a detour," Jamie stated.

Meg looked up. "Yes it is, isn't it?" Meg took in a lungful of air. "I saw Dad last night." Meg stared at Jamie.

"Dad?"

Meg nodded.

"Where?"

"At Kate's sister's party, would you believe." Meg shook her head again like *she* still didn't believe it.

"What?" A frown appeared on Jamie's face. "What was he doing there?"

"Eating quiche and shagging Kate's mum." Meg closed her eyes.

"At the party?"

"He might as well have been." Meg paused. "The upshot is that our dad is now seeing Kate's mum, so Kate and I might become step-sisters and I'm just so pissed off. I mean, he fucks up our lives once, now he's trying to do it again." Meg stood up and began to pace the room.

Jamie bit his lip. "And what did he say?"

"Say?"

Jamie stroked his chin. "Yeah — did he say anything? Anything about me?"

"Why would he say anything about you?" Meg frowned.

"Because I've been kinda seeing him. Over the past few months. I was going to tell you."

Meg's eyes widened. "You've been kinda seeing him? Seeing him or kinda seeing him?"

Jamie looked down at the carpet. "You know..." he began.

"No, I don't," Meg said. "Please fill me in."

"He... We met by accident in the Bull & Bush a couple of months ago. We had a pint, then we've been meeting there every few weeks. Taking things slowly. I didn't want to tell you because I knew how you'd react. *Like this.* But now he's seeing your girlfriend's mum, I mean — that takes it to a whole new level." Jamie shook his head slowly.

"I can't believe you didn't tell me." Meg's voice was full of nails.

"I was going to, but then what with Mum and Kate and everything — and I didn't want to put anything else on you. I wasn't lying — I was just waiting for the right time." He gave a weak smile.

"I could have saved you the trouble — there's never going to be a right time with him. *Never, Jamie*. How could you do this to me and Mum? I thought we were a team?"

Jamie stood up and faced Meg. "We are — you know that. But we're all getting older and I've wanted to talk to him for a while now, to get his side of the story. To find out why he just left us. Surely you've wanted answers, too?" Jamie spread his palms before Meg.

Meg stuck out her bottom lip and shook her head. "Not really. I've no need to hear his side. I know what I need to know — that he ran out on us. That Mum did the best she could. And that he's a useless piece of shit."

Jamie touched Meg's arm, but she shook him off.

He ploughed on. "He's not, though — he was depressed and he couldn't deal with us, with his family. He's regretted it every day since and he wants to make amends. He's not a bad man, Meg, he just couldn't cope and made some wrong turns. He's human." Jamie paused. "So did he say anything else when you saw him? You must have had a conversation?"

Meg sighed. "Not really — I walked out before he could say anything."

Meg sat down and Jamie sat beside her, taking her hand. "And what did Kate say?"

Meg shrugged. "She was as baffled as I was — neither of us knew our parents were seeing each other." She shook her head. "It makes things ten times more difficult now, though, doesn't it? And just when we'd cleared everything up." Meg exhaled. "Why does life have to be so hard?" Meg leaned in to Jamie and he put his arm around her. He smelt of fresh rosemary.

"You know, this doesn't have to be an issue. It's only an issue if you make it one." His voice hummed through Meg's body, the vibrations surging down to her toes. "I mean, you and Kate — that's a definite goer. Nothing's going to change that, right?"

Meg shrugged.

Jamie frowned. "Take it from your wise brother — you shouldn't let anything get in the way of that."

"She told me she loved me last night."

Jamie looked down at Meg. "And what did you say?" He raised his eyebrows waiting for the response.

"I told her it was too messy and walked away." Meg hid her head in Jamie's shoulder again.

"You just want to keep sending her flowers, is that it? Keep pissing her off and then winning her back?" He smiled as he spoke.

"Apparently," Meg mumbled.

"Well, get another bunch ready and prepare to grovel. But if she loves you, she'll forgive you. And then there's Dad."

Meg untangled herself from her brother and sat back. "I don't want to see him or deal with him. It would upset Mum too much."

"I think she might surprise you."

Meg eyed Jamie. "Really? After she's just had a heart attack, you want to drop this on her?"

Jamie narrowed his eyes. "You know what I think?"

Meg shook her head. "No, but I think you're going to tell me."

"I am," Jamie said. "And you won't like it one bit. You should give Dad a chance — he wants to make amends. He wants to be a part of our lives and I think we should let him. Mum will deal with it and we have room for both of them." He stroked Meg's thigh. "And Mum will cope. This will *not* give her another heart attack."

"How do you know?"

Jamie shook his head again. "You're using Mum's situation as a shield, to deflect away from the fact it would help you move on if you spoke to Dad, heard what he had to say and tried to make sense of it all. He's a nice bloke, he really is."

"You clearly take after him then, being a nice bloke too."
Meg's voice was laced with sarcasm.

Jamie smiled. "We both take after Mum. Dad missed the
boat on claiming any of our characteristics, that ship has
sailed. But we could make some new memories with him now,
perhaps ones that might make up for the lack of them in all the
previous years. And you're not betraying Mum or forgiving
Dad — you're just putting yourself first for a change."

Meg looked at Jamie for a long time before speaking.
Finally, she said: "When did you get so self-helpy?"

Jamie nudged her, before smiling. "Sweetheart, it's in the
gay rulebook, you know that. You just skipped those pages."
He paused. "Now are you going to stay for lunch? I'm trying
out a new recipe and it involves *a lot* of cream. I mean, *tons*.
And you won't find *that* in the gay handbook."

Meg considered his question. "You got wine, too?"

"Course."

"Sold." She paused. "But I'm still mad at you."

Jamie smiled. "You won't be after you taste the food."

35

It was a gunmetal Tuesday at Fabulous Flowers, and Meg was out the back when she heard the front door go. Her heart sped up — was it Kate this time? What she was going to say to Kate after ignoring all of her texts so far, she wasn't sure. The rest of her life was moving ahead, with Olivia showing signs of improvement and the house getting two second viewings over the past week.

Kate was the only cloud still bruising Meg's horizon.

And Kate loved her.

Meg emerged into the shop to be greeted by Tanya, barrister-fresh with leather briefcase in hand. She smiled broadly at Meg.

"To what do I owe this honour?" Meg walked around the counter and folded her arms across her chest.

Her ex carried on smiling. "I thought you'd want to hear this news in person — the estate agent just called and the second couple have put in an offer — and then so did the first. They're in a bidding war and the upshot is, we've been offered 20 grand over the asking price."

Meg's mouth formed an 'O'. "You're kidding."

Tanya shook her head. "I wouldn't joke about stuff like this, and I wouldn't come all the way here to tell you, otherwise." She walked up to Meg and put her arm around her. "We're going to be rich, kiddo. You and me both. You should go on holiday — you could do with a break."

"That's true." Meg leaned into Tanya's embrace. "I can't believe it, though — we really might be moving." Meg paused. "And I really might be homeless."

"Sooner than you think too — the first couple are cash buyers."

"Shit."

"Shit indeed," Tanya replied. "You fancy dinner to celebrate? End of an era. Just you and me, like old times?"

Meg gave Tanya a look. "Not exactly like old times, I hope."

Tanya cocked her head. "Yes, exactly like old times. We'll go out for dinner, we can snipe at each other and not have sex at the end of it. Sound good?"

Meg nudged Tanya, chuckling. "Sounds perfect. Only not tonight. I'm meeting Jamie and my dad for dinner tonight. Much against my better judgment." Meg bit her lip.

"*Your dad?*" Tanya sounded incredulous.

Meg nodded. "Believe me, I'd rather be having dinner with you, and that's something I never thought I'd say."

Tanya crumpled her face. "Thanks, I think." She paused. "Another night, then? Thursday or Friday?"

Meg nodded. "Definitely. It'll be good to mark the end of such a grand era."

"It will." Tanya stared at Meg. "Good luck tonight."

"Thanks. I might need it."

* * *

At Female Health & Fitness magazine, Kate was sat in her chair frowning at her screen. She couldn't get this current article to work and it was beginning to annoy her. Mind you, after the past week, that didn't take too much. After the debacle of last weekend, Meg had gone into radio silence with her, and that was despite Kate's ill-timed declaration of love. Then this weekend, Jess was moving out. Life had a funny way of twisting the knife, didn't it?

Kate moved the image of a woman in Lycra to the left of the spread to see if that worked any better. It didn't. She sighed and got up, walking down the row of desks towards the coffee machine, where she bumped into Dawn.

"Morning sunshine."

"I think you'll find it's raining and actually the afternoon now." Kate looked out the window at the damp October day, before showing Dawn her watch which read 12:41.

"Oh dear. No word yet?"

Kate frowned her best frown. "Nothing. And I can't get this Ten Ways To Get A Fitter Core spread to work. And I'm going to die alone. Anything else you need?"

Dawn's face remained impassive. "No, I think that about covers it. Only, I do have some news that might cheer you up."

"It's going to have to be mega to cheer me up." Kate pushed past Dawn and thumped the panel on the coffee machine.

"So this issue, the one with your girl... I mean, the one with the Princess Emily on the front and the lesbian runners and all of that."

Kate picked up her drink, took a sip and winced as it burnt her tongue. "I know of it."

"Well," Dawn continued, exuberance sweeping her words along. "It's already our best-selling issue. *Ever*. Ben just told me. And there's still a week to go." Her face lit up. "So this means it'll be up for Cover Of The Year in the next awards too, with the numbers to back it up." Dawn swept her hand through the air to illustrate her point. "I can picture it now — Cover Of The Year for the second year running and Magazine Of The Year for the first time." Dawn clapped her hands together quickly and Kate worried she might burst with excitement.

Kate stared into her coffee, then at Dawn. "The power of lesbians, right there."

"I think you might be right. We should have lesbians in the magazine every issue!"

Kate winced. "I'm not sure I'm up for meeting any more." She sighed. "But that's great news, honest. But sadly, not enough to cheer me up. Because it means the magazine with the one that got away will be winking at me for the next year or so, give or take."

Dawn pulled Kate into a hug and squeezed her so hard, Kate coughed.

"You'll be fine. Meg'll come round, you'll see."

Dawn released Kate and she staggered sideways.

"And if all else fails, I'll take you out this weekend and get you really drunk. How does that sound?"

That forced a smile from Kate. "It's the best offer I've had in a while."

"That's the spirit," Dawn said, before linking Kate's arm and walking with her back to their desks.

Kate sat down and stared at her screen, the steady hum of the office all around her. Next to her, Henry was tapping his hand on the desk to the tune playing through his headphones. Across from her, staff writer Daisy's face was gnarled with concentration as her fingers stabbed her keyboard. Meanwhile, Hannah looked tired and had an eyebrow raised at her screen; and the sales team were on the phone quoting inflated circulation figures to possible advertisers. So far, so normal.

But nothing felt normal to Kate today, nothing felt right at all. She and Meg had come so close, and then had imploded again through no fault of their own. Logic told Kate that Meg would come around, but logic had long since left the building. Her stomach rumbled with the injustice of it all — she hadn't eaten yet today, but it wasn't high on her priorities. She sipped her coffee and felt it hit her empty stomach, the hot liquid the lonely dweller inside her.

Should she be so easily defeated? She decided she should not. Yes, Meg had said it wasn't up to her, but she wasn't going to just take that lying down. However, if Meg wasn't returning her calls or texts, what was she to do? Kate twirled a blue biro in her fingers and cupped the back of her neck. She flicked onto the Fabulous Flowers website and an idea came to her. Flowers. Meg never got sent flowers. And she'd sent Kate enough to last a lifetime.

Kate made a decision and clicked on the Interflora website.

* * *

Meg was the first to arrive, so she ordered a bottle of Cobra lager and fiddled with her phone, checking the door every few seconds. She texted Jamie to ask where he was, as he'd assured her he'd be early. Clearly, her brother had lied.

Meg's worst fears were realised five minutes later, as Lawrence pushed open the door to the Indian restaurant. No matter what she thought of him as a person, Meg had to admit her dad was wearing well and the fact he had a full head of hair was something Jamie was terribly excited by. Hair was important to Jamie.

Lawrence smiled, but his eyes showed anxiety. He indicated the chair opposite Meg and she nodded curtly, pursing her lips.

Where the hell was Jamie? She was going to kill him.

"Hi," Lawrence said, sitting down and fixing Meg with his gaze. "Been here long?"

Meg shook her head and clicked her phone off. "Five minutes."

They both stared.

Meg searched her mind for something to say that might nibble at the endless silence, move it along a little, but nothing sprung to mind that could make up for her dad's absence throughout her life. All she could think about were all the things he'd missed out on — the school plays, the summer holidays, her first boyfriend, her first girlfriend. He didn't know her at all, so what the hell were they doing here?

Lawrence cleared his throat. "Before your brother gets here, I just want to say thanks for coming. It means a lot." He paused, studying his cutlery for a couple of seconds, before looking back to Meg. "We've got a lot to catch up on and I'm pleased you're giving me the chance."

Meg stayed silent, taking a swig of her lager while her dad ordered his own. She looked at her watch. She really was going to kill Jamie.

Lawrence looked at her expectantly. "How was the florist today?"

Meg nodded. "Good. It's going well." She bit her fingernail.

"Your mum did a good job there," Lawrence said.

"She had to, didn't she?"

Lawrence smiled weakly. "Yes, she did." He paused. "I'm not denying that."

More silence.

"How about you — how was your day?"

Surprise registered on Lawrence's face. "It was productive — had some good meetings to get some projects going, so…" He ran a hand over his chin. "But I've been looking forward to this all day. Looking forward, while also being scared witless."

Meg's face remained stoic. "Why scared?"

"That you might not turn up. And that if you did, you'd scream at me." Lawrence gave a faint shrug. "You've got every right."

Meg leaned back in her chair and grasped the back of her neck, exhaling as she did. She took a while to answer. "You can thank Jamie — he persuaded me." She paused. "And now it's down to you to persuade me further."

Lawrence laced his fingers together in a dome and took a deep breath. "I really am sorry for everything I missed and I'm sorry for being an absent father. But if you'll let me, I'd like to make it up to you." He paused, looking Meg direct in the eye. "I don't want to lose you again. Whatever it takes, I'm willing to do."

Meg sat up in her seat and tapped her knife on the table. "Whatever it takes, huh?"

Lawrence held her gaze. "Whatever it takes," he repeated.

Meg let a smile creep onto her face. "Well, you can start off by paying for dinner. I think you owe me a few."

Lawrence risked a smile back. "Done."

36

Wednesday night and Kate was at her mum's for dinner. There was an uneasy truce in the air after the Lawrence debacle and neither of them knew just what was going on with their relationships. Lawrence had been in touch with Maureen to tell her he needed to sort 'the situation' out first before seeing her again, and Maureen was optimistic that wouldn't take too long and things would soon be back to normal.

Kate wasn't quite sure where normal began and ended, so her take on matters was quite different. She was currently slumped over Maureen's kitchen table, her chin resting on her hands, the weight of the world on her shoulders.

"They met up you know — Lawrence and Meg." Maureen was chopping the tips off of green beans to go with their salmon and potatoes, currently baking in the oven.

Kate's ears perked up. "They did?"

Maureen chopped, then turned around to face Kate. "They did. And he said it went okay. She brought her brother along and they went to the Indian place on the High Street. It's a start, and hopefully it'll smooth the way forward." Maureen paused. "Her brother's gay too, did you know?"

Kate nodded. "I did — I've met him. He's nice."

"Lawrence says so, too." Maureen paused. "You never know, we might all be going on a double date and laughing about this before too long. Me and Lawrence, you and Meg."

Kate smiled wanly. "How do you stay so positive? I feel like I've been thrown around on a spin cycle since I've met Meg."

"But despite all that, you still want to be with her, don't you?"

Kate shrugged, then nodded slowly. "I do. But I'm not sure if we're meant to be. There's too much change in the air and maybe the universe is trying to tell us something. That it's just not the right time."

Her mum put the beans on to steam and put the plates in the microwave to warm — it was one of her mum's habits that she'd passed on to Kate — always warm your plates.

"You youngsters and your stars aligning nonsense. You're in control of your life, love. If you want it to happen, you make it happen — listen to a wise old crone like me." Her mum chuckled. "I was like you once, very c'est la vie." She put the last comment in finger brackets. "But then your dad died and I thought, where does c'est la vie get you? Lawrence is in no doubt what I want to happen and he's in agreement. I'm giving him time to sort things out. And he will."

The microwave pinged and her mum took the salmon and potatoes from the oven with a sky blue silicon glove shielding her fingers from the heat. She dished up the food, scooped the beans onto the plate with a large metal spoon and sat down opposite Kate.

"Have you been eating?" Her mum didn't wait for an answer. "You look thin."

Kate smiled. "I've been eating — Jess has been cooking for me."

"And when she moves out?"

"I'll start cooking again, don't worry. I've just had more pressing things on my mind." Kate speared a potato.

Maureen let a few seconds pass. "And I meant what I said — about the double date. It'd be good for Meg and Lawrence to know they have our support." Maureen put her cutlery down and waited for her daughter's response.

Kate chewed some salmon before speaking. "Let's get her talking to me first before we start organising double dates, shall we?"

37

"My loneliness is killing me — oh Britney, if you only knew!" Meg was swaying her hips and singing along to Britney's stellar hit with some gusto this morning. "When I'm not with you I lose my mind, give me a sign!" She paused and let out a huff of frustration. "A sign would be good, Britney, a sign would be *really* good." Meg nodded her head in time to the music. "Give me a sign, universe!" she shouted into her empty shop.

This week had surely been one of the weirdest of her life. In the past seven days, she'd gone out for dinner with her dad and shut out her girlfriend, when it would normally have been the other way around. However, much to Meg's surprise, the dinner hadn't been a total bust and Jamie had performed his role to a tee, once he'd actually arrived. He smoothed the ground for her dad to speak, filling the gaps as Meg and Lawrence struggled to take in enough air. It had been a start, Jamie had told her, and they should do it again.

Without Jamie there to assist, though, Meg wasn't sure how such an evening would play out. However, Jamie was there and would continue to be, until Meg and her dad felt able to wade out of the shallow end of their relationship and start swimming unassisted.

Meg had waited her whole life for her dad to appear. Now that he had, he'd better be prepared to go at her speed. She had enough other change going on with Kate, her mum and the house. She should spend this weekend looking at possible flats, but her heart wasn't in it yet, being pulled as it was in so many directions. Maybe moving in with her mum as a temporary measure would suit them both right now.

The radio began blurting out Ricky Martin's most famous hit and Meg took the bait, determined to charge up her good mood battery. Livin' la vida loca? She could do that, just for today.

She was just belting out the final verse of Ricky Martin's opus when the tinkle of the shop bell made her look up, the final *la vida loca* sticking in her throat. Meg frowned at what she saw. In front of her was a man standing with a bunch of white roses and three alert sunflowers in the middle of them.

Standing in her shop with a bunch of flowers *not from here*.

The man looked at Meg with more than a hint of confusion on his face, then consulted his delivery address, before looking back at her again.

"Meg Harding?" He was wearing a shirt emblazoned with Interflora.

"That's me," she said.

The man strode over to her and handed Meg the bouquet with a grin. "I've never delivered flowers to a florist before."

"And I've never received any either, so that makes two of us."

They exchanged a 'whatchagonnado' grin, with Meg signing for the roses and the man wishing her a good day.

When he'd gone, Meg couldn't resist plunging her nose into the roses' fresh bouquet — they were beautiful. She ripped the envelope from where it was stuck to the stems. If this was from her dad, it was a highly misguided gesture. She plucked the card from the envelope and her heart stuttered. She held her breath as she read.

'You said you never received flowers, so I thought I'd remedy that. I miss you. Kate. Xxx'

Meg gulped in air and dropped her head, before scanning the card again. No hidden message, no cryptic clues. Just a plain and simple 'I miss you'. And this was quite the romantic gesture. Something brave. Something bold. Kate was being bold and Meg was welling up.

Meg was being wooed.

38

Saturday dawned with wearisome predictability and Kate lay in bed listening to the rain cascade down her windows, breathing in the fresh laundry smell of her clean sheets. Fresh bed linen was one of life's little perks you could count on. Her brain was bone-dry, her tongue furry. She wouldn't have minded, but Kate hadn't even had a drink last night.

Outside her door, Jess was singing along to the radio as she packed her stuff into boxes. From the sound of the clanking, she was packing up her kitchen stuff. Kate would have to buy some new baking trays and tins.

The flowers had been sent, but Kate had heard nothing — so she had no idea what to think anymore about Project Meg. Perhaps fate was trying to tell her something. Perhaps the goddess of love was taking a well-earned break and had washed her hands of any more lesbian love affairs and drama.

She should get up and help Jess pack, but Kate couldn't move from her bed. Instead, she grabbed her phone from her bedside table and checked her inbox. Still nothing. She looked at Meg's Facebook page — it stood unchanged, the same as it had been for the past week. It was as if Meg's life had stopped turning the night she met her dad again, even though Kate was well aware she was still very much alive. Kate was grateful for that at least, if not for all of the ill-fated connections the pair shared.

Kate's mum was seeing Lawrence tonight, exactly one week after the party.

Kate, on the other hand, was having a meal for one in her newly solo home. Her current failure at life and love was so obvious, she worried there might be a neon sign erected by her front door: 'This Way To Loserville'.

She threw her phone back on her bedside table and flung back the covers. She made a decision on the spot.

"No wallowing, Carter," she said out loud. "Today you're going to do something just for you." What that was, Kate wasn't sure, but it was a decision, and that was something. She grabbed her jeans from the floor and pulled them on, together with her favourite purple sweatshirt. She brushed her hair and opened her eyes as wide as they would go. Then she went in search of her soon-to-be-departed flatmate.

She found Jess in the lounge, looking out of the window and hugging one of Kate's cushions to her chest. Kate yawned before speaking. "You can take it if you like." She walked over and rested her head on Jess's shoulder. "As a keepsake, a souvenir of our time together."

Jess didn't turn her head. "You're giving me a cushion? But you love your cushions."

"And I love you, too," Kate said.

Jess turned her head. "This is a fine time to declare your love for me — the day I'm moving out to be with another woman."

Kate walked around the sofa, before dropping onto it with a sigh. "Apparently timing isn't my strong point. Just ask Meg."

Jess gave Kate a rueful smile. "She'll come round, you'll see." She sat down beside Kate. "And even if she doesn't miss you, I will. I've loved living here. I was just standing there thinking that."

"I know," Kate replied.

"And I worry you won't eat if I'm not around."

"I *can* cook, you know." Kate waved a hand. "And if I don't feel like it, I'll come to the café every day to pick up supplies." She stroked her chin. "And I was thinking I might redecorate. Do something different. I might even go freelance and turn your room into an office — who knows?"

Jess laughed and threw the cushion at Kate. "Charming. At least wait till I'm out the door before you start making any changes."

"I'll try." Kate cleared her throat. "What time's Lucy due?"

Jess pulled her phone from her pocket. "About an hour."

"And is there lots left to do?"

Jess shook her head. "Just a few bits — I need to pack my clothes. Besides, I can always come back. It's not like you're going anywhere is it?" Jess yawned and stretched, her arms extended fully above her head.

"I dunno, it depends," Kate said. "I might have turned your room into a wet room by next week."

* * *

Meg lay on her side in her bed, curled up in the foetal position. She'd spent last night with her mum, talking things over. Olivia was being surprisingly calm about the situation with her dad, even the bit about Jamie seeing him behind their backs. Apparently, that's what two near-death experiences will do.

"You can't control every aspect of your life, and the sooner you learn that, the better," she'd told Meg.

Meg had simply eyed her with suspicion over their M&S meal deal dinner — lasagne, profiteroles, salad and wine. You couldn't go wrong for a tenner.

Olivia had also told her to get over herself and give Kate a call, because wouldn't life be better with her than without her? Meg had grudgingly admitted that of course it would, but every time something had happened with them so far, some other obstacle had been thrown in her path. She was tired of building her hopes up and seeing them dashed, as she explained to Olivia.

Her mum had told her in no uncertain terms that she needed to toughen up, her disapproving look telling Meg she hadn't raised her to give up so easily. Meg knew it was the truth. However, giving up was *so much easier*.

Meg got up, threw on her soft cream dressing gown, stepped into her slippers and padded down the stairs to the kitchen. On the table sat some of Kate's roses in a glass vase; the sunflowers and the rest of the roses were in a vase in the lounge. Meg put the kettle on, picked up a rose and inhaled its scent. Outside, the rain was lashing down again — at least her plants would be happy.

"Can I have one of those?"

Meg glanced up to see Tanya in the doorway, dressed in pyjama bottoms and a hooded sweatshirt.

"A rose?" Meg asked, before putting it back in the vase.

"I'd prefer a cup of tea." Tanya sat down at the kitchen table. "What are you doing here, anyway? Who's at the shop?"

"Jamie and Greg — I'm getting my first Saturday off in forever."

"About time too. And did you over-order on the white roses? Never seen so many in the house when I came in last night." Tanya yawned and ran her hand up and down the back of her head.

Meg shook her head as she added two teabags to the pot and turned around. "They were a gift actually — from Kate."

Tanya raised an eyebrow. "Sending flowers to a florist — that's brave or stupid, depending on how you look at it." She pursed her lips. "Which way are you going?"

Meg smiled. "I think more brave." She paused, then nodded. "Definitely brave." She turned back to make the tea.

"So are you giving her another go?"

Meg chuckled. "You make her sound like a fairground ride."

"I didn't sleep with her, so I can't possibly comment." Tanya paused. "But are you?"

Meg didn't say anything, instead making the tea and carrying the pot to the table, along with the mugs and the milk. She sat opposite Tanya and locked eyes with her.

"I don't know, is the honest answer. Jamie thinks I should. Mum thinks I should. Even my dad has an opinion, which is *really* weird. But they're not the ones in the firing line, are they?" She squeezed the teabags and shook the pot.

Tanya reached over the table and stopped Meg's fiddling. "What are you waiting for exactly?" she asked. "I mean, we've been over for a while and *you rejected me*. I accept that. But now you meet someone who you like — *and I know you like her* — and you're not willing to truly give it a try?"

"But look at how it's gone so far."

Tanya shrugged. "Pretty well, I'd say. So your dad's seeing her mum — so what? You didn't tell her about us — it happens. None of this is about me or your dad, though; it's about you and what you want. And she clearly wants you if these roses are anything to go by." Tanya sucked on her bottom lip. "We're about to make a fresh start, and you could do that with Kate. Wouldn't that be better? Better than sitting here in the rain, making endless pots of tea and wondering 'what if'? And this isn't something I say lightly — I'm just sick of seeing your moping face."

Meg stared at Tanya and exhaled. She looked up at the clock on the wall, then back at her ex. Then Meg poured the tea and pushed a mug over the table to Tanya, before pouring her own.

Tanya clicked her fingers together and jumped up. "I nearly forgot," she said, disappearing. She returned moments later with a small white envelope addressed to Meg. "I picked this up with my mail yesterday and only realised last night." Tanya handed it to Meg. "No idea what it is."

"Me neither." Meg frowned, holding up the small envelope to the light, peering to see if she could solve the mystery. She didn't recognise the writing. Meg sliced it open with her finger and pulled out a Sainsbury's receipt with a Post-It note attached. The Post-It note read: 'Never Forget x'. Meg's breath caught in her throat and the corners of her mouth edged upwards.

Tanya screwed up her face. "What is it?"

"You know what, for the first time in a long time, you might just be talking sense." Meg drummed her fingers on her mug, before standing up abruptly. "I have to get showered and get going." She picked up her mug of tea, kissing Tanya on the cheek as she passed her.

* * *

An hour later and Lucy was carrying Jess's final suitcase out to her car, groaning under its weight as she bumped it down the stairs.

Jess was standing in the kitchen, washing up her favourite black-and-white spotted mug.

Kate stood at the kitchen doorway, a favourite position where they'd shared many conversations in their time together.

"You really have been my favourite-ever flatmate, you know." Kate didn't want to get misty-eyed, but thought it might happen anyway. She fiddled with her white belt and sucked in her stomach.

Jess looked up at her sister-in-law. "And you mine. But we will see each other again, so let's not get too maudlin, okay?"

Kate smiled. "I know." She paused. "But now you're heading off to live with your girlfriend, you do remember the faults you need to work on, right? Emptying the dishwasher, cleaning toothpaste off the sink, emptying the toaster-crumb tray. These are things that can irk a lover."

Kate heard the steps being taken at double-quick speed and turned to see Lucy, whose hair was stuck to her face from the rain, her black coat shiny with rain drops.

"What's irking me?" she asked, poking her head under Kate's outstretched arm and squeezing past her to stand next to Jess.

"Jess's many faults — but I'll leave you to find them out in good time," Kate said.

Lucy waved her hand. "It's fine — we had this discussion and Jess assured me she was perfect, as am I, so it's all good." She paused, before turning to Jess. "Shall we get going with the first load? I've given up hoping the rain's ever going to stop, so let's just get this show on the road." Lucy dangled her car keys from her thumb and index finger.

Jess bit her lip as she looked to Kate and then back to Lucy. "Let's do it."

Kate stepped back and ushered them out. "No tears this time around — we'll leave that till you return, okay?"

Jess stepped forward and gave Kate a hug. "Deal." But she gave Kate an extra-tight squeeze for good measure anyway, before grabbing her coat from the rack.

"Mind the bike!" Kate shouted at their backs.

* * *

Kate waited for the sound of Lucy's engine to fade and then wandered out of the lounge and into the kitchen. She opened the fridge, where Jess's shelf stood empty. Then Jess's cupboard — same thing, bar a single can of baked beans. Had Jess decided beans were no longer in her diet now she was co-habiting with her girlfriend rather than her sister-in-law?

Kate scratched the back of her head as she walked down the hall and stood in the doorway to Jess's room, bed stripped, wardrobe bare. A black bag of clothes and another of shoes stood waiting to be collected, along with two other boxes by the door. The room smelt of vanilla and coconut, Jess's go-to scents.

Kate recalled Jess moving in, just back from Australia, sad, jobless and single, her possessions then easily fitting into the back of her dad's car. But nearly two years in London had seen her acquire a job, a girlfriend and possessions that required two trips even with Lucy's back seat down — that's what putting down roots meant. More stuff to cart about.

Kate walked down the hall and made herself a cup of coffee — just instant now there was only one of her to make it for. She walked through to the lounge and switched on the TV, listening to the rain hurl itself onto the pavement in violent patterns — it wasn't giving up today.

So what could she do to cheer herself up? What would do the trick? Her mind was blank as she stared at a football show on the TV.

A bike ride perhaps? Too wet.

Go up to see her sister? But that would go dangerously near to Fabulous Flowers, where Meg would be. Sure, she couldn't avoid the area for the rest of her life, but perhaps just for today.

Perhaps she'd get the tube and visit Dawn and Nick — they could go for a pub lunch. She picked up her phone and sent Dawn a text.

A shower, a coffee and a bacon sandwich. It was a plan.

Kate would make today a success if it was the last thing she did.

* * *

Meg clip-clopped down the stairs, her black tote bag banging against her hip as she did. Her hair was springy, her make-up perfect, her attitude gung-ho. She had everything crossed that this bubble didn't burst before she turned up at Kate's front door, because Meg was going to need every ounce of courage to follow this one through. As she grabbed her jacket from the rack, Meg heard a chair scrape back in the kitchen.

Tanya appeared in the doorway, a half-eaten piece of toast in her hand. "Look at you," she said, sweeping her eyes up and down Meg. "Ready for battle?"

They exchanged a knowing glance.

"As I'll ever be." Meg paused. "How do I look?" Meg puffed out her chest.

Tanya smiled. "Like a million dollars." She stepped forward and hugged Meg to her, planting a kiss on her cheek. "Now go get your girl."

Meg put up her umbrella — this weather was getting worse by the minute and was definitely not part of the script. But seeing as she'd yet to write the script, she figured it was all part of life's rich tapestry. Today, she was going with her heart, trying to drown out the panicked voice telling her not to take a chance. And it was Tanya, her ex, of all people, who'd finally persuaded her — that, and the Sainsbury's receipt. The house was sold and they were moving on. But would Kate be ready to move on with her? Meg could only hope.

Water splashed around Meg's leather boots as she skipped along the pavement, the bricks of the surrounding houses weeping in the damp grey morning. A fine mist hung in the air and swiped her face as she walked towards the tube — her hair was going to be a flat mess by the time she arrived at Kate's place.

She got a seat on the tube and sat in silence as the train rumbled its way through London's basement tunnels. Meg's eyes flicked over adverts for religious conventions, takeaway meals and online dating sites, but her brain took none of it in. All she was thinking about was Kate, what she might or might not say, how she would react to Meg finally deciding she wanted in. Kate had to say yes, didn't she? It was the only outcome Meg's brain was entertaining today.

Meg reached Kate's stop and rode the giant escalators up to street level, jostling shoulders with tourists and Londoners alike. Once outside, she put her umbrella up and strode purposefully towards Kate's flat. Within seconds, a gust of wind took hold of her umbrella and turned it inside out. Meg swore and tried to turn the umbrella back the right way. It refused. She wrestled with it for a few minutes, before giving it up as a bad job and depositing the umbrella in a nearby bin. So much for her carefully coiffured appearance. Her heart sunk, but then she rallied as she rounded the corner of Kate's road, rain running down her face.

One thing was for sure — Meg was about to find out how much Kate *really* liked her.

* * *

Before she knew it, Kate heard the doorbell ring — Jess must have left her keys. Typical.

Kate rolled her eyes and trotted down the stairs. "Trust you to forget your keys!" she said, pulling the door wide.

But instead of Jess and Lucy standing on the doorstep in the rain, she was faced with Meg. Getting wetter by the second as the rain dripped down her face in tiny little rivulets.

Kate simply stared. "What are you doing here?" As first lines went, it wasn't her most romantic, or even original.

Meg stared right back, before rubbing her face. "I've come to give you a rose. We had a rush on in the shop yesterday — we got an extra 24 delivered." She rummaged in her bag and produced one of Kate's roses. "So I brought you one. The rest you'll get when you come over to mine."

Meg's hair was flat against her face and she was soaked to the skin. In Kate's eyes, she radiated beauty.

Kate took the rose. "I'm coming over to yours?"

Meg nodded. "If everything goes according to plan. Which of course it *totally is*. My first plan was to come here, break my umbrella, get soaking wet and stand on your doorstep in the rain looking bedraggled — and that part has gone like *absolute clockwork.*" Meg gave Kate a lop-sided smile, before wiping some rain out of her eyes.

Kate stepped back. "Sorry — do you want to come in?"

"I don't know." Meg stumbled over her words. "Do you want me to?"

There was silence on the doorstep, the only sound being the steady boom of the rain on the pavement, the outside traffic and their hearts stamping an insistent beat.

Before Kate knew what she was doing, she was nodding slowly. Her heart had taken over, and seeing Meg looking like such a drowned rat only made her melt that little bit more. Warmth oozed through her body like hot chocolate.

"Do I want you to come in? I'd like nothing more. But seeing as you're so soaked, I might as well get wet, too."

Before Meg could protest, Kate kicked on her trainers and stepped into the morning rain, splashing in a puddle for extra effect.

Meg's laughter pierced the air, her smile flooding her eyes.

And as Kate laughed too, the rain got more insistent and a brittle crack of thunder rumbled not too far away.

Both Kate and Meg peered upwards, before turning back towards each other.

"I think you might have mystical powers." Meg turned her full-beam smile on Kate.

Kate was suitably dazzled. "You should know that by now." Kate searched Meg's almond-shaped eyes and found what she was looking for. "I missed you so much."

Then Kate stepped forward and took Meg's face in both hands. She kissed her on one cheek, then the other, and finally on Meg's soft mouth. As their lips fused together again, Kate's heart swelled. She steadied herself and they pulled away, staring at each other as the rain showed no sign of abating.

Meg trailed her hand down the side of Kate's face. "Thanks for the flowers." She put her lips to Kate's again.

Kate smiled shyly, her lips never leaving Meg's. "You said you never got any."

Meg shook her head. "You're the first."

"I'm glad."

Their lips touched again.

Kate took hold of both of Meg's hands and they stood face to face, lip to lip, water running down both their cheeks. "But what about your dad and my mum? How's that going to work?" Kate breathed in the smell of petrol and wet tarmac as the rain slackened a little.

Meg shook her head slowly, dropping one of Kate's hands to run her fingers through her wet hair. "I don't know — but our parents aren't what's important right now. What is important is us — you and me." She gave a single, defiant nod. "We'll deal with the rest together. Good enough for now?"

A smile creased Kate's face. "More than good enough."

They kissed again, a long, deep, passionate kiss. When they pulled back, Meg's eyes had clouded over with emotion. "There was one other thing," she said. A tear tracked its way down her cheek, mixing seamlessly with the rain.

"Don't cry," Kate said.

Meg sniffed and wiped the tear away. "It's a happy tear." She sniffed and wiped the back of her hand across her nose. "I must look a right state."

"You look beautiful," Kate said. "What was the other thing?"

Meg smiled hesitantly. "Just to say… I love you too — and I'm sorry I never told you before. And I'm sorry I ran off when you told me — it wasn't the best response." Meg winced, never taking her eyes off of Kate.

"I've had better."

Meg let out a bark of laughter. "Am I sharing too much on your doorstep?"

Kate smiled, then shook her head. "Not at all. I think it's perfect. You're perfect. This is definitely my most favourite doorstep moment ever."

"You've had a few?" Meg raised one eyebrow.

"Never with so much rain and such a gorgeous woman."

Meg laughed and held up her palm. "And the rain seems to be stopping — at last."

Kate turned her face to the sky and just at that moment, a massive drop of rain landed on her face. She spluttered and Meg laughed.

Kate wiped her face, before turning her full attention back to Meg. "And just so there's no confusion, I love you, too. More than you know."

They kissed again and Kate's head swam. She sunk into the kiss, revelling in its warmth and how right it felt. But after a few seconds, it was interrupted by a shout from nearby.

"Oi, you two — take it inside!"

Kate and Meg stumbled apart, their bubble pierced. They turned to see Jess and Lucy slamming their car doors.

"What's going on here, apart from you two looking like you've just been for an impromptu swim?" Jess grinned as she walked up to them.

Kate smiled right back. "We're having a doorstep moment."

"Oh, really?" Jess said.

"Well, don't let us stop you — we'll see you upstairs." Lucy dragged a gawping Jess away and into the flat.

Kate laughed, then turned back to Meg. "Now where were we?"

Meg moved forward and planted her lips onto Kate's. "Right about here," she replied.

39

Two months later and Christmas was upon them. The week had been a busy one at Fabulous Flowers, with festive orders booming and Olivia officially retiring. Anya had agreed to come on-board at least three days a week, more when required, and their new delivery driver was working out a treat, so Meg wasn't daunted. Rather, taking on the shop as the official boss was something she was looking forward to — but, as she'd told Olivia, she'd still need her on the end of the phone for making some decisions, which had pleased her mum. Olivia might be retiring, but she wasn't redundant.

And now, as Meg packed up the last of the flower remnants at 4pm on Christmas Eve, her mind turned to the coming festivities and what they might bring — this year was so far removed from the last. Back then, it had been Meg and Olivia having dinner alone, with Jamie and Greg away skiing. This year, however, the boys were cooking Christmas dinner for Olivia, Meg and Kate, and tonight Meg and Kate were going out with Kate's mum and Meg's dad — their first date as a foursome.

Meg's thoughts were interrupted with a rat-a-tat-tat on the door. She looked up and saw Lawrence — he gave her a wave. She walked over and unlocked the door.

"I thought we were seeing you at the pub?" Meg stepped aside so he could come in.

Lawrence rubbed his hands together, shivering as he came in from the cold. "Freezing out there!" he said. "And you were — but I thought I'd stop by to pick up some flowers for Maureen. I was going to buy them from Waitrose, but then I thought, why don't I buy them from my daughter? Seemed a better option." He smiled broadly at Meg and shivered again.

"Anything in particular?"

Lawrence shook his head. "Whatever the lovely florist advises." He paused. "And the more expensive, the better."

Meg laughed. "Big spending will get you everywhere."

She spent the next few minutes putting together a colourful, seasonal bouquet she knew Maureen would love, squatting to select the flowers while Lawrence watched her every move.

"You're good at this, you know," he said.

Meg raised an eyebrow as she wrapped the bouquet. "I should hope so by now."

She presented Lawrence with the bouquet and he gave a low whistle, before reaching inside his jacket.

"Just perfect," he said. "How much?"

Meg waved a hand. "On the house — consider it a Christmas gift."

But Lawrence already had his wallet out. "No, I insist — I would have paid for them from anywhere else." He took two £20 notes and put them on the counter.

However, Meg pushed them back towards him and shook her head. "It's on the house — honestly. My gift to you."

Lawrence shifted on his feet, his mouth twitching uncomfortably.

Meg wrapped her hand around his. "It's what families do."

His head dropped slightly and she saw tears glistening in his eyes, before he nodded at her. "Thanks."

The bell tingling broke the moment, and Meg looked up to see Kate striding into the florist. "Thought you were closing up early?" She walked over and kissed Meg on the lips, then nodded at Lawrence. "I hope those are for my mum," she told him, smiling.

Lawrence sniffed, then nodded. "Of course — and I'd better get them to her." He straightened up, pulling down his grey winter coat. "Thanks again for these — see you at the pub at seven?"

Meg smiled at him. "See you there."

He kissed her on the cheek, then Kate, before leaving the shop.

When he was safely out the door, Meg stepped into Kate's embrace, wrapping her arms around her neck, breathing in her perfect scent. Meg could happily live right here, in this very spot forever.

Kate kissed her cheek. "You okay?"

Meg nodded, then lifted her head and stared into Kate's exquisite face, before kissing her perfect lips. "I'm more than okay." She kissed Kate again. "I have you, I have Mum and Jamie, and now I have Dad." She swallowed down a wave of emotion. "I never thought I'd ever say that. My dad. Isn't life weird?"

Kate nodded, a smile warming her face. "Life is weird and wonderful. Luckily for me, you're more wonderful than weird."

Meg threw back her head, laughing. "Glad to hear it." She kissed Kate again, heaving a contented sigh. "And you know what you are? You're some kind of wonderful."

Also by this author...

If you enjoyed *This London Love*, read where it all started for Jess & Lucy in the original rom-com, London Calling!

PRAISE FOR LONDON CALLING...

"Well-paced, fun and genuinely engaging. A very likeable debut from this talented author."
Eden Carter-Wood, Diva Magazine

"Amazing chemistry & a beautiful romance. I read this twice, that's how much I loved this book!"
Caroline Domenech, Curve Magazine

"A top-notch rom-com that will keep you rooted to your seat with realistic characters that make you want to know what happens next. Well crafted, well written – well done!"
Velvet Lounger, The Lesbian Reading Room

"Clare Lydon's London Calling is as strong as any straight chicklit from a major publisher."
Katie Bennett-Hall, Planet of the Books, Planet London

"A fast-paced warm & witty debut, whatever your sexuality."
Gary James, Entertainment Focus

Secrets. Lies. Sex. Intrigue. When a group of friends rent a house by the sea, there's excitement in the air. Fresh air, sandy beaches and historic friendships – what could possibly go wrong?

The catch is, university sweethearts Vic & Stevie are on the rocks, their three-year marriage floundering, while Kat & Abby's combustible relationship looks set to ignite at any second. Meanwhile, Tash & Laura have downed responsibilities & kids for the weekend and are ready for some fun; single CID sergeant Geri can't wait to get away from the London scene to reboot her slumbering love life and that's not to mention Stu & his boyfriend Darren who bring their own man-sized baggage...

Add in laughs, simmering tension, romance & no shortage of wine and you've got all the ingredients for a rollercoaster ride of a long weekend...

PRAISE FOR THE LONG WEEKEND...

"From the very start I felt engaged with these characters and their lives, a part of this fun-filled, but very dramatic long weekend."
Sanya Franich, Curve Magazine

"Clare Lydon's second novel sets out her stall as a fixture in the modern lesbian lit canon."
Katie Bennett-Hall, Planet of the Books, Planet London

"Interesting observations, well drawn, engaging characters and realistic, well-done dialogue made this an enjoyable read."
Velvet Lounger, The Lesbian Reading Room

My Top Five London-Based Rom-Coms

I loved writing this rom-com, and I'm a sucker for a rom-com film too. My top five rom-coms starring London also suffer from a permanent case of Hugh Grant...

5: About A Boy
Hugh Grant is the feckless singleton who tries to woo single mums with his make-believe son Marcus, a young Nicholas Hoult. About A Boy is heart-warming and life-affirming, with North London taking a starring turn.

4: Run Fatboy, Run
Simon Pegg is the runner as he tries to woo back his ex from her smarmy new American boyfriend. Cue tight shorts and hilarious running around the capital's streets, but the even tighter script and acting make this an assured London hit.

3: Four Weddings And A Funeral
The breakout British rom-com that set the standard for all those who followed. Four Weddings has a stellar cast, rich screenplay and is packed with just the right balance of romance and cheese to make it deliciously irresistible.

2: Bridget Jones's Diary

Ahhh, Bridget! Renee Zellwegger gives the performance of her career as the bumbling heroine in this gorgeous London rom-com. Turkey curry buffet, a delicious fight scene, fancy dress and lashings of white wine. What's not to like?

1: Notting Hill

A dazzlingly pretty Notting Hill is the perfect backdrop for this tale of bumbling boy meets famous girl — and who does bumbling better than Hugh Grant? This is writer Richard Curtis's finest hour, with perfect lines planted throughout the script. Beautifully re-watchable.

Connect with Clare

If you'd like to know what I'm up to and never miss another book release, sign up to my mailing list at **www. clarelydon.co.uk**

If you have a moment, I'd greatly appreciate you leaving a review on the site you bought this book on — or any other reading site you use. Plus, any mentions on Facebook, Twitter or any other social media would be greatly appreciated by me. Better yet, if you want to let me know what you thought, tweet or Facebook me — details below.

Twitter: @ClareLydon

Facebook: www.facebook.com/clare.lydon

Find out more at: www.clarelydon.co.uk

Contact: mail@clarelydon.co.uk

AND FINALLY, THANK YOU FOR READING!

6918451R00172

Printed in Germany
by Amazon Distribution
GmbH, Leipzig